Praise for *Rebecca of Salerno*

Rebecca of Salerno gives voice to one of literature's overlooked heroines, the courageous, intelligent, big-hearted Rebecca of Walter Scott's *Ivanhoe*. . . . Esther Erman deftly weaves. . . detail about the lives of Jewish women in medieval Europe into a gripping, fast-paced tale of vengeance, love, and healing. . . Rebecca battles with anti-Semitism, misogyny, and her own heart, as she pursues justice for a man wrongly accused of murder. . . . a novel for our time: while acknowledging the worst tendencies of our shared humanity, it also affirms our capacity for resilience and renewal. Erman's masterful achievement left me feeling moved and inspired.

—Professor Juliet Shields, Dept. of Humanities,
Northumbria University, author of *Nation and Migration*

. . . a lively classic romance with a modern twist. . . after 200 years, Walter Scott's Rebecca. . .gets a second chance for true love but also finds a brilliant career in medicine, in progressive Salerno. . . . By following Scott's heroine to Barcelona, Salerno, and (in an exciting medieval version of a car-chase) Palermo, Erman brings to life the. . . age-old story of established Jewish communities forced. . . to leave their homes. . . . For all the colorful details that make the book such a pleasure to read, the plot on a deeper level is driven by Rebecca's determination. . . A life-affirming narrative with deep cultural roots.

—Emily Klenin, Professor Emerita, Department of Slavic,
East European & Eurasian Languages & Cultures,
University of Southern California

. . . a superb work of historical fiction. It is everything the genre begs for: romance, intrigue, and a captivating mystery. Set at the end of the 12th century and the dawning of the 13th. . . a lively picture of life for Jews, especially Jewish women, in much of Southern Europe, including colorful and historically accurate descriptions of clothing and food preparation. . . not only an enjoyable read, it is a history lesson for Jews and gentiles alike.

—Sara Zeff Geber, Ph.D., free-lance author

. . . a compelling story of a passionate Jewish heroine solving a murder mystery in the brutal setting of the Crusades. The depth of her knowledge of the customs and language of this period is unsurpassed. A book to be read with relish by lovers of historical fiction.

—Neil Kaplan, author of *Acquiring Polish Citizenship by Descent*.

. . . meticulously researched and populated with a cast of engaging characters . . . Rebecca must pit her intelligence and resourcefulness against the forces of anti-Semitism and misogyny to solve a murder. This historical novel boasts witty dialogue, a fast pace, and an ingenious plot.

—Roberta Rich, author of *The Midwife of Venice,*
The Harem Midwife, and *A Trial in Venice*

Rebecca
of
Salerno

Rebecca of Salerno

A Novel of Rogue Crusaders,
a Jewish Female Physician,
and a Murder

ESTHER ERMAN

SHE WRITES PRESS

Published 2022
Printed in the United States of America
Print ISBN: 978-1-64742-247-9
E-ISBN: 978-1-64742-248-6
Library of Congress Control Number: 2022902216

For information, address:
She Writes Press
1569 Solano Ave #546
Berkeley, CA 94707

She Writes Press is a division of SparkPoint Studio, LLC.

For my parents, Gucia and Mulek, and for all refugees in their search for a home

One

BARCELONA, 1225 CE

O*n the eve of your betrothal, my beloved daughter, Ana Luisa, I am answering your oft-repeated request to tell you the complete story of my time in Salerno—including the parts I have been previously reluctant to share. Remembering the many questions that were never answered about my mother's life and even the secrets Papa kept about his, I have decided to honor your wishes by writing it for you. I have told you of my early life in England. Now here is the story of the time in Salerno. I hope it satisfies your longing to know about this period in my life. Most of all, I hope it is of value to you, and, someday, God willing, to my future grandchildren.*

BARCELONA, 1195 CE

"How beautiful you have grown, Rebecca." Uncle Carlos, my father's younger brother, had rushed to greet us when, after a long, harrowing voyage from England, our feet at last touched land in Barcelona. "But you, Isaac, you have only grown older."

Both men laughed and wept as they embraced. "Finally, we have you here—away from that hell for Jews in England." My face must have reflected my turmoil at recent events because Uncle Carlos immediately changed the subject. "Let us not permit sadness to mar this joyous day. Oh, Rebecca, wait until your Aunt Liora gets her hands on you. She wants to fatten you up, turn you into a proper match for the bachelors here. She has already alerted the matchmakers that the loveliest of Jewish maidens will soon fall into their eager hands." *Any such match is the last thing I desire at this time, but look how Papa's face is lighting up at this prospect.*

Papa wiped the tears from his eyes and broke into a larger smile than I had seen since long before we left England. "Matchmakers, you say? I hope they work quickly to find the perfect husband for my Rebecca. I am more than ready to see her settled and to be a grandfather."

Both men laughed as I blushed. "Papa, better you should have the matchmaker find a wife for yourself." He had been a widower since my mother's death, days after my own birth, nineteen years before.

"No one could ever take your mother's place." I had heard this response far too often.

With our things loaded into Uncle Carlos's wagon, we climbed on for the short trip to his home. As the men conversed and the rhythm of the wheels lulled me, I sank into a reverie about the man who was never far from my thoughts—the Christian knight I had given my heart to in England. Ivanhoe. But that was one match that would never happen. By now, he was wed to Rowena, the woman he had pledged to marry before following King Richard on a disastrous Crusade east, to Outremer. The Holy Land.

During my entire voyage over land and sea, I had wept, decrying the power and pain of disappointed love. I resolved never to marry. Instead of marriage and children, I vowed to devote myself to a life in the healing arts, which I had studied since childhood—first with a skilled aunt, then with wise women we had met in previous travels.

Had I not healed Ivanhoe from a grievous wound? I pulled myself
back from this dangerous idea. Thinking of Ivanhoe was hazardous
to my well-being.

When I reflected on my thirst to work as a healer, I envied Christian
women. They could turn their backs on the world of marriage and
children, free to perform good works. Not an accepted option for
a Jewish woman, who is commanded to stay in the world, to wed,
and to be fruitful. How alive and fulfilled I had felt when I healed
Ivanhoe. . . . Of course, those same skills nearly saw me burned at
the stake, accused of sorcery—rescued just in time by Ivanhoe, even
though he was not yet completely recovered from his wounds when
he fought the duel that freed me. The duel against Brian de Bois-
Guilbert, the Knight Templar who expressed his so-called *love* for me
by kidnapping me—and almost costing me my life.

I sighed. My life had been spared, and I now resolved to live that
life as I intended to. So, in the days to come, I would have to avoid
matchmakers dedicated to seeing me fulfill the Jewish woman's list of
commandments. And, to avoid despair, I had to believe God was not
completely displeased with my chosen path.

₰

As promised, Aunt Liora and the family fairly overwhelmed us with
the warmth and abundance of their welcome. Food, drink, and,
above all, love. How easy it would have been to wrap myself in the
blanket of their affection and caring and just sink into the life my
family so much wanted for me. But I was determined to hold onto my
vision of a life devoted to healing.

We were sitting down to dinner on our second night when Uncle
Carlos announced that an additional guest, Rafael Lopes Dias,
would be joining us. Inwardly I groaned. *Was this already the first*

matchmaker's candidate? But Uncle Carlos went on to say, "He is visiting his sister here. He is from Salerno, in the Kingdom of Sicily, which too has a thriving Jewish population. It also is home of the great medical school where all can study together—even Jews. For the Hebrew hospital we are building here in Barcelona, we hope we can employ physicians trained in Salerno, such as Senyor Lopes Dias."

My excitement grew with each word Uncle Carlos said about the medical school. *Can this be the miracle I long for?*

When Rafael Lopes Dias arrived at the table, it was all I could do not to leap at him with my questions. A childless widower in his thirties with family ties in Barcelona, although Senyor Lopes Dias had indeed completed the course at the Scuola Medica Salernitana, he was not a practicing physician. Instead, he was translating texts from Arabic, Latin, and Greek into Hebrew. *How can someone achieve such a level of education and then not use it for healing? He throws away what I yearn for with all my soul.*

Perhaps it was something about his presence—and he was a most handsome man—and the way his dark eyes immediately took my measure that made my heart tremble a bit and my breath catch. Or perhaps it was just that he might be a link to my heart's greatest desire.

When I could no longer bear to wait, I asked him so bluntly about the school in Salerno that I was almost to the point of being rude. "Is it true that such a school exists?" Fortunately, he merely raised an eyebrow and appeared to take no offense.

He smiled. "Yes, difficult as it is to believe."

"And can women study there?" I had to struggle to keep my voice and demeanor calm. Decorum demanded that I restrain my eagerness.

"Yes, women and men together. Jews, Christians, and Moslems, all at the same school." He nodded in a way that encouraged me to ask more.

"How did this miracle arise?"

"Salerno, until recently, has enjoyed a climate of tolerance for all." His brows drew together and he frowned. "Alas, under its latest rulers, the Hohenstaufens, who conquered the Normans, it is unclear how long this atmosphere will continue. The school is thriving despite the political upheavals. At least for now."

"Let us hope that continues," I murmured. *This school cannot cease to exist just when I have learned about it.* "Please, Senyor, tell me more."

He smiled, charming me, and my heart once again fluttered.

"I can tell your interest is genuine. How intriguing." He paused and sipped his wine. "Very well, Senyorita Rebecca. The studies are based on the texts of the ancient Greeks and on the most recent medical advances from the learned Arabs. But this school is not new. It dates from the eighth century and was founded by four masters: the Greek, Pontius; the Arab, Adela; the Jew, Helinus; and the Latin, Salemus."

"You sound like a professor talking about this school." Uncle Carlos was starting to look a bit bored. I hoped our guest would nonetheless continue.

Senyor Lopes Dias shrugged. "People who spend time in Salerno become well acquainted with the lore of the school's history. But perhaps we should talk of something else?"

Before that could happen, I needed to know more. "Senyor, what are the requirements for one to enroll in the school?"

Papa now eyed me with suspicion. "Daughter dear, why are you asking for such information? Our visitor has already been generous enough to tell us so much."

I blushed. "I am curious about this unusual place."

Our guest responded quickly. "It is quite rigorous. Though women can study at the Scuola, few do. Few have the preparation. Then, too, such studies are not easily compatible with the duties of a wife and mother." He smiled at me with bemusement.

Please, Senyor, respond to my questions without adding to the usual criticisms.

As if he had heard my thoughts, he continued, "There have definitely been some women. For example, the woman known as La Trotula, the most renowned, wrote a book about female disorders. To answer your main question, in order to be admitted, one must have an extensive education, usually university based. Languages, mathematics, rhetoric and disputation, astronomy and geometry, and, of course, history and literature."

"I have studied in all these areas, though not at a university." Wherever we went in our travels for his business affairs, Papa had always insisted that I study with masters.

At that point, Uncle Carlos forcefully though politely changed the topic of our conversation by asking Papa to speak of the situation for Jews in England.

As we left the table, Rafael Lopes Dias quietly offered, "Senyorita, if you would like to discuss more about the medical school, we can do so."

"Yes, please."

There was no further conversation about the school that evening, but the next day Senyor Lopes Dias, who had promised to bring my aunt herbs from his sister's garden, visited again. Along with the herbs, he provided me with a document listing more fully the requirements for the entrance exams. I eagerly read these and felt confident I would be able to pass those exams. The question became, how could I present myself in Salerno to take them?

Over the next few days, as I settled into the life of a newly arrived guest with far too little to do, I carefully plotted my campaign to attend the school. Benign providence—or perhaps the God of Abraham Himself—continued to smile on my plans. After three failed attempts at matches and many tears from Aunt Liora, even Papa had to admit I would not marry now.

And, almost as if a miracle, we also had a connection in Salerno— Uncle Chaim, brother to Aunt Liora. Uncle Chaim and his lovely wife invited me to stay with them in Salerno. So, traveling there would not overly horrify Papa, nor my Barcelona relatives. Little by little, I gently kept talking of going to Salerno, until it became familiar, almost inevitable. Finally, several months after the first conversation with Senyor Lopes Dias, our entourage left for Salerno. It included Uncle Chaim, at the end of a visit of his to Barcelona, and Papa, who had some business in Salerno.

My first challenge was the sea voyage. At least this would be a shorter crossing than the one from England. Three days on the Balearic Sea to the island of Corsica, then another day and a half on the Gulf of Salerno, part of the Tyrrhenian Sea. *Perhaps a medical education would help me better tolerate sea voyages?*

Even after a rough crossing, from the moment I arrived in Salerno, despite the evidence of recent battles, I felt at home. The narrow streets and tall, narrow houses and shops that had escaped destruction charmed me.

I was unfortunately surprised to find that, even here, echoes of my old life in England gave shape to the current conditions. King John. Whenever I saw evidence of battles, I thought of him. Even now, the memory of that awful, petty-minded tyrant made me shiver. John, whom we called "Lackland" and other derogatory names, was the younger brother of King Richard, Coeur de Lion—to whom Ivanhoe pledged loyalty. John seized power and began his reign of misrule while Richard was on Crusade. Then John extended his unjust rule when Richard, en route back across Europe after the Crusade, was captured and imprisoned by the Hohenstaufens. John refused to ransom his brother until their mother, Eleanor of Aquitaine, intervened and raised the money. Ironically, the Hohenstaufens had been able to conquer the Kingdom of Sicily—which included Salerno— with the help of that very ransom money.

I shook off these thoughts. I was resolved to move forward with my new life, and so I did not allow the destroyed buildings or the rubble-strewn dirt roads to discourage me. In fact, I was encouraged to see men working to rebuild the damaged parts of the city, a fitting parallel with my own life.

I worked to find a way to demonstrate my knowledge to the appropriate professors at the Scuola. This involved both oral and written exams, some administered individually and some in small groups. Despite the school's reputation for tolerance, not every professor seemed equally inclined to accept female students. Or Jews. I conferred often with Rafael Lopes Dias, who was an invaluable guide to the different professors and what they required. After months of showing myself to be adequately prepared, I was finally accepted and then enrolled at the Scuola Medica Salernitana.

During my very full student days, I continued to live in Uncle Chaim's household, with Papa as a visitor three to four times a year. Nina, their servant, kept the household well fed and well taken care of. She immediately took the role of mother hen and doted on me.

At the school, we students attended lectures, watched demonstrations, and learned to use different implements. Under the supervision of our physician professors, eventually we worked with patients. There were two other women studying then. Despite the religious differences—they were Christians—we three became good friends.

Anatomy class was both a special challenge and source of fascination. Because it was against Christian law to work on human cadavers, we worked on pigs. I ached to participate hands-on on the pig but hesitated because we Jews regard pigs as impure. By that time, Rafael and I had become good friends who could talk about many topics. I asked him what he had done.

He laughed, which I did not appreciate. "My dear Rebecca, how quaint that you would be so troubled on the question of learning anatomy from a pig."

"What do you mean?"

He shrugged. "I never gave it a moment's thought. Cutting the pig, examining its organs—I viewed that all as an essential part of my education. I would never think to allow my being a Jew to conflict with those needs. I thought you had worked that out already, you a Jewish woman who would touch men—even Christians and Moslems—to heal them."

"I did not think to make an equivalency between touching men and cutting up pigs," I muttered, which caused him to burst into gales of laughter. In truth, I knew I must have been blushing like a roasted pig over how young and naïve my question made me sound.

When he stopped laughing enough to talk, he said, "I think you have your response." And so I, the good and faithful Jewish daughter that I tried to be, often found my hands and arms immersed in pig's blood as I studied the animal's heart and entrails, wondering how different a human's might be. Fascinating work. Of course, I did not dare tell Uncle Chaim, Aunt Aster, or my dear papa about this part of my education. Or Nina.

Four long, hard, exciting years after I arrived in Salerno, I had completed my studies and earned the professional licenses to be a practicing physician. Though Papa could never completely mask his disappointment about what I did not provide him—a son-in-law and grandchildren—he took pride in my accomplishment.

Remaining in Salerno, I accepted the title of *Magistra*, conferred upon female physicians, and began both to practice medicine and to teach at the Scuola—in the same place that had provided me with the fulfillment of my dreams. I was able to care for both Uncle Chaim and Aunt Aster and offer comfort during their final illnesses, which came one soon after the other.

After their deaths, I discovered that they had bequeathed their home to me and, in light of the property laws, to Papa. At that point, Papa felt he should stay with me more and not leave his only "child" of twenty-four years alone. However, as an independent woman, a doctor, and a teacher, I longed to run my own household. Fortunately, I was able to convince him I would be fine, even in his absence. Also convincing was that, along with my owning the house and garden, I had retained Nina to run the household. Now that it was only the two of us, she took me even more closely under her substantial wing, which increased Papa's willingness for me to remain in Salerno without him.

An even greater blessing, though sometimes a mixed one, Rafael Lopes Dias proved to be a faithful friend and colleague in many ways. Less welcome were his repeated proposals of marriage, which started about six months after we met, and which I rejected with a constancy equivalent to his offerings. I had, after all, taken a vow precluding marriage—even if I was the only one who knew about it.

I had to admit, also to myself, sometimes it was not so easy to resist Rafael's proposals. Not only was he handsome and agreeable, but something about him always caused my insides to warm. And then, once Papa learned of my suitor's efforts, his entreaties joined Rafael's. It became increasingly difficult to put both men off, but I was as determined as they were. More determined. I stayed faithful to my early love—wanting to protect my heart from further pain, which was, as far as I knew, inextricably entwined with loving a man—even when saying yes to Rafael would have been an easy path.

In fact, I became ever more cautious when it came to Rafael when I realized the increasing intensity of my reaction to him—how strongly I responded to his voice, his smile, his appreciative glance. I knew instinctively, if I gave myself wholeheartedly to him and our love did not endure, I would not survive another blow to my heart such as I had taken when leaving England and my first love. I could not face the risk of such devastation a second time.

Compared to dealing with Papa and Rafael, my professional life presented fewer challenges. I indulged in the dream that I had found a way to lead a simple life—as a healer.

Simple?

Two

SALERNO, 1205 CE

"Shabbat Shalom!" Greetings flew as we women hailed each other and settled in for Sabbath morning services, punctuated with a bit of gossip. It was a glorious spring, directly after our celebration of the Passover holiday. Even indoors, the day's brilliant sunshine, filtered through the stained-glass windows of the ancient synagogue, brightened our moods.

Sometimes obligations to my patients kept me from attending services, so I was grateful when I could. I gazed about at the other women from Salerno's Jewish community. They would have to rush home to oversee meals for their families. I had the leisure of going home to the simple meal Nina had prepared the day before and hurried home to set on the table before I, walking more leisurely, arrived.

The men's voices in prayer rose to the balcony where we women sat sequestered. Despite the *mechitza*, the intricately carved and painted wooden screen separating our section from the men's, I could easily see the weekly portion being read from the Torah scroll in front of the centrally placed altar, the bimah. We may have been separated from the main activity, but there was also much to observe in the women's section. Here we could show off our finery to our peers. The sumptuous fabrics of most of the ladies' clothing along with their sparkling jewels were meant to enhance the spirit of the day. I wondered how the display of wealth was supposed to support the spirituality of our prayers—one of the many questions I pondered as my mind persisted in wandering.

At the end of the Torah service, we always heard a sermon. Today, instead of one from our own revered rabbi, we had been told we would hear the words of a visitor. Glad for the novel distraction from my restless thoughts, I sat up straighter on the hard wooden bench and smiled in expectation.

At first glance, however, the guest speaker, a rumpled-looking man of some forty years, did not appear impressive. Small and wiry, dressed in shabby garments that were decidedly inappropriate for a Shabbat service, he regarded his listeners with a frown, as if affronted by a foul odor.

Our rabbi, however, presented the guest speaker as if he were visiting royalty. "We are indeed blessed to have Rabbi Isaac ben Shmuel from Egypt. There, he was a colleague of Rabbi Moses ben Maimon, our beloved departed Maimonides, *the Rambam*, revered by Jews everywhere. May his memory be a blessing."

A communal gasp of astonished delight greeted this announcement. Before his recent death, the Rambam had been court physician in service to the successors of the Saracen leader Saladin, an office that showed his greatness extended beyond the Jewish people. The Rambam was widely considered a genius for writing many works of great philosophical and scientific import, both for Jews and others. Because of this visitor's connection to the Rambam, I believed we all were now prepared to overlook the newcomer's appearance.

I admired the Rambam's erudition and, as a healer, had found his scientific works of great merit. As a Jew, I considered that much of his writing on the holy scriptures also had great merit. As a Jewish woman, however, I wished he could have done more for us.

Despite my mixed feelings, I was as thrilled as my neighbors to have a chance to hear the words of someone who actually had known and worked with the Rambam, expecting that our visitor might share some secret wisdom from the master. Perhaps while the Egyptian rabbi was here in Salerno, I would have a chance to find out more about the great man. *Too bad Papa is away from Salerno now, as I am sure he would be thrilled to hear this speaker.*

Once the visiting rabbi began to orate, however, my initial delight gave way to disappointment and worse. "Jews of Salerno," the little man thundered, "take this holy Shabbat to halt your evil ways and return to righteous paths! Or else prepare to suffer the worst punishments for your abominations!"

It was not unusual for a speaker to be understood by only a few congregants because we Jews spoke an assortment of languages in addition to Salernitan, the local vernacular. Our visitor addressed us in Arabic, a language that only a small number of Salerno's Jews understood well. A few gasps, this time of shock, greeted the rabbi's opening remarks. Silence followed by confused glances showed that some of the congregants had not understood what was said, only its effect on those who did. I had had the good fortune to learn Arabic. More was the pity—I wished I did not understand these particular utterances. The whispering explanations of those who did understand to those who had not led to more gasps of shock.

Rabbi ben Shmuel went on to explain how much he disapproved of the free and easy relations amongst the diverse groups in Salerno. "God commands in the holy Torah that we Jews must not take up the sinful ways of others, and yet you mingle with the non-Jews.

And it is to this immoral, unholy land that my wife ran, taking my children to live with her Christian lover, breaking up our family and our home." He nearly choked on the last word. "This vile pair knew they would have a warm reception in this city that defies all the laws of righteousness. Jews mixing with Gentiles is an abomination that God should destroy as He did Sodom and Gomorrah!" He waved his arms about like a madman swatting at a swarm of flies.

Dear Lord, please do not heed the unlovely and unloving words of this man. It appears his family tragedy has shocked him into unreason. Please continue to bless Salerno with peace and tolerance for all. The unhappy rabbi speaks from his ignorance of how wonderful this place is—even despite the challenges of the current day. He is clearly in pain, and he blindly blames others for his personal losses.

"What is he saying?" Nina pressed me to continue interpreting. Much as I sympathized with her desire to understand, I loathed filling her ears with such hatefulness. Nonetheless, I satisfied her need to hear the words and turned her day sour.

Abandoned at birth here in Salerno, Nina did not know which group her ancestors hailed from. Her coloring—olive skin, dark hair now tinged with silver, and big dark eyes—could have marked her as belonging to any of the groups in the Kingdom of Sicily. Yet it was a Jewish woman who had taken Nina in and raised her, so Nina came to identify with the Jews, converted formally, and was, as is the case with many converts, a most fervent member of our congregation. Though many people believed servants and their masters should sit in separate places, my relationship with Nina was yet another way I forged my own path.

"He does not like the way the groups here mix," I whispered. "He thinks Jews should interact only with Jews unless it is for unavoidable business."

She sniffed. "He clearly is a stranger. If he is here long enough, we shall set him straight."

I almost smiled at her optimism. I feared, however, that the rabbi would not be so open to revising his opinions. Though Salerno had traditionally been a place of peace and prosperity, in the past few years, changes had eroded these blessings. For me, the most immediate and obvious was the arrival of crusaders, the accursed "holy" warriors en route to and from the East, supposedly for reasons of faith.

As if he had heard my thoughts, the rabbi continued, "The crusaders are a curse to our people and whatever land they cross. They are our enemies, prepared to destroy us and everything that stands in their path."

I agree with him on this. Too bad he started off on the wrong foot by denouncing the Jews here. The crusaders who used Salerno as a stepping stone to the four Christian states of Outremer in the Middle East or a pass through on their way home were of the roughest, most ragtag type. The largest group here now was from a Crusade that had sacked Constantinople despite its being a Christian city. If even their fellow Christians were not safe, we Jews had good reason to fear them.

At least they had not destroyed our city—yet. From their base in a shabby camp on the outskirts, they committed acts of vandalism, robbery, and, according to horrified whispers, rape. And there seemed to be no way to stop them.

After the Hohenstaufen victory in 1195, Duke Henry, a relative of the Hohenstaufen family, had been granted his castle and title, subject to the court in Palermo, and the right to govern Salerno. Except for the crusaders, he had effectively kept the peace. When delegations from the different Salerno communities protested the crusaders' crimes, Duke Henry explained that political needs dictated he turn a blind eye. Since both Pope Innocent III and William of Capparone, regent of our young king, Frederick II, supported the crusaders, Salerno would suffer if we were seen as inhospitable.

Still, Duke Henry valued order and, therefore, advised us to be extra vigilant in staying out of our unwelcome visitors' way. He assured us any disturbance was only temporary—the foreign knights would eventually move on to other destinations. For our part, the citizens of Salerno, Jews and Gentiles alike, could only hope they would leave before they wrought too much more damage.

The rabbi's voice grew more forceful as he piled commands upon condemnations. "You must rid your land of this pestilence!"

If only. I wished he had taken the trouble to be informed about the political realities of our city before he spoke. And, of course, what power did we Jews have in such matters? In full ignorance, he went on with his tirade.

"It has come to my attention that some members of the Jewish community have allowed their daughters to be defiled by contact with the crusader scum. To any woman who has any such contact, I call down the wrath and curses of the Almighty on her and her family to seven generations!"

His voice reached such a fevered pitch, I expected him to bring down the roof upon his own head. And I, for one, would thank God for such a show of divine justice.

I heard whispered conversations, a loud hiss, and then one woman rose and shrieked, "No!" She fainted, landing across the laps of several other women. What could have caused this? Was it in reaction to something the rabbi said?

On the bimah, when the shriek was heard, the rabbi stopped for the briefest moment before blustering on. Had he any sense that he might have been the cause of the disturbance?

The stricken woman had fallen two rows in front of where I sat. My physician's instincts roused by her plight, I squeezed through the crowded pews to see how I could help. The women she lay upon were murmuring amongst themselves in surprise and discomfort.

Everyone there knew me to be a healer. The woman cradling the fainted lady's head in her lap slid over so I was able to sit beside her. I now recognized the woman who had fainted as Malka Freya, wife of Natan Mendoza, a leader of the Jewish community. I put my hand on her forehead to feel for fever, of which there was none. Slowly, she roused from her swoon.

"What is wrong?" I asked her. "Are you ill?"

She blinked several times and clutched her throat. She tried to speak but could not.

"Take your time. Breathe. Would you like a bowl of water?"

She frowned then found her voice, albeit a rasp. "Need you ask? Of course."

Her impatient tone told me she was returning to herself. I stroked her arm and saw her regain color. Her breaths became even. All indicators were good. She and I had become the center of attention in our section, which did not affect any further the activity on the bimah, where the rabbi had finished his address and where the cantor was now intoning the *Musaf* service—the additional service for Sabbath and festival days.

I squeezed her hand. "Can you tell me what happened? Why did you faint?"

She moaned. "That dreadful man said such horrible things. My daughter . . ." She tried to sit up but slipped back. Along with another lady, I helped her to sit and lean against the back of the bench. Then

Malka Freya snapped at me, "Forget what I said. Go away and leave me alone."

"With all due respect, Signora, you fainted. That is not something to be overlooked."

Two other women had slipped in next to her, one with a small bowl of water. Another member of the Mendoza family smiled in an unfriendly manner. "Your services are not needed any further. If my sister needs medical attention, I can care for her," a woman I recognized as Leah Sara Garcia said. Since she was one of the few other local women who had studied at the Scuola, I knew Malka Freya was in competent hands.

I returned to where Nina sat. "The Mendozas and the Garcias are so self-righteous," she muttered. "They are in with the duke, so they think they are quite grand. More important than us ordinary Jews."

This thought did not feel especially appropriate for our holy day. With an effort, I turned my mind back to the prescribed readings and prayers.

At the end of the service, we filed from the synagogue. As usual, Nina insisted on rushing home ahead of me to have food waiting on the table when I arrived. And, as usual, I appreciated having a few quiet moments to myself. However, nearly as soon as I stepped outside into the sunshine of the spring day and started toward my home, Rafael made his way to my side and began walking with me. Since he almost never attended services, I was surprised to see him.

"Why did you come to synagogue today?" I looked up at his face while raising a hand to shield my eyes from the bright light. With his tall form and thick dark hair graced with some strands of silver, he drew admiring glances from the women who passed us.

"Would you believe because I had heard that a disciple of the

Rambam would be speaking and I wanted to hear his words of wisdom?"

"Ah, the Egyptian rabbi. Not what you were expecting?" We shared a laugh.

"No. But all is not lost. I get to see you on this lovely Shabbat morning."

I could not help the smile that spread across my face. I was thirty years of age. Rafael, some fifteen years my senior and a long-time Salernitan, had become, over the course of ten years, my sometime adviser as well as my dearest friend. Of course, our relationship was far more complex than that word can describe. Though Jewish women and men were not meant to have close relationships other than those by blood or marriage, still, the two of us did.

Professionally, I often conferred on his translation projects. Rafael had not pursued a medical career and instead devoted himself to translating medical and scientific works into Hebrew. He was passionate about this work—and I shared his determination to keep the Hebrew language alive and vibrant by creating vocabulary to keep up with new knowledge.

Most of all, though, Rafael challenged me—my ways of thinking and how I looked at the world. The biggest challenge was where he actually coincided with community standards and I did not. Although often a rebel regarding much of Jewish practice and tradition, as a widower, he still firmly intended to marry me.

I cared for Rafael, of course. How could I not? He was a lovely man, with wonderful qualities. Many women would be happy to accept him as a husband. Widows. Maybe even younger women. But, as unrealistic as the possibilities might be, my English knight still had my heart. Not that I had ever told Rafael about this. I merely turned him down whenever he proposed and encouraged him to stop proposing. Yet, he persisted. And of course Papa made no secret of his desire to have Rafael as his son-in-law.

From time to time, I wondered how I would feel if Rafael did take another woman for his wife. Certainly, we would no longer be able to have the close friendship I cherished. So far, I had not had to face such a disturbing possibility. Deep down, I hoped that would never happen.

After the intensity of the worship services, we strolled at a leisurely pace in the warmth of the day. He asked, "What happened up in the women's section?"

"Oh, so you heard that? I did not think you men paid attention to what went on in the clouds, where our balcony perches."

He chuckled. "Even hidden away as we try to keep you, we have great curiosity about what goes on amongst you womenfolk. We heard a noise that almost sounded like a scuffle. Did you ladies come to blows while the Egyptian rabbi chastised us all?"

I winced at the recollection. "The rabbi's words so affected one woman that she fainted."

"Really? How fascinating. I suspect the incendiary rabbi would be thrilled to know his words had such a strong effect."

I nodded. "I never learned what caused her extreme reaction, though before she came fully around, she did make mention of a daughter. Alas, she and her family were less than eager for me to explore the cause of her fainting once she came to, so any opinion I might have is a guess."

"Ah. And may I ask who our fainter was?"

I shook my head. "Though she is not my patient, I feel bound by notions of confidentiality, so I will not say. I expect the episode will bring forth a torrent of gossip, so you will probably soon know. But not from me."

He stopped abruptly and looked at me full face. "Was it one of the Mendoza women? I saw several members of that family leave the synagogue in greater haste than usual."

"Please do not ask me any more questions on this topic."

"All right. As you say, the gossip will soon make short work of secrecy, though the Mendozas are adept at keeping quiet what they want to."

"As are most families, I think."

"Perhaps." He shrugged, and we resumed walking toward my house. "So, what did you think of the rabbi from Egypt?"

I let out a deep breath. "To be honest, like you, I was more impressed before he began to speak. Although I certainly agree with his assessment of the crusaders, as to his opinions of Salerno, I believe he was speaking from personal pain about his family. Worst of all, his ignorance in that area made it difficult to hear his thoughts on other topics."

He nodded. "Pity about that. I have to agree regarding his unfortunate sermon, yet there is more to the man. There must be, for he could not have worked with the Rambam without having some substance and also without having learned something."

"Perhaps the rabbi was a better man before he lost his family." I shook my head. "I would hope you are correct and that in the near future we will benefit from what he has learned." Especially on a day like this, I tried to have a positive view of my fellow beings.

"I wanted to talk to him about several of the medical pieces the Rambam wrote in Arabic—of course, the *Regimen Sanitis*—the *Guide to Good Health*. But my next project will be to translate into Hebrew the *Treatise on Cohabitation*, which is said to include recipes for aphrodisiacs and anti-aphrodisiacs. This was supposed to be the Rambam's treatise of sexual advice to the sultan's son. I am hoping the Egyptian rabbi can give me valuable insight because he knew all the people involved."

I stopped and glared at him. "What? Why will you translate *that* work next? There are so many other medical and scientific texts of greater importance to translate into Hebrew before you turn your attention to that one. Why not the *Guide to Good Health* first?"

Rafael held up his hands as if to stop my words. "All will get done in good time. But I figure this one is timely to do while I have access to the Egyptian rabbi, who might provide extra information about the Rambam. Though now that I have actually heard the man, I have some doubts—"

"You are not listening, Rafael. I do not believe this piece has sufficient merit to take precedence and be translated first—" I needed to put forth effort to express my argument calmly.

He continued not to listen. "It would definitely be challenging. Especially since the Hebrew patois lacks the precise vocabulary for a full translation. We would once again have to create new vocabulary that accords with the rules of the language."

When he got caught up in a project, it was difficult to get through to him. Then his words caught up with me. "We?"

His smile lit up his face. "Oh, yes. I definitely want to include you with your knowledge of medicine and languages."

"You also trained as a physician," I pointed out.

"Yes, but my studies are far in the past, and because I have not practiced medicine recently, what I learned is most likely less useful."

"Of course I shall be willing to help if I can, though as I said, I have misgivings as to your choice." Despite my concerns that this work would displace others more worthy of being translated sooner, his project did pique my curiosity.

"I hope to convince you these misgivings are misplaced. And, of course, I will once again look to the Mendozas for involvement, including funding. They are committed to advancing the Hebrew language with a variety of topics and have been most generous in the past."

"I hope you get your funding, though I reserve judgment on this piece of writing." By now, we had arrived at my house, although Rafael seemed reluctant to say goodbye.

"Thank you for being willing to consider this project. Something to look forward to." After a slight pause, he went on, "Who knows? By next year at this time, you may have finally consented to be my wife, and our walk after services will be to *our* house."

"I expect not," I said. "Perhaps by next year at this time, Rafael Lopes Dias, you will have learned to appreciate me as your friend and your colleague for translation and be satisfied with that."

Nina, who must have been looking out the window, opened the door as we approached and then stood back. Before I entered my house, I heard Rafael's words quite clearly. "I expect not."

Three

Never in the dreams of my younger years had I imagined that I might be asked to teach after completing my own education. So when this honor was offered to me, I humbly accepted. However, much as I loved sharing my knowledge with students, the work of engaging with all their eager minds took a great deal of energy. On Tuesday, I had forgotten about the disturbance at services the previous Shabbat. As I was returning home from a worthwhile but intensive session after tutoring one of my students, I found Nina quite fretful.

"What is it?"

"Signor Lopes Dias has been waiting for you. He is in the parlor, anxious to tell you of some grave matter."

Abandoning my plans for a quiet evening alone, I rushed in to him. Might his visit be related to the meeting held the previous evening about translating the Rambam's piece? I had gone with Rafael, despite my misgivings about his proposed project, in part because I hoped these possible funders would convince Rafael to choose a different topic. He had set up the meeting with the wealthiest supporters, Baruch and Natan Mendoza, and also with the Egyptian rabbi. It quickly became clear that the rabbi would not consent to my presence. When Rafael refused to ask me to leave, the rabbi stormed out, and our discussion came to an end.

Had something about the project changed? Had Rafael convinced the Egyptian rabbi to allow me to participate? Surely Rafael would not agree to the rabbi's demands without speaking to me first, would he? Pacing like a caged wild boar, Rafael looked ready to burst. I had never before seen him so agitated.

When he saw me, he put his hands on my shoulders. Rafael and I did not follow the Jewish dictates that strictly governed how and when men and women could touch, but this abrupt contact startled me.

"What is it?"

"Prepare yourself to be shocked."

"Tell me."

"The duke's guards have taken the Egyptian rabbi into custody." His words came out in a rush.

"What? Why? What does that mean?"

He took a deep breath. "He has been arrested and is now imprisoned in the duke's dungeon." He then seemed to realize he was clutching my shoulders tightly and released his hold.

"Why?" I shook my head. "Verily, this must be some mistake. Only people who have committed a crime are imprisoned."

He scrubbed a hand over his face. "Unbelievably, he is accused of having murdered a crusader." He swallowed hard.

It took a moment to glean any sense from his words. "Accused of murdering a crusader? The little rabbi?" I must have misheard.

He held both hands up to demonstrate his own bafflement. "I cannot believe it either. The Egyptian rabbi was found in a Frankish tavern holding a knife stained with blood and standing over the corpse of a crusader."

"Impossible," I whispered. "Rabbis do not murder, not even crusaders. It is always the opposite."

Rafael snorted and shook his head. "A crusader has been murdered in Salerno. Once people hear the accusation against the rabbi, let us hope the duke can prevent a pogrom against us Jews. I have heard that a spokesman for the crusaders has already demanded that the duke act quickly to provide justice in this case. Meaning, the punishment must be visible and harsh and swift. The spokesman invoked the support of the pope and the king's regent. This is trouble that can destroy our community. From the crusaders or from our non-Jewish neighbors. Or both."

"The situation is surely not so bad as to threaten our good relations with other Salernitans?" I half-asked, half-stated.

He pursed his lips and shook his head. "It is so bad. The Mendoza brothers are conferring with the duke in the hope of protecting the Jewish community."

I shivered. "Even here in Salerno our sense of safety is so thin? A false accusation can put a whole community at risk?"

He sighed. "We need to be vigilant and prepared, the best we can. We have seen often enough in the past how little it takes for those we felt some ease with to become our enemies. We cannot take for granted that any group will not turn against us."

His words reawakened my insecurities. Had I not seen what happened in England?

"Is there anything we can do?" The worst would be to feel utterly helpless.

Rafael nodded. "We have to do two things at once. First, we must secure the duke's support to keep our people safe. Second, we must solve the crime so justice is done and the rabbi freed."

How could I help in either? "Neither is a small task."

"True. Most importantly, we must not lose sight of who we are and of what we value. We cannot allow the rabbi to endure injustice." He began to pace again. "Though he came as a stranger, he is now part of the Jewish community that we must safeguard. Even if our Salernitan neighbors do not rise against us, the crusaders are more than capable of staging pogroms, as they have proven too many times elsewhere. And since it was one of their number who was murdered . . ." he trailed off, the implication obvious.

"How do we start?"

"I will go to the castle as soon as I can to meet with the duke to determine more directly his view of all this and, hopefully, help him see he must look for the real murderer. As you know, on several occasions I have been able to provide His Grace with translations of Arabic documents that were highly helpful for matters of state, for which he has indicated great gratitude. Thus he has granted me the privilege of having access to him. I shall also find out how the negotiations are going with the Mendozas. We Jews must present ourselves as united on the issue of justice for Rabbi Isaac ben Shmuel. Otherwise, he is subject to a swift trial and execution in Palermo."

"Trial and execution? Are you not jumping ahead? What if he is innocent? Not what if. He *must* be innocent. Nothing else is possible."

Rafael's sad, harsh laugh chilled me. "Given that he is being held in the dungeon, the rabbi is lucky if he lives long enough to go to trial."

I shivered at this dire prediction. "This is insane. How could the Egyptian rabbi have killed a crusader? He is no warrior. And why? Although he hates the crusaders, that does not mean he goes around killing them. Killing anyone."

"Innocence of the crime may have little effect on the outcome of this case." Rafael's voice sounded flat. "Not when those in power have a suspect they consider suitable."

I shook my head. "Clearly Duke Henry has the wrong suspect. We must convince him. He will not have his guards search for the real murderer if he believes he already has him."

Rafael made a harsh noise. "Consider all this, Rebecca. As I said, the rabbi was in a *Frankish* tavern, a place frequented only by crusaders. The rabbi was found near the dead crusader, who was stabbed several times. It must be that the real killer dropped the knife to the ground, and then, for some reason, the rabbi must have happened along right then. Who knows, maybe he got lost. He is, after all, a newcomer. Then for some even more unknown reason, he picked up the knife and was standing by the body when the duke's guards arrived."

I could not believe my ears. "Something is very wrong. In his sermon he condemned any mixing with Gentiles. Why then was he in a place frequented by the ungodly, unclean Frankish?"

"I agree, not that my opinion matters." Rafael ran a hand over his eyes. "But we have to look at the situation from other views. The duke is in a difficult position. He normally does not have to deal with Jewish criminals or crime amongst us. Any time there is trouble within our community, he is more than happy to let our rabbi or other leaders handle the matter. However, this being a crusader's death complicates everything. Since the king's regent and the pope are politically allied to fully support the crusaders, the duke must act quickly. Either that, or Salerno will again face retribution from powerful outside forces. That murder must be expiated very soon in a very visible, very public way."

"Does the duke not have some obligation to uphold justice? And the regent and the pope, for that matter?" My voice cracked with indignation.

Brow raised, Rafael studied me for a moment. "Are you really asking such a naïve question?" His expression was kinder than his words.

Of course not. I know better. "So now we have to go to great effort to save the ill-mannered Egyptian rabbi and ward off any vengeance that may spawn pogroms." I shook my head in an effort to bring order to my thoughts.

Rafael's laugh contained no amusement. "There is the added matter of the so-called relics."

"Relics? What do you mean?"

He shook his head. "Evidently, along with sacking Constantinople, many of the crusaders looted the churches and other sites for objects, said to come from the bodies or possessions of saints. As they are highly sought by priests and other holy men, some fetch a high price."

I tried to understand Rafael. "How does this relate to the accusation of the rabbi?"

"I have heard speculation that the rabbi was involved in some sort of dispute over such merchandise, hence motivating the murder."

"The rabbi was involved with trafficking such goods?"

"You know the reputation we Jews have in such matters. The duke and his followers, and indeed all the Gentiles, do not see the rabbi as a holy man, but merely as a Jew. He is the object of the same prejudices as are all of us."

Rafael was, of course, correct. Had I not witnessed my father laboring under similar ugliness during his many years as a merchant? How often he had been accused of baseness and worse.

I wanted to weep that we were now encountering the all too familiar accusations and offenses against us Jews in this once more amiable, tolerant place. However, even with regard to the most fundamental laws, our society was in a constant state of flux. The Kingdom of Sicily, long a crossroads for conquest, had flourished under each previous conquering power. Byzantines conquered the early Latins and Jews, and they in turn were upended by the North African Moslems. While a band of Normans, led by William, was conquering England, another group of Normans, under a leader named Roger, laid claim to Sicily—with much happier results for its existing residents. Whereas William's royal Norman descendants such as Richard, the Lion Heart, and his brother John tried to eradicate all traces of what came before, the Norman conquerors of Sicily treasured and preserved the best of what was here, leading to a relatively peaceful and culturally rich time.

Then Henry VI, the Hohenstaufen Holy Roman Emperor, defeated Sicily's Normans. When he died, his young son by Queen Constance of Sicily's royal house ascended to the throne, and Sicily found itself under the control of a regent, William of Capparone. Unfortunately, the latest conquest brought new nobles and soldiers from Henry VI's lands, men with little regard for Sicily's traditions of tolerance, and so we in Salerno were now subject to this new regime's justice.

"I still do not know how I can help."

"For now, take tonight to reflect. Tomorrow morning, we will visit the rabbi in the dungeon and get whatever information we can get from him. We will also bring him food and supplies. After all, I doubt the hospitality of the duke's dungeon extends to providing food acceptable under our codes."

Curfew had sounded by the church bells. Until now, the curfew had not been strictly observed by anyone. But now, at such an unsettled time, I hoped Rafael would not encounter trouble as he went out and about.

Once he departed, I asked Nina to organize a package with sustenance for the Egyptian rabbi. He would refuse to eat anything the prison provided because it would certainly not be kosher. As

I thought more about the rabbi in the dungeon, I realized I knew nothing of how a prisoner there would fare. Clothing? Furnishings? Was there a bed in the cell? And what—if any—facilities were there for hygiene?

How astonishing that I had never considered the details of imprisonment. Papa, who had been imprisoned several times in England, refused ever to talk about those experiences. Not wishing to cause him pain, I never pressed the point. I also remembered being in England at the time of King Richard's brutal imprisonment—at the hands of the same nobility who now had custody of Rabbi Isaac ben Shmuel.

My skin crawled as I imagined the horror he might be facing, and then I stopped myself. No sense spinning tales that might have no connection to reality. Tomorrow, I would join Rafael on a visit to the dungeon and see the rabbi's condition for myself and, I hoped, be able to alleviate it somewhat.

⁂

After a difficult night during which I woke several times, I eased my way out of bed and braced myself for the day ahead.

With the basket of food prepared by a distraught Nina—enough for three days, which was, we hoped, more than the rabbi would need—we set off. Rafael's servant Manuel, a small, quiet man of about forty years, drove Rafael's carriage to the duke's castle. Rafael and I sat under the shade cover on the bench seat behind Manuel.

I shivered despite the warmth of the day. Never in my life had I imagined I would approach this imposing castle for any purpose, let alone that I would be bringing food to a member of the Jewish community in its dungeon. When we stepped down off the wagon and sought entry via the castle's massive portal, the attendant demanded, "What is your business here?"

Rafael spoke in a neutral tone. "Good day. We are here seeking access to Rabbi Isaac ben Shmuel, lately of Egypt, who has been detained in the prison quarters."

"You must speak to the duty guard. Follow me." The man led us briskly ahead, across the grand entry to a smaller room that was partitioned off.

I bowed my head in thanks as the attendant showed us into the room. Today, I had chosen to cover my hair in an ordinary white wimple and to wear the simplest linen garment I owned. I wore these clothes for comfort and to give myself an air of plainness. The man who led us indicated we should be seated in low chairs. Our guide whispered a few words to the guard.

"You are inquiring about the Egyptian Jew, Isaac ben Shmuel. Is this correct?" He directed his question at Rafael.

"I have conferred with the duke on this matter, which is why we are here. We have been told we can bring the prisoner food and supplies and see how he fares."

"Who is the woman? Your wife? The wife of the prisoner?"

"No. I am a physician and a colleague of Signor Lopes Dias." I spoke before Rafael had a chance to respond.

The guard looked bored. "Since you have the permission of Duke Henry, you and the *lady* physician can bring the prisoner food and such, which, of course, we must first examine."

"Why do you have to do that? We will tell you exactly what we are bringing," I said. The idea of his going through Nina's provisions revolted me.

He actually laughed. "Perhaps you can explain reality to this woman," he said to Rafael. "I have no more time to waste."

Rafael signaled me to remain silent, which I did at great cost to the balance of my humors. The guard carried the package to a small table and, with a distinct but unsurprising lack of fastidiousness, pawed his way through the bread, cheese, fruits, and wine, putting aside a goodly portion of each, his eyes gleaming with gluttonous desire. At least he left the small pile of linens and clothing alone.

"You do know there is a toll to be paid for the service I have provided."

"What service?" I asked and then bit my lip. Not only was he going to maul the goods we brought, he would steal from us too. Steal from the rabbi, who was in need of these supplies.

Rafael shook his head slightly. Too bad I did not bite my lip sooner. The guard's eyes sparked anger before he resumed an attitude of disinterested smugness. "I am only trying to accommodate you and the prisoner. If I must continue to dispute with you, the toll will go up to three quarters of the goods. I am not about to haggle with *Jews*."

I bristled at that, and I knew Rafael burned hot at the insult. However, poised where we were, with the rabbi in the dungeon, a Jew under suspicion of a crime, we had to tread with wariness. I hated this.

I clamped my lips tight. If this blackguard continued to extort from us, we would go to the rabbi empty-handed. Or, worse, we might not even get in to see him. In the future, I would know better how to comport myself. Having helped himself to a generous portion of all we had brought, the guard sloppily closed the bundle, which he thrust back at Rafael as if bestowing a great gift, and "escorted" us to the cell where the rabbi languished. The guard unlocked the entry and ushered us in. "When I return shortly, you will have to leave."

The rabbi, who did not convey much of a figure even when preaching on the bimah in the synagogue, now looked exhausted to the point of illness. Though he came from a place where people's skins were dark from the touch of the sun, his skin appeared nearly as gray as his beard and the bit of hair on his head. His eyes were dull, almost lifeless. I wanted to examine him for any signs of disease with the hope that I could treat him if needed, but I knew better. Surely a strict adherent to all the Jewish teachings about touch between men and women, he would recoil from contact with me.

I had a penchant to diagnose people based on which of the humors their behavior exhibited, though this was not, strictly speaking, an exact science or even good practice—especially since I scarcely knew the man. However, following in the footsteps of the great ancient physicians Hippocrates and Galen, I believed knowledge of the four humors could be useful in helping understand people. Though it could be difficult to classify some whose particular behavior might result from a strange combination of the humors, others were easy.

So, even without an actual examination, I could see some aspects of the rabbi's condition. Rabbi Isaac ben Shmuel was clearly a melancholic, relating to the element earth, and prone to moodiness and severe unhappiness. Of course, his current state was certainly influenced by the recent traumas in his life—including the need to quit his homeland. My instincts told me, though, he would have exhibited gloom and discontent even in the midst of joyous celebration. A melancholic, by nature cold and dry, he had a preponderance of black bile.

In addition to depression, people of this type were, at the extreme, prone to being cowardly and envious. I believed in the need for balance to deal with one's humors. So, with proper diet and appropriate clothing, the rabbi might be able to achieve the healthy balance needed for a satisfactory life. Clearly, that would not happen at present with him in prison and at so great a risk.

In any case, I would have had to be a dreamer to imagine the rabbi would listen to advice from a female physician. I wondered if

Rafael, almost entirely choleric in his nature—yellow bile, hot and dry, related to the element fire, prone to belligerence and irritability—shared in my observations. At least with Rafael, I had been able to help him toward moderation and balance, especially with food suggestions to his servant, Manuel.

Trying to put the best possible face on our current situation, I placed the now paltry bundle of food down on the pile of straw, belatedly realizing it must serve as the rabbi's bed. I hoped it did not shelter many vermin.

"The guard helped himself to the greater portion of what we brought for you," Rafael said when the rabbi looked askance at the sloppy bundle.

"Thank you for even this meager meal. I have had nothing to eat or drink since—" he trailed off. "Thanks be to *Hashem* that the guard did not take it all." His voice was a mere whisper, hoarse and thin.

"So the guard assured us," Rafael continued.

There was nowhere to sit in the cell except the straw or the ground. The place smelled of damp and far worse. I shivered.

"How are you managing? This is awful," Rafael said, then shook his head. *So much for wanting to help the rabbi remain of good cheer.*

"I thank you for your kindness." The rabbi looked mostly at Rafael but with a sideways glance or two at me. "Never did I dream that this could happen to me." He shook his head. His hand brushed away what might have been a tear—or a bedbug. "Will this miserable hole in the ground be my last abode in this world?" he continued in a choked voice.

"Rabbi, we hope not. But we have to get you out of here," Rafael said. "The best way to do that is to know the truth. Once we find the true murderer, then you can go free. Can you tell us how you came to be with the crusader and holding the knife in your hand?"

Rabbi Isaac ben Shmuel grew paler and shook his head. "I cannot tell you that," he rasped.

Great. How were we supposed to solve this crime and save his life if he would not answer our questions? I started to speak, but Rafael quickly signaled me to be quiet.

"What *can* you tell us?" Rafael asked. "Were you really in that place with the crusader?"

"This I can tell you. God forgive me for my sin—I *was* at the accursed place with the accursed crusader," he hissed. "He should only burn in Gehenna forever with all the rest of his putrid companions. And the Good Lord should only forgive me for my folly for being with the unclean."

His admission took me aback. So he had been with the crusader intentionally, not merely passed by at the wrong moment. But why?

"Where were you exactly?" Rafael maintained a calm tone. "And what did you see?"

The rabbi closed his eyes and trembled. "At the *Frankish tavern*." He said that last phrase as if it might as well have been the lowest cesspit of a brothel. A rabbi intentionally going to a Frankish crusader tavern? What was our world coming to?

Rafael winced but kept his face neutral. "You were at the tavern and became involved in a conversation with a Frankish crusader? Why?"

The rabbi shook his head. "As I have already stated, I cannot tell you more than this. I can never tell you." His voice now faded away, not at all like the thundering tone of his sermon.

"Tell us what you can of what happened."

"I was talking with the crusader, may his kin be cursed to seven generations. At a table outside the tavern, a distance from the others. He had a drink. Of course, I partook of nothing in that filthy place.

Suddenly, someone jumped on him and stabbed him with a knife. Someone hidden in a cloak who let forth an unearthly shriek and dropped the knife to the ground with a clatter." He grimaced and shook his head.

"Then, as I tried to take in what I saw, another cloaked figure drew the first away. In confusion and shock, I picked up the knife. A thing dripping blood I should never have touched." His face contorted into a frown of disgust. "At that exact moment, the duke's guards fell upon me and arrested me."

We sat in stunned silence. I had a thousand questions, and I expected Rafael did too. Yet no one said anything.

Hands trembling, the rabbi took the cork from the remaining small jug of wine the guard had not confiscated, mumbled a blessing, and took a long draught. Though the guard had taken the largest of the loaves of bread, the rabbi intoned another blessing and bit hungrily into one of the others and sighed. Then, with a dirty, shaking hand, he brushed crumbs from his lips and beard.

Rafael paced in the small space. "From the duke's point of view, for political reasons, the murder of the crusader must be expiated promptly. You might not be aware, Rabbi, but these warriors have the support of the regent and the pope."

He groaned. "That does not surprise me. There are politics everywhere, whether the leaders are Christian or Moslem. Still, I did not kill the man. I did not murder. I would never murder anyone." His voice broke. "The cloaked figures—"

Rafael snorted. "A mysterious cloaked figure who came out of the dark and stabbed a man with such force as to kill him, dropped the knife to the ground a moment later. Another mysterious figure drew the first away. And then a third person, standing over the dead one, knife in hand, claims he is innocent." He shook his head. "The magistra and I believe you and will try to help you. We will seek others to join in this effort. You must understand, though, it is difficult for some to lend credence to such a tale. The duke, for one, refuses to entertain the possibility of your innocence."

"It is the truth," the rabbi said softly.

"It still does not supply a reason as to why you were there, with that person, at that time, in a place where no Jews, let alone rabbis, tarry," Rafael explained in a most reasonable tone. "If you can tell us this, perhaps the duke will listen. As to the rest, let us face the situation squarely, Rabbi. The crusaders are our enemies. Even among the Jewish community, you have not made many friends here in Salerno. It will not be simple to see justice done."

"I have good reason to be angry with this city, with your claims of tolerance and acceptance," he muttered. "Even with the Jews."

At that moment, and on that ominous note, the guard demanded we end our visit.

Four

After we left the dungeon, Rafael escorted me back to my house where, before anything else, we washed the filth from our hands. Then, over mint tea, we discussed the precious little we had learned.

Rafael's expression was grim. "As if we did not face enough challenges, the rabbi is not helping at all by refusing to tell us the whole truth about what happened."

I set my cup down. "Do you think it is at all possible that, God forbid, he actually did murder the crusader? That he is making up this tale of mysterious cloaked figures looming out of the dark?" My instinct told me that his story was so preposterous, it just might be true.

My friend made a face. "No. Whatever else he might be, the rabbi is not a killer. Unlikely as his tale sounds, I believe someone else murdered the crusader, although the fact of the rabbi even being at that tavern adds a layer of confusion."

Rafael leaned back in his chair. "It will be difficult to convince the duke to look elsewhere. I did not tell you this before, but it appears the Mendozas are in agreement with His Grace. I was hoping to convince them otherwise, though I have as yet not been able to."

"You mean they think the rabbi committed the murder?"

He nodded. "The whole tenor of the Mendozas' discussions with the duke is about ensuring that the situation be handled swiftly, in a manner suitable to safeguarding the Jewish community. To see the rabbi convicted and executed, and thus to close the books on this matter."

"At the expense of truth and justice?" I cried. "This goes against our values. As written in our Torah: 'Justice, justice shalt thou pursue.'"

He reached out and placed his hand on mine, providing welcome comfort. "I agree and told them so, even before we saw the rabbi. They argue that we must be practical, that the lives of the many outweigh the life of one man. Especially when that man is an unappealing, uninvited stranger."

I shook my head at the enormity of the wrong direction my community's leaders were choosing. How could we allow such a lapse in our pursuit of what is right?

Rafael continued, "Frankly, we are alone in this battle. To my knowledge, other than us, the Egyptian rabbi does not have even one supporter in our community."

"He is a stranger alone," I pointed out. "How often we have lamented our ill treatment when we were such. Our Torah requires us to treat wayfarers with kindness because 'we were strangers in a land not ours'. If only he had not preached that sermon."

He nodded. "That sermon! Yes, usually, his being a newcomer would count in his favor."

"I am committed to seeing truth and justice served with the rabbi cleared, even if the man makes caring about him a challenge."

Rafael touched my hair where it had slipped out from under the wimple. "You are a very caring woman. The rabbi at least has the good fortune of your support."

I warmed to the compliment and blushed. "And yours," I murmured.

"Usually it would be a simple matter to unite the community in the pursuit of the truth and of justice. Alas, this time, the politics of our people here is against us. And in addition to his sermon, the rabbi has quarreled with several people in his short sojourn here, as he did with us on the matter of the translation. He has set the Mendozas against him, and they are powerful foes." He shook his head.

"He did not limit his contretemps to arguments but also made threats and appeared more than ready to cause trouble for anyone not in agreement with his rigid ideas. And then he was permitted to give his sermon, even though our rabbi warned him it would not be well received."

I was taken aback. "So *our* rabbi was not surprised by the tirade. I wish he had found a way to prepare us or, even better, to deter the visitor." I wondered if our visitor had such trouble getting along in his native land, and then an idea struck me. "Do you think we should send a messenger to the sultan's court in Egypt? Perhaps someone there can come to help."

Rafael pondered momentarily and then shook his head again. "In usual circumstances, I would say yes, if we could dispatch a messenger quickly. However, I have heard the rabbi was forced to leave after the death of the Rambam."

"If I did not know better, I could almost believe he is trying to bring punishment down upon himself. Yet he says he did not commit the murder. Of course, I have sympathy for him as I would for any prisoner in that foul place. But his difficult personality and lack of candor make it so difficult to help him."

"There are those who might believe that, in precisely such cases, it is even more imperative to seek justice." Rafael's voice was barely above a whisper.

"Tempting as it would be to debate intellectually the morality of these circumstances, we need to focus on solving this crime. I do not expect the duke and his men to provide any assistance for that."

Rafael scrubbed a hand across his chin. "None at all, since the duke is satisfied his men have caught the killer, and he can fend off pressure from the regent and the pope. And with the agreement of the Mendozas, he can feel confident that the Jewish community will not object."

"All right," I said. "You have summed up several almost insurmountable obstacles. Any ideas of how to make progress toward our goals?"

He smiled despite the gloom. "I can always count on you, Rebecca, to keep things clear."

A compliment I was happy to accept. Clarity should lead to solutions, should it not?

He thought for a moment, then his eyes lit up. "One of my apprentice translators might help."

"Which apprentice? Why do you think he might be of help?"

"I think you have not met him, in part because he is often busy with many jobs. Moshe ben Shlomo is very smart and very poor. If I remember correctly, he is originally from Egypt. Maybe he knows something of Rabbi Isaac ben Shmuel that can help."

"How do we contact him?"

"Not so easy because he has no actual home. I understand he often sleeps in the bread bakery near the school of medicine. His payment for helping with the baking is shelter in the kitchen when the weather is too inclement for him to sleep under the stars."

"He is that poor? Why not invite him to stay with you? You have extra room."

Rafael huffed. "Do you not know me better than that? Of course I have invited him. Numerous times, especially when we have a spell of harsh weather."

"So?"

"So, along with being very smart and very poor, Moshe ben Shlomo is extremely proud. He refuses any offer of what he considers charity."

"Have you worked with him much?"

Rafael shook his head. "No, but he made a strong impression. Let us try to talk with him tonight."

❦

It was quite late when Rafael and I went to the bakery most of the Jewish community frequented for bread and challah. The shortest way there, as well as to the school of medicine, was to cut through the Greek section, which dated back to before the arrival of the Normans. As we walked through the dark, empty streets, we made plans.

"Will the bakery not be closed and empty so late?" I asked.

"Closed, yes. Yet from what I understand, not empty. Evidently, there are people besides ben Shlomo who spend the night there, at least some of the time."

In another few minutes, we were at the bakery's entry. Our first taps brought no response, but we were not about to give up and so grew more spirited in our attempts. Finally, a tired, ill-tempered man came to the door and cracked it open.

"Do you not know we are sleeping? We have to get up early to bake, so disturbing our sleep is wrong. Why do you do so? Be quick."

We apologized, and then Rafael said, "We must locate Moshe ben Shlomo immediately. I understand he sometimes stays here with you."

"Only when it rains," the baker barked back. "Does it look like a rainy night to you?" He gumbled about annoying people as he started to close the door.

I insinuated myself into the doorway before he could bar it. Even now, when the ovens stood idle, the delicious aroma of good baking perfumed the air. Unfortunately, the sweetness of the surroundings appeared to have little effect on the mood of this inhabitant of the place.

"Signor, please listen. We would not bother you if it were not critical. Please, can you give us any idea where we might find the young man tonight?"

The baker glared at us. "Who are you and why are you bothering good, honest folk at night? You say it is urgent, but if you ask me, there is only one kind of business that would send a woman out on the street at night."

His accusation distressed Rafael, who pulled me back and physically put his body between mine and the baker's, as if that would protect me from his slanderous words. Then in several terse sentences, Rafael outlined the situation.

"Leave me out of the duke's business," the baker said, "but I will tell you this. Young Moshe will be here before dawn to help fire up the oven and bake the bread. Come back then."

I was about to protest when Rafael forestalled my response. "We have done all we can for tonight. We shall return to the bakery then to meet with ben Shlomo."

⁂

Back home, I had scarcely fallen asleep when it was time to rise. In the early morning chill, Rafael, who had also returned to his home for a brief rest, and I rushed to the bakery. I was grateful to have the warmth of a beautiful blue wool cloak Rafael had brought back for me from a voyage to France. So soft and warm, often too warm for our mild climate, though perfect now. *Rafael.* I smiled at him even though it was too dark for him to see. Later that morning, he and I would take more food and other supplies to the rabbi. Suddenly, my days were filled with spending time with Rafael, a surprisingly pleasant circumstance to come out of this terrible occurrence.

As we neared the bakery, we reviewed the questions to ask Moshe ben Shlomo. When we reached our destination, we could see the lamps lit inside. Soon, the bakers would be preparing loaves of bread and pastries for Salerno's Jews. Another stab of sadness sliced through me. The rhythms of ordinary life never seemed so sweet as when disrupted. Even Rafael, doubter though he was, loved the rituals and symbols of our faith that gave a texture and flavor to our days.

Once again, we knocked at the door, this time with immediate results. A pale young girl opened the door a bit.

"You are too early for bread, my lady." She lowered her eyes.

"We spoke with a man here last night. We are looking for Moshe ben Shlomo, who I understand works here."

"Ah, yes. My uncle told me about you. Moshe ben Shlomo is at the ovens, helping to light them for the day. Then he helps with the bread. You cannot talk to him until the dough is mixed."

It would not do to fluster this child further or argue with her. "Very well. But my companion and I are cold. Might we come in while we wait to speak with him?"

She turned and called to someone for permission, which, thankfully, was soon forthcoming. Rafael and I slipped into the warm room where, despite sitting on a hard bench, both of us began to doze.

"I understand you are asking for me." A male voice brought me out of my stupor. Rafael was already awake beside me, and I realized my head had drooped sideways onto his shoulder. I sat up straight and tried to regain a sense of decorum.

In the dim light of the room, I could hardly make out the features of the tall young man except that he had a dark beard.

Rafael spoke, "Is it you, ben Shlomo?"

"Who is asking for me?"

"It is I, the translator Rafael Lopes Dias." Rafael stood up and then reached down and took my hand, drawing me to my feet. "And my companion, the magistra, Rebecca."

As my eyes grew accustomed to dimness, I saw ben Shlomo's brow crease with suspicion. "Signor Lopes Dias, why have you come here now?"

"On a matter of utmost importance. The Egyptian rabbi, Isaac ben Shmuel, has been charged and arrested for the murder of a crusader, and the magistra and I are trying to clear him of the charges."

The young man peered at us with a look that seemed to be assessing us. After a pause he seemed to have made up his mind and so spoke. "So the rumors of the murder and his arrest are true."

"Yes. The bad news has traveled."

He snorted with disgust. "Do you think any sort of news remains quiet for long? This rabbi has made such a strong first impression everywhere he has gone. To be seen with a crusader who was murdered! There are many in the community who would not be unhappy to see you fail in your attempt to help him."

"Then part of our task is to show our fellow Jews why they should pray we do not fail. Let us hope, for all our sakes, that our community comes through this difficulty unharmed. If a Jew, even a disliked stranger, is found guilty of a crime he did not commit, all in our entire community—even those who feel too powerful to be vulnerable—are at risk."

His face seemed to harden. "I do not have much time now. What is it you want from me?"

Rafael looked the young man in the eye. "We hope you might be able to provide information about the rabbi because you also come from Egypt. Do you have any idea why he would be uncooperative in helping us to help him? Also, who might be involved in this murder?"

The ghost of a smile animated his face. "I am from Egypt, yes, but left when I was very young. My family had little involvement with the court or the Rambam or any of the rabbis who flocked around him. That said, I have a dim memory that this accused rabbi was known for his meekness."

"Hmm, that is certainly not his behavior now. Did you have any contact with the rabbi after he arrived here in Salerno?" I asked.

"No. There is no reason why I would have." He thought for a moment. "I did hear his sermon this past Shabbat. I am not surprised that he upset many people with his cursing of the Jews of Salerno." He shrugged. "There are a few of us Egyptians here. We like the traditional ways, although we know it is not the way in Salerno. Look, I have told you what I know about his once being meek. If that memory is accurate, something must have happened to make him change."

Nothing less than the loss of his family. Once again, I feel a small tug of sympathy for the rabbi.

"Anyone who heard that sermon would have difficulty imagining the rabbi as ever being meek. Do you know anything more? Did the death of the Rambam and the rabbi's need to leave Egypt turn him into an angry denouncer?" Rafael asked.

"How can I know this? The local scholars would know more about this than I."

"Which scholars do you mean?" Rafael asked.

"Of course the Mendoza brothers. Also, Reuben and Benjamin ben Joseph, the brothers who live near the medical school. They have many materials from my country in their library. They might know about the rabbi's being in the Rambam's circle, though I doubt he was worthy even of much notice. That is all. Now, I must get on with my work, Signor, Magistra." With that, he walked away.

Back outside, Rafael and I conferred. "Let us add the ben Josephs to the Mendozas as people to speak with. We cannot overlook any opportunity."

Fatigue and frustration roughened his voice. I could sense that I would need to balance those tendencies with optimism. As it was too early to call on the men Moshe ben Shlomo named, we parted ways and went to our own homes in the early morning chill.

Five

As soon as I arrived home, Nina insisted I break my fast. After being surrounded by the good smells of the bakery, I readily agreed. My day would be quite busy, since I also had to tend to a patient with a stomach ailment, tutor a student, and deliver a lecture at the Scuola. This in addition to trying to solve a murder and save the rabbi.

"This morning you will eat a dish of warm grains for extra strength," Nina dictated.

I frowned. The grains would make a heavy meal, and I preferred something light. Sometimes my preferences prevailed, but Nina stamped her foot. "I made this dish, and you shall eat a decent serving."

So much for enjoying a dish as appealing as the smells of the bakery. She filled a bowl with the warm grains. "Eat it all." If only I could love warm grains, I think Nina would be the happiest of women. That, and if I married Rafael.

As I forced down this hearty and, I thought grudgingly, healthy meal, I considered the day to come. Being more familiar with the Mendozas than the ben Josephs, perhaps we should start with them, despite it being clear that they were against the rabbi. It would be useful to know why they were so determined to see him punished for this crime.

Perhaps the leading Jewish family in Salerno—certainly one of the most powerful—the Mendoza brothers lived next to each other in a group of residences in the center of the Jewish quarter. In addition to their businesses here, they owned some ships, and they had connections to other merchants and ship owners in Venice and Genoa.

Why were the Mendozas supporting the duke's position on the rabbi's guilt? I liked to believe myself not so naïve when it came to the ways of the world, and I recognized that sometimes compromise was unavoidable. However, we Jews needed to hold strong to our belief in justice, as well as our solidarity as a community.

I sipped my barley tea. Rather than try to guess what I might learn from the Mendozas, I would go to them with an open mind. However, seeing my patient, tutoring, and my lecture were fixed commitments for today. So, I now planned to see the Mendozas with Rafael after my patient and tutoring and before my lecture. At a later time, we would look into the library that belonged to Reuben and Benjamin ben Joseph. At the Mendozas' and the library, we would also seek to learn if there was anyone else to include in the investigation.

My patient, *Avvocato* Marco di Rienzo, was a Christian lawyer of close to fifty years—a good, intelligent man who somehow could not believe an accomplished healer such as myself could not find a way to let him eat and drink whatever and however much he desired without growing fat and having stomach discomfort.

"I am not a miracle worker," I told him time and again.

"You are to me. Without you, I would be even fatter and more uncomfortable."

"You are lucky on both those counts." I dosed him with

peppermint and ginger, with the hopes of calming his stomach upsets after especially indulgent feasts. "Still, moderation is the key for you, my friend. As for everyone. A bit of self-control in eating and drinking will bring what you most crave. It is the way to get your humors in balance. Moderation is the only miracle. That and a bit of exercise."

"Moderation? What language is that you speak? Some ancient, thankfully forgotten tongue, no doubt." And he laughed.

Sometimes, though I should not have, I laughed with him. He was so charming a figure—hard to resist. But today, I had too much else on my mind.

He studied me with his large dark eyes, sensing my state. "What is it, Magistra? You are not yourself today."

I had not intended to bring up the rabbi's situation with my patient. However, it now occurred to me that, as a man of the law, perhaps he could help. So I told him of the murder, the Egyptian rabbi's subsequent imprisonment, and the threat to the Jewish community.

A frown distorted his handsome face. "I heard of this crime. I thought it was simply another unfortunate murder by brigands intent on robbery. Usually the duke does not trouble himself in such matters. Is it the political consequences of the death of a crusader? I think so."

I nodded. "If the true murderer is not caught soon, the rabbi faces execution."

The avvocato shuddered. "A swift end that has little to do with justice. It is said Duke Henry has orders from the regent to reduce crime, though he has taken little action in that area. It all comes down to the arrival of the crusaders. Like other port cities, Salerno is easy prey for such travelers. If only they received the chastisement their offenses merit! These unholy holy warriors!" He shook his head. "And then with one of their number getting himself murdered—"

"The rabbi is not a murderer. He is innocent of this act."

He scratched his head. "Alas, in the workings of law, innocence is sometimes irrelevant." After a slight pause, he went on. "I try to stay away from any politics that involves the crusaders. A dirty business. However, if you would like, I will see what I can find out about this arrest. But I am not optimistic that I can be of much help."

"I would so appreciate whatever help you might provide."

He offered to inquire within the Christian community and among his fellow lawyers to see what, if anything, might arise.

Buoyed by this bit of possibility and the avvocatto's general bonhomie, I felt less heavy-hearted when I left to meet with my favorite student. Involvement with these normal activities of my life helped my body and mind come back to a balance. It was only when I was so immersed that I fully realized how much I loved my life here in Salerno. How much I would miss it if I ever had to leave. Unfortunately, the rabbi's situation reminded me of the constancy of Jewish fragility in communities that are never really our own.

Here in Salerno, in the Kingdom of Sicily, we had a relative paradise for women such as my student, Laura di Petrocelli, and myself. We thirsted for knowledge, using both new and traditional lore for healing. And here we had been able to flourish and even to expand the boundaries of medicine. I regretted that this path was closed, indeed unknown, to most other women elsewhere, and every day thanked God for having directed me to this refuge.

Paradise? In a way. But much as I wished to hide away from harsh aspects of reality, even I had to admit our school, embedded in the actualities of a changing society, was facing a subtle though frightening decline from the best days of its history. As I let myself into the small chamber in the university's library where I met Laura, I wondered how long this refuge would continue. And where would seekers such as myself go when Salerno could no longer be home? Where else could even a Christian woman like the lovely blonde-haired Laura find a place to study the latest in medicine? Not even a convent could provide that.

"Magistra, you seem a bit preoccupied today," Laura said.

With a start I realized I had been so lost in thought, I had not noticed her arrival. I smiled, meeting her green eyes and hoping the attempt appeared bright rather than half-hearted. Laura, an intelligent, inquisitive young student had the talent, skills, and personality to become an excellent healer. Although she had a fiancé and a family who insisted that she marry soon, she was determined to finish her studies first, because after marriage, usually children come quickly. So she managed to resist her parents' pressure, proving she was strong-willed.

"Forgive me," I said. "My mind was elsewhere for a moment. If I remember correctly, you were going to start reading the text of La Trotula."

She made a face akin to eating overly sour soup. "I find it so difficult reading. I must remind myself it was quite miraculous for any woman to have written such a text."

"Yes, but it is often the difficult task that yields the most fruit. Tell me," I persisted, "what do you find to be so difficult about this text?"

As was her wont, she thought before speaking. "One problem is, I wonder about La Trotula's contention that the healer might ease the pain of the mother during the time of childbirth. But is it not true that this pain must be borne because of women's sinful natures?"

I tried to hide my dismay at these words. As a Jew, I knew I had to tread lightly when my beliefs conflicted with those of Christian students and colleagues. Though La Trotula had made little progress in attempts to meet her goal of reducing women's childbirth pain, I admired her for trying—and for not accepting the doctrine that such pain was not only inevitable but also deserved. However, I had to proceed delicately with Laura on this point. "Please explain more to me about your view, as a healer, of childbirth."

She frowned. "I never questioned why women suffer in childbirth or thought healers should try to intervene to lessen the pain."

"Is this what you continue to believe?"

She nodded.

"I understand. Laura, as you know, I am of a different faith than you. There have been times for me also when there has been a conflict between my faith and my work as a healer."

"And what did you do then?"

I sighed. "I took the time to give the matter deep thought, to see which side in the controversy appeared to be truer for me."

"So you cannot tell me that La Trotula is right or wrong."

"For me, she is right. For you, that is a matter to consider."

And I knew she would.

With my full concentration on the healing topic, as often happens, the allotted time for our study flew by. As we were finishing up, however, I found my thoughts turning once more to my concern about the rabbi.

Laura regarded me with curiosity.

"Yes?" I asked. "Is there something else?"

She swallowed hard. "Please forgive me if I am being too forward, but I feel there is some matter worrying you. Is it something to do with me?"

"Oh, no! I am, as always, immensely pleased with you and your work."

"Is it a matter I might be able to help with?"

Should I tell her about the arrest of the rabbi from Egypt? What would a Christian woman, even in a place like Salerno, care about rabbis and other Jewish matters? I did not know if his arrest for the murder of the crusader was common knowledge in the wider community yet, though I expected the news would soon spread.

"Great powers of observation—one of your skills as a healer. What specifically do you notice?"

She blushed with evident pleasure at the compliment. "Something in your expression, in your eyes, around your mouth. Would you care to tell me what it is? Has it to do with your humors? You are of a sanguine humor, are you not? As am I."

She said the last shyly, speaking of matters of such a rather personal nature. On the other hand, her sharpness to suspect an imbalance of the humors marked her talent as a future physician. I allowed myself a momentary smile of pleasure in recognition of her well-considered question.

"Good question about my humors, which, of course, always bear regarding. Yes. I am afraid something puzzling and disturbing has happened in my community."

"I am sorry to hear that. Can you tell me?"

"I suppose there is no good reason not to tell you, though I fear there is nothing you can do. One of our holy men, a rabbi newly arrived from Egypt, has been arrested for the murder of a crusader. Perhaps the news of this has spread? The rabbi is innocent, and yet Duke Henry appears convinced that the right man is in custody."

She frowned. "How is it possible for a holy man to meet such a misfortune?"

I almost laughed at the naïveté of this statement, but I remembered with a tinge of sadness the days when I, too, had been so naïve. If we were to look to God to protect the holy, we would all be in for great disappointment—a lesson repeated far too many times.

I gazed at her with fondness. "To my understanding, the holy of all faiths are subject to the same physical laws of nature as the least pious. And similar quirks of behavior or misbehavior, as well as the imbalance of the humors."

"You must think me very young."

I patted her shoulder. "We were all so young once. A refreshing reminder of the passage of time. It is good to be able to retain at least a bit of that hopefulness and optimism as one gets older." *But so difficult . . . perhaps impossible.*

"I hope you soon find the answers to bring this case to a just conclusion," she said.

"As do I. As do others." *Though, alas, not all.*

࿇

Rafael and I had arranged to meet at the Mendozas' shop of fabric. He and I arrived at the same time.

"In light of our plans today, I sent Manuel to the prison to bring the rabbi a bit of food," he said. "Tomorrow, we will have to make sure he has supplies for the Sabbath."

"Good," I said. In the shop, the fabrics of many hues and textures filled wooden shelves on three walls. The customers chose the fabrics that interested them and had lengths cut on long wooden tables. Though the shop was quite busy, it turned out neither Baruch nor Natan Mendoza was there, so we continued along the street toward their homes.

We arrived first at Baruch's house, the larger of the two. The façade was quite ornate, with intricately cut metal work providing a pleasing decoration to the entrance.

"Signor Mendoza, please," Rafael announced to the servant at the door.

"I shall see if the master is in," the dour-faced elderly man responded as he showed us into an anteroom where we could wait. The room, festooned with sumptuous draperies and tapestries in shades of gold and blue, clearly belonged to a man of great means. Baruch Mendoza himself entered moments after the servant had let us in, which surprised me, as I had expected the merchant to keep us waiting.

"Lopes Dias, Magistra, what brings you to my home on this day?"

"It is the matter of the arrest of Rabbi Isaac ben Shmuel for the murder of a crusader. I understand the Mendoza family agrees with Duke Henry, that you believe the rabbi to be culpable." Without waiting for a response, I rushed on before he could interrupt. "We know that you and others are working with the duke to prevent retribution by the crusaders on our community, and we appreciate that."

Rafael caught my eye and shook his head. I had probably started off by saying too much.

A flash of color darkened Baruch's cheeks before his face resumed its usual pallor. "I am indeed aware of these matters, as is all of Jewish Salerno. Why have you come here? I do not understand your involvement. Please explain quickly as I have other matters to see to."

"The magistra is working with me to help investigate the situation. We have taken on the task of gathering information to prove the innocence of the rabbi. We also mean to find out what really happened and who the guilty one is, so justice can be done."

Signor Mendoza looked at Rafael as if he were speaking a strange tongue. "Why do you come to me in this way when you already know I disagree, Lopes Dias? In addition to your mistaken, futile efforts to prove the rabbi innocent, it is most unseemly for a woman to be involved in this matter." His mouth went into a tight, grim line.

Before I could share my opinion of his opinion, Rafael replied. "We do know that our views on this matter differ from yours. I respect your position, and I hope you can extend us the same courtesy. One reason we are here is because Moshe ben Shlomo, with whom I have worked on translations, thought you might have some helpful information."

Baruch Mendoza grimaced as if the question made the food with which he had broken his fast that morning curdle in his belly. "Ben Shlomo? That irksome pauper should know better. Well, leave him to me. He forgets his debt to our family, although I shall remind him." He coughed, which sounded painful. "Your self-appointed mission is counter to the interests of the Jewish community."

"With all due respect, Signor, you and I disagree. I believe that justice is always a compelling interest of a Jewish community. Once we have learned what we can, we hope to put together the picture and solve the crime. For the ultimate good of all."

Signor Mendoza studied us as if weighing something in his mind, coughed, and said, "My brother and I met with the Egyptian rabbi only during the same brief occasion as you yourself, Lopes Dias. However, despite his personal relationship with the Rambam and his knowledge of the Egyptian court, we were disappointed and felt there was not a good opportunity for a translation after all."

He gestured with his hands in dismissal. "We do not know anything more about him. And we certainly do not know what happened to the accursed crusader whose death is causing so much trouble, but we want to make short work of the disruption and danger to the Jewish community it has caused." Wiping a small spray of spittle from the corner of his mouth, he finished, "That is all I have to say. I hope you do not intend to go next to my brother's house to bother him and his family."

That was exactly what we intended. "Sometimes people pick up information they are not aware of until they start to answer questions," I said.

He grunted with derision. "Intelligent people always know what they know."

Another point on which to disagree, but this time I held my tongue. The sour servant escorted us to the door with a speed that skirted the edges of courtesy.

"Well, what did you think of that?" I asked Rafael.

He shook his head. "No surprises. Baruch behaved in his home exactly as he does in Duke Henry's presence. But at least we have now established your involvement in our efforts, Rebecca. And that there is an effort to pursue the truth."

"It must require great patience to sit in councils with the duke and our Signor Mendoza," I observed.

He smiled. "And you know that I am not a patient man."

We made our way next door to Natan Mendoza's abode. Although slightly smaller than that of his older brother, it was equally impressive.

I knocked and we were shown in by another surly, forbidding retainer—was there a central source for dour-faced servants whose primary duty lay in discouraging any but invited guests?

"I shall see if Signor Mendoza is in," this one repeated. "Please have a seat while I look."

To my surprise, when we went into the light-filled anteroom, two young girls were deep in conversation. When we entered they stopped, looked at us, and arose as if to leave.

"Please, do not let us chase you off," I said.

The older of the two, who must have been around thirteen or fourteen, regarded me warily. "Who are you?"

I explained, adding that we were there to see Signor Mendoza.

"Papa." Naming her father did not appear to give her any pleasure. "Are you not the magistra? Are you here because he is ill? That cannot be. Papa would never allow any but his regular *medico* to treat him or any of us."

While she spoke, I had a good look at her. I could see the child was pale and seemed to lack the vigor expected in someone of her age. "What is your name, child?"

"Esperanza," she whispered. "And this is my little sister Deborah." The younger girl, who coughed quite a bit, looked ready to run off in the manner of a frightened rabbit.

"Esperanza and Deborah," I repeated. "Tell me, Deborah, have you been ill? Have you been coughing for some time?"

Esperanza shook her head. "She coughs when she is scared. We miss our mama. She is away with Gabriela. Deborah and I are in the best of health," she said as if reciting a memorized line.

When I was about to probe further, a voice broke in.

"Why are you asking my daughters questions?" A distressed Natan Mendoza bustled into the room. "I have not given you permission to enter my home and interrogate family members."

The girls cowered in a manner so cravenly, I feared that, despite the finery they wore and the wealth of their surroundings, he somehow mistreated them. And what was it they said about missing their mama and sister? Malka Freya, she who had fainted in the synagogue. Why did they miss her? Had she gone on some sort of travels? I could not recall hearing word of that.

I nodded to Rafael. "We are here because of the arrest of Rabbi Isaac ben Shmuel, from Egypt. We know you have been involved in handling this matter."

The girls turned more ashen when I spoke these words. "Go to your room, girls." They ran off without so much as a backward glance.

Once we were alone, I repeated my words, adding, "Perhaps you can provide some information that will help to solve this case."

He shook his head and frowned. "It is a tragedy that the Egyptian rabbi has brought this accusation down on the Jewish community after he came seeking refuge. The murder of a crusader—they should all disappear from the world—endangers us all."

"Yes. So surely you must agree that we want to find the guilty culprit with all possible speed. Both to restore our sense of safety for Jews in Salerno and to see justice done." The signor glared at me as I expressed my view.

Rafael spoke up. "I have spoken of this matter in the castle with the duke. I have expressed my concerns and doubts and hoped you might be thinking the same way, now that I have raised my concerns."

Natan drew himself to his full height, displaying an impressive carriage. "Here we do not agree. I did not realize you were so mistaken as to my stand, Lopes Dias. Hard as it appears to be for you to accept, I believe the guards have arrested the correct man. My brothers and I are in complete accord on this. I am sure justice is being done."

What? How can any intelligent adult believe so? As I was trying to organize my counterargument, a female version of the dour servant came to escort us out. In moments, we were back on the street, accompanied by Signor Mendoza's strongly worded directive to stay away.

Fortunately, there were not too many people on the street at that time to witness our involuntary exit from casa Mendoza. Although now was not the time to meditate on this inhospitable behavior, it did bear thinking about—why were the Mendoza brothers behaving so stubbornly? Could they really believe Rabbi Isaac ben Shmuel guilty of the heinous crime of which he stood accused? I knew they *appeared* to support Duke Henry in this view. Did this support reflect their actual belief?

I regarded Rafael. "Is this how they always are to work with?"

He shrugged. "Since I have worked with them only as funders for translation, and they regard me as an expert in that, they have been more respectful and more courteous in the past."

"I hope the current hostility does not impair their future funding of your work."

He laughed. "Fortunately, I have other means to fund my work. But I am distressed at the disrespect they showed you."

"Perhaps this disrespect and breach in courtesy are a sign that the Mendozas are more troubled than they would have us know," I said.

"What do you mean?"

"After this visit, I have a question for us to explore. The little girls say they miss their mother. Why? Where is Malka Freya Mendoza? And why is her absence being kept a secret?"

$\mathcal{Six}$

I still had my lecture to deliver at the university that afternoon. I had done far less than my usual thorough preparation. Fortunately, the topic of digestive health and the humors was one I had deep familiarity with. Though I did not like to rely on previous lectures, the past few days had been extraordinary, and so I gave myself permission to use my earlier lecture notes.

Despite my lack of preparedness, as always, seeing the twenty or so students fill the room lifted my mood. During my own student days, I was avid to attend every lecture I could, and I very much appreciated that my continued connection to the university allowed me to still attend such sessions by others as often as my busy schedule allowed.

"So," I concluded, just as I had told my patient that morning, "moderation and balance are the keys to good health, including digestion. It is a question of managing the humors—with food, with herbs, with activity, and with rest—in the ways we have discussed."

Alas, moderation and balance would not be the keys to solving the murder and safeguarding both the rabbi and our community. What would be the means for that?

❧

I woke early the next morning, Friday. Sundown would be the start of our Shabbat. Hard to believe—just six days before, the Egyptian rabbi delivered his stinging rebuke to our community in his ill-conceived sermon. How much change this week had brought to our community!

Even though it was still several hours until sundown, all the families would have begun their preparations well in advance, it being a transgression to be caught up in the ordinary work of the world at the hour designated to welcome the Sabbath. Rafael and I needed to plan accordingly for ourselves, and for the rabbi.

I sometimes found myself tempted to nibble away at the edges of the time commanded to observe the Shabbat—tempted, though I did not give in unless faced with a crisis. For one thing, Nina would never let me hear the end of it. Also, at this time each week, I especially thought of Papa, who always insisted on honoring the full Sabbath. Whether at home or when traveling for business, he treated this as a sacred commandment. I also recognized the value of setting aside time for being, rather than for our constant doing—a deep wisdom of our ancient tradition fully consistent with my understanding of balance that was a foundation of all my studies of healing.

It distressed me that the accused rabbi would spend the Sabbath in the dungeon. Thank goodness we could supply him with some small comforts.

To do that, early in the day I collected provisions that Nina prepared, including cheese and fruit as well as a challah, fresh from the bakery. Hoping that most of this would not end up as part of the guard's dinner, I was ready when Rafael arrived and we set off for the dungeons.

Soon we were at the castle gate. This time we were able to get past the guard without incurring loss. A quiver of nervous energy skittered up my spine, and my stomach clenched at the notion of approaching the disapproving rabbi once again. When we arrived, however, he seemed grateful to Rafael and to me for giving him a chance to observe a bit of Shabbat in his miserable cell. He closed his eyes and mumbled a prayer. "Blessed be the Lord, who watches over us. *Baruch Hashem,* thanks be to God that the guard did not keep the challah."

I sensed a shift in him, which Rafael also seemed to detect. We regarded each other with some satisfaction. The rabbi looked better than I had expected. Perhaps due to the magic of the challah and the approach of Shabbat, even in this dark place.

Turning to the rabbi, Rafael asked, "Is there anything more that you can tell us that might be helpful?"

He shook his head. "It is hard not to succumb to despair in this accursed place, cut off from the world. Though I know that to do so would be yet another sin to add to all my transgressions."

What are these transgressions?

"I am so recently arrived in Salerno. I wish to God I had never come to this place." The rabbi began to sob softly. "It was a fool's quest that brought me here. I thought somehow I could find my wife," he shuddered. "The woman who is mother to my children. If only I could convince her to let me be with my children. . ." he trailed off.

A wave of pity tugged at my heart. To have lost his children. Perhaps he truly loved his wife and felt her loss too. "One thing at a time. First we must clear you of this accusation and secure your release from this place. Then, who can know? Do not lose heart."

At that moment, the guard interrupted our discourse.

"Out," the guard ordered. "You have been here far too long."

In moments, Rafael and I were out on the street now filled with the bustle of folk going about their daily lives. Since Rafael and I both had busy schedules, we went in our separate directions.

❧

After I returned home from seeing my last patient of the day, I took time to change into my Sabbath garments. This was part of the practice of leaving behind the other six days of the week in order to enter into the proper mood to greet the Sabbath. Tonight, because of my busy day and the lateness of the hour, I would not attend the evening service at the synagogue to welcome the Sabbath. Unless an emergency called me away, tomorrow morning, I would join the other women in our gallery as I had the week before, and almost every week.

I was grateful for the comfort of sharing my Shabbat dinner with not only Rafael, but also Nina, and, often, Manuel. It had taken me a good deal of persuasion in the past to convince Nina to join Rafael and me weekly for our Sabbath meal—no matter that she often served as an excellent confidante when she was not being a mother hen. Yet she would never join us at the table when Papa was in residence. When we were alone in the house or with Rafael and Manuel as our only guests, having her as our companion for this fundamental Jewish practice felt right.

Though Nina no longer made her own challah—I had finally been able to convince her not to perform this demanding task when we had an excellent Jewish bakery in Salerno—she insisted on making all the rest of the dinner from the freshest ingredients and best herbs available.

Both from my work and Papa's generosity, I was blessed with riches beyond what I could possibly need. Still, I saw no need to fill my table with the finest, rarest, or richest of foods when, most times, I preferred simpler fare. So though many chose to celebrate the Sabbath with stews of lamb or beef, I asked Nina to center meals around fish or fowl, so abundantly available in Salerno by the sea.

Rafael and Manuel arrived. As I lit the candles and recited the ancient blessing, I added a silent prayer: *Dear Lord, let the rabbi be freed. And let our community be spared injustice and violence.*

We said the blessing for the wine and sipped, then performed the ritual washing of our hands, with its blessing, before blessing and partaking of the challah. Nina rose. "I will go and get the greens to start our dinner."

Many of our vegetables and herbs came from our garden, which Nina lovingly oversaw while the gardener weeded and watered. Tonight, she mixed lettuce with mustard greens, a combination I especially liked, and included salt, balsamic vinegar, and olive oil as well as basil, dill, and chives.

Nina frowned. "You did not take the rabbi any greens."

"Manuel, would you please take the rabbi greens with the rest of the bundle tomorrow?" I asked. Since Rafael's servant was not bound by the Shabbat commandments forbidding work, he could treat the day as any other.

Nina appeared to consider that, then nodded. "At least maybe the guard will not try to take the lion's share for himself."

I smiled at the image of a lion eating a lot of greens. I attempted to focus on feelings of gratitude and joy—to have arrived at another Sabbath of blessings and prayers, and keeping hope for the time to come. However, I felt uneasy, perhaps because the table was too quiet, and also because we were self-conscious about eating with any degree of levity or gusto while Rabbi Isaac ben Shmuel was not able to savor the Shabbat.

While at the table, Rafael said, "In addition to the pleasure of joining you for a sweet dinner, I have some news to impart. Duke Henry told me he has identified a crusader who appears to have some authority in their camp. He is now to be included in the talks. For the moment, it does not appear he and his men are about to maraud and pillage the Jews of Salerno."

"They are content to limit themselves to assaults and robbery?" I muttered, the pall of the situation never far from my thoughts.

"Since they have not been charged with murder and one of our community has, it serves us best to tread lightly. Especially when it is clear to those outside, like the duke, that there is disagreement within our Jewish community as to the rabbi's guilt." He pursed his lips.

This disagreement complicates an already difficult situation. Perhaps we should focus attention on achieving agreement among us Jews.

Nina served our next course, chicken with broth, a special favorite of mine and Rafael's. He gazed around him with a relaxed and contented expression. "Tonight, let us take a respite from the current travail. Let us savor the feast before us. Nina, you continue to amaze me with your wondrous meals."

Rafael's praise set Nina to blushing. This time our silence felt comfortable as we all indulged. We paused contentedly before the next course. However, Manuel ruptured the peace as he set down his wine glass and spoke of what we were all thinking about. "The master says you will speak with the ben Joseph brothers next?"

"Yes. Since the Mendozas were not forthcoming, I am still hopeful about the ben Josephs. But tell us, Manuel, has there been any talk in the streets?"

He shrugged. "Almost everyone believes that the rabbi, holding the bloody knife, was the murderer. And there is revulsion for the stabbing despite the unpopularity of the crusaders."

Nina grew pale at this mention. I decided to delay until later to delve further into what Manuel knew. In particular, I would ask him if the crusader's body had been seen yet by anyone from the Scuola.

There were physicians whose specialty was to examine the bodies of the dead to learn their secrets. Some even claimed the dead "spoke to them". I shivered at the prospect of working with dead people, a practice I would find most difficult.

Nina got up from the table and went into the kitchen. She returned with the next course very quickly, perhaps not wanting to miss anything that was said, or, perhaps, hoping to stop more discussion by filling our mouths.

She had prepared partridges according to her foster mother's recipe. Nina made both a stuffing and a topping for the birds. Her unique stuffing included many ingredients—cinnamon, lavender, and a juice made from cilantro, pine nuts, almonds, and diced hard-boiled eggs. To this she added a drop of pennyroyal, olive oil, pepper, cassia, mint, cider vinegar, and salt. The topping included cinnamon and sugar, pepper, pignoli, pistachios, and almonds.

At the end of such a feast we usually had refreshingly light fruit for dessert. Tonight, that certainly would have been enough, but Nina considered the dessert course her star turn. She brought out a tray of nougat candy and pastries.

Though no one thought they could eat another bite, the appetizing sweets looked too delicious not at least to sample. Further, no one would have dreamed of offending Nina by turning down her dessert.

I had taken my first delicious bite when a fierce knocking came at our door. Emergencies were no respecters of Shabbat.

"Permit me to answer," Manuel offered.

I could see Nina was torn about letting a guest perform her duty, yet I nodded to indicate she should allow him to do so. Meanwhile, I brought myself to mental alertness.

We heard men's voices, and then Manuel rushed back to the table.

"What is it?" Rafael spoke first.

"Rabbi Isaac ben Shmuel has been attacked in the dungeon," Manuel spoke rapidly, making a clear effort to maintain some sort of calm. "He is grievously wounded."

"No!" Both Nina and I cried out our distress at the same moment.

"The duke has asked for the magistra, accompanied by Signor Lopes Dias, to attend to the rabbi." Nina had an excuse for her emotional response. As a physician, I did not. I would much better serve the rabbi by going to minister to him with a calm resolve that allowed for high-quality, rational treatment. Assuming I could help him. Assuming his injuries had not already, in the interval since the messenger set off, killed him.

By this time, Rafael and I were standing too. "What do you know about the injuries? How serious?" Even while asking, I rushed from the room.

"Magistra, I cannot answer your questions. The rabbi was discovered when the guard made rounds. He was barely able to talk."

If the rabbi was capable of even a bit of speech, maybe the injury was not devastating. With a prayer on my lips and many questions buzzing in my head, I grabbed my satchel with the medical supplies I always had ready and followed Rafael, Manuel, and the men who had come to fetch us. For one second I thought about this happening on Shabbat, when we are forbidden from many activities—including both traveling on a horse-drawn wagon and practicing medicine. But I marvelled, as always, at the deep morality of our traditions and laws. In this case, there is the concept of *Pikuach Nefesh*—preserving life—which makes clear that doing what is necessary for saving a life takes precedence over the laws of Shabbat. Indeed, we are *commanded* to do this "work."

As we were transported at high speed, I hoped we would arrive in time.

The castle area around the dungeon appeared much quieter at night than during the day. Quieter, and also more sinister. What would I find when we arrived at the rabbi's cell? I trembled with a fear that I could not let master me.

If I arrived at the rabbi's cell. A snarling, hostile guard met us at the entrance. "What took you so long? Oh, wait. Now I remember. The Jews stay huddled behind closed doors to hatch their schemes on their so-called *Sabbath*." He spat when he finished speaking.

Rafael, Manuel, and I all shuddered, but, thank goodness, we refrained from responding.

"Please," I beseeched, my tone soft, as I was desperately trying to get to my patient as quickly as possible, "show me and these men to his cell. Afterward, we can settle up and show you our gratitude."

The guard scowled at me, but with a bit more cajoling, a threat from Rafael to involve the duke, and the promise of the bribe, the guard led us to the rabbi's cell.

Dear God! If the first sight of the Egyptian rabbi, crumpled and bleeding on the filthy ground, did not throw me into despair, nothing would.

"Rabbi," I called in his Arabic tongue, which he would most readily understand. "Rabbi Isaac ben Shmuel. Please, speak to me!"

He groaned and opened his eyes to mere slits. "You again," he whispered. "The woman doctor."

"Can you tell me what happened?" I asked, wanting to keep him conscious, as I held his wrist to check his pulse, counting while I attempted to evaluate his condition. He had an injury on the left side of his head, which clearly had bled a lot but had now, blessedly, stopped. How long ago had he been struck?

Weak as he was, he tried to pull his wrist from my hand—so deeply ingrained must have been his beliefs about touch between the sexes. In his dire state, with his body more at risk than his soul, the rabbi would have to surrender to the necessity of allowing my touch.

I had held his wrist long enough to determine what I needed to, so I let go. His pulse, though rapid—I would have been surprised if it were not—was relatively steady. I directed Rafael and Manuel in carefully lifting the rabbi off the floor and onto the sleeping pallet.

The rabbi weakly shook his head, his dazed expression telling me he had a long way to go before he recovered his wits. "What happened to me?" he croaked.

"We shall soon find out." I gingerly touched his head wound with my fingertips, and he winced before recoiling. The blood was barely dried, so the injury was recent. Apparently the guard had discovered and reported the attack in good time. Of course, perhaps the guard was complicit in the attack, in which case his timely reporting would merely provide him with the appearance of proper behavior.

These are complicated thoughts worthy of a Talmudic scholar. I need to focus on the rabbi and not let my mind meander.

He sucked in his breath as I probed the wound. "Cannot someone else do this?" he whispered. "You are causing agony both to my body and soul."

At least he now sounded more like his cantankerous self, at which I took heart. "In respect to your bodily agony, I am doing the minimum required to assess and treat your injury. No one else here can do this, so by the principle of *Pikuach Nefesh*, my touch is not injuring your soul."

The rabbi's wordless response of relaxing into my touch signaled to me that he was at last compliant with my attending to him, which tempered my annoyance with his constant resisting my help. I also felt so much gratitude that the combination of my Jewish heritage and medical training provided me the powerful and precious ability to bring healing to others.

I set about cleaning the wound, using a cloth moistened with salt water, which caused more pain but was also necessary. I then applied honey for further cleaning, and then bandages from my kit. Finally, I had the rabbi swallow some poppy, mixed in honey, to soothe his pain.

The rabbi's heartbeat remained a bit rapid and his breathing too shallow—all consistent with shock and injury. "Bring some blankets," I ordered the guard who had remained hovering at the cell door. "Clean. Not the filthy rags around here."

He bristled yet refrained from saying anything before wandering off, I hoped to do my bidding. I was pleased and surprised that, in a fairly short time, he actually returned with some reasonable blankets—an act which no doubt would exact a price later.

"Do you have any idea who attacked you—or why?" Rafael asked the rabbi once I had him settled on the bed with blankets the best I could.

"He is probably weary and maybe not in his full senses," I told Rafael quietly.

However, the rabbi was alert enough to respond. "No." He started to shake his head, then thought better of it. "From behind. One minute pacing, and the next . . ." he trailed off a moment. "Do not know. But the strangest feeling. Another Jew hit me. Crazy, no?"

"Why do you think it was a Jew who hit you?" Rafael asked.

The rabbi made to shrug then stopped mid-gesture. Any such movement would cause discomfort or worse. "The smell. A Sabbath smell. Challah and sweet wine. Happened so fast. Maybe a dream."

Indeed. Or maybe a real scent. Very strange. "So someone came into your cell?" I whispered.

He nodded, with the same painful result as his headshake. "Yes. Someone was in here."

Then the guard must have let him in. *And, of course, all it would take is a bribe—not even a large one.*

When the guard returned again, Rafael asked him the question of an intruder.

He shrugged. "I just arrived back on duty. I had my own dinner. Several other men were on guard duty during that time."

"I want to find out who was let into this cell—and which guard made it possible for this prisoner to be grievously attacked," Rafael said. "I shall speak to Duke Henry of this matter, including that you are not willing to help uncover how this happened."

The guard appeared unconcerned by this quest. I found him especially vexing, despite his having brought a few blankets. We would do well to steer out of his way, for certainly, it would do our cause no good if, out of pique with us, he treated the rabbi even worse.

After a few minutes under several blankets, the rabbi's shivering subsided. He began to regain his color and resume more normal breathing. His eyes appeared to focus correctly. Head wounds could bleed a great deal and yet not be very serious. Alternatively, what appeared superficial could turn out to be of the utmost seriousness.

I announced, "I will need to stay with the rabbi all night. If he were to fall into a stupor or begin to bleed again, he would need immediate attention."

"A woman cannot stay in a prisoner's cell," the guard retorted. "This is not a brothel."

Both Rafael and Manuel bristled. The rabbi blinked with seeming incomprehension.

"You will watch what you say with a lady present," Rafael said, and with such authority, the guard backed off.

"Are you sure, Magistra? I can stay with him and summon you if there is a problem," Manuel said.

Before I could reply, Rafael surprised me by saying, "The magistra said immediate attention. I will stay here with her."

"Are you sure?" The notion of our being together for the long hours to come shook my composure.

His eyes locked with mine. "Yes. It is more important for me to be here with you than anything else I might accomplish. After all, there was one attack already. I want to keep you both safe this night."

I wanted to thank him for this, but instead, I decided to react in my most professional manner. "Very well." I turned to Manuel. "Please let Nina know what I am doing so the poor thing does not tarry all night in a vigil for me."

Manuel agreed, and he and the guard left.

Rafael and I settled in for the night—if one could settle in such a dreadful place. Rafael and I exchanged a bit more about our current situations, and then we decided to take turns attempting to sleep. He had closed his eyes only a minute when our patient stirred. He looked straight at me and said, "Abraham ibn Hasdai, from Barcelona." And then, before I could question him as to who this was, he too closed his eyes and appeared to be instantly asleep.

Surprised, I turned to Rafael only to see that he was already fast asleep and had, no doubt, heard nothing. Despite my curiosity, I chose not to awaken Rafael to relate the rabbi's words. So, with nothing to do other than stay awake in case the rabbi's condition changed, I found myself having the opportunity to study the placid expression on Rafael's face. I had never before seen him asleep. He appeared to be at complete peace, causing him to look younger than his years. Was it possible for him to be even more comely in his slumber than when awake?

A strange sensation stirred my heart, a welling of something warm in my chest. I shook my head and stopped staring at my good friend. *I must think about other things.*

Abraham ibn Hasdai. I repeated the name to myself so I would not forget. Though apparently he was from Barcelona, where I had spent a short time with my family, the name was unknown to me. Papa was often there because he shared in his business with men from our family residing still in that city. Maybe Papa or other of my kinsfolk would know something about this ibn Hasdai. Could he possibly have had something to do with what had happened? It seemed unlikely, but I was determined to follow every clue.

I surveyed the tableau of the rabbi and Rafael sleeping deeply in the straw and filth of the cell. I felt assuredly that what I was doing was acceptable in the eyes of God. In spite of that, I could not keep my mind from skittering to all the rules I was violating, now adding on spending a night with two men, neither of whom I was related to. I shook my head, realizing that for many members of my community, more important than my good intentions was the disgrace that I, a woman, had broken community conventions—yet again. Though he would have struggled not to judge, dear Papa would have been hurt. Perhaps my aunt in Barcelona had been right to regard me as hopeless and beyond despair.

Much as I would have preferred to let Rafael continue to sleep, my eyes were closing with fatigue. I roused him awake so that I could rest for a bit. He smiled at me and wished me a good rest.

❧

"Rebecca," Rafael's voice cut through my uneasy sleep. "It is almost dawn. The guard will be here soon with extra soldiers. You and I must leave here right away."

"My patient?" I asked. When I saw he was awake and I did a quick examination, I added, "How do you fare, Rabbi?"

He groaned. "I have been better. I will be better."

I wished I could agree with confidence that he would manage. Still, I had done all I could for now. "We will return. With good food, so you can build up your blood again, replacing what you have lost."

The rabbi nodded and winced. He should not be moving his head so much.

I asked, "Before we go, last night, you said something about a man I do not know. Abraham ibn Hasdai."

The rabbi peered at me through narrowed eyes. "From Barcelona?"

"Yes, you mentioned that too. Who is he?"

He shook his head and winced again. "A translator from Arabic to Hebrew. A supporter of the Rambam." He sighed and touched his head. "Abraham ibn Hasdai claims Moslem influence and eloquence as expressed in the Arabic language has a corrupting effect on Jews and thus on our use of the Hebrew language. He says we no longer create with style and elegance in Hebrew because we have been seduced by Arabic." By the last word, the rabbi's voice grew faint.

"Try to rest," I told him. "Stay as still as you can. And try not to worry." I would have liked to learn more, especially why the rabbi had mentioned this name, but a guard arrived to remove Rafael and me.

"Surprising about Abraham ibn Hasdai. Do you know of him?" I asked Rafael once we were outside the prison. Like most educated Jews in our part of the world, I had become quite accustomed to thinking and working in Arabic and Latin. Rafael, whose Hebrew was much better than mine or anyone else's I knew, was one of the few who did sometimes compose in Hebrew.

"I think I have heard a vague reference to him. I must admit I am curious to know more. Once we free the rabbi, maybe we can fulfill the early promise we attached to his arrival and learn more about the Rambam and his followers."

Rafael took me directly home to resume my observance of the Shabbat while Manuel would take supplies back to the rabbi and let us know if his condition worsened. I would have to wait until sundown, the end of Shabbat to pursue further answers. I prayed that by next Shabbat, one week away, the current experience would have been transformed into a memory.

Seven

I often found peace and a connection to my fellow Jews at Shabbat services. That sense of comfort was missing on this particular Shabbat because of the rabbi's situation.

Though tempted to bypass the services because of the investigation, doing so would have unnecessarily offended my fellow Jews, which I did want to avoid. Meanwhile, with a bit of luck, I might hear something of value as I sat in the women's section of our synagogue. I dressed with care. Nina fussed over me even more than usual, making sure no detail of my costume went unexamined. "You must be especially well dressed since you will arrive so late. But it is good that you are going to services so you can pray to God for forgiveness and mercy after the way you transgressed His laws for the Shabbat."

Though Nina's words sounded harsh, I knew profound love and caring lay behind her scolding.

"Spending a night with two men in such an unholy place. Bad enough at any time, but on Shabbat—"

"Nina, I assure you what I did was in accordance with the Lord's most important commandment, that we preserve life."

"So you say. But I fear you will be the death of me. Soon."

I regarded her with affection and finally convinced her to forgive me. Her lecture resulted in our being even later for the services. The women's section was packed this Saturday morning, so we found space on one of the pews in the back.

Seated next to me was Miriam, the aged matriarch of the Mendoza family. A quiet, dignified woman, she never entered into the lively gossip that often tempted us away from prayers and Torah readings.

"Shabbat Shalom, Signora," I greeted her.

She lowered her eyes, avoiding my gaze. She merely nodded and appeared absorbed in her prayer book. On her other side sat her daughter-in-law Raquela Susanna, wife of Baruch Mendoza. Following her mother-in-law's gesture, Raquela Susanna also averted her gaze.

Why this distancing? Was it because of the questions I had asked Natan and Baruch? Was this something the men would even have discussed with the women in the family? Had the women somehow come to understand that I had joined Rafael Lopes Dias in opposing the Mendoza stance on the murder of the crusader?

The Torah service ended, and then our rabbi delivered a sermon very different from that of the visiting rabbi the previous week—about the need for us to be vigilant about our reputation and well-being in the larger community. That we were a people known for peaceful ways, that violence was abhorrent to us. He insisted that we must move quickly to put the scandal and the horror of the murder of the cursed crusader behind us, and that we should pray for these men and all their ilk to leave our city forever. Soon. Without inflicting any more harm on us or our fellow Salernitans.

Based on the sermon, it appeared our rabbi had sided with the Mendozas and judged the newcomer guilty—and was quite willing to condemn and abandon him, a sacrifice for the "greater good" of the whole Jewish community without any further effort to find the truth. Certainly, the Egyptian rabbi had not earned our rabbi's good will with his hostile sermon. Still, were people not entitled to not be judged harshly before the full truth is known? How much did actual innocence count?

All around me, there were murmurs and whispers of agreement—and some surreptitious looks in my direction. I could not help wondering what about me was currently attracting less than friendly attention? If it was not about my fighting for the accused rabbi, might it be my relationship with Rafael? I had heard from Nina that, even here, in tolerant Salerno, people were troubled by any relationship that violated the usual patterns. Not a marriage. Not merely professional colleagues—itself a relationship not known to include partners of the opposite sex. I did not have a husband and Rafael did not have a wife. Somehow, if we each had a spouse, our particular relationship might be a bit more acceptable.

A chill came over me as I again realized how alone Rafael and I were in our efforts to save Rabbi Isaac ben Shmuel. As I looked around at the other women, none met my gaze. I wanted to stand up and, here in this house of God, proclaim the Egyptian rabbi's innocence.

That, of course, would do nothing to relieve the hostility around me. The good Lord might be forgiving and merciful but much less likely this congregation. Yes, it was a fearful time, and it was easy to understand why people would yearn for a simple and quick solution to the threats we faced. I also hoped for a solution that was simple and quick . . . but, most of all, just.

I could scarcely focus on the final parts of the service. Usually, as we left, people stopped to enjoy a bit of conversation—expected behavior on a lovely spring Sabbath. Today, however, few people partook. The whole community seemed to have closed in on itself in a way the peace of the day belied. Wherever a few women had gathered and begun to chat, as soon as I approached, their conversation halted and they looked anywhere but at me. If I tried to strike up a conversation, they awkwardly scattered.

Nina rushed home, as was her usual habit, to lay out the after-service meal. I was about to give up on any social exchanges when Leah Sara Garcia came up to me.

"Shabbat Shalom, Rebecca," she said. Older than me, Leah Sara had many qualities I admired. Although not a practicing physician, she had also been educated at the Scuola. And, it was she who had taken charge of Malka Freya when she swooned during services the previous week. Unlike me, Leah Sara was a native Salernitan, married to another native. She had managed to live the true Jewish ideal with a large, thriving family—in addition to or, perhaps, despite her education. Most impressively, she made her accomplishments appear easy—a woman I wished I knew better. Maybe after Rafael and I could put this murder behind us, I would take the time to pursue a friendship with her. If life ever got less busy, which, granted, never seemed to be the case. However, at this moment I imbued her presence with the hope she might be helpful for my immediate concern.

"And to you too, Leah Sara. Please, may I ask what might you know about the murder of the crusader? Have you heard any information Signor Lopes Dias and I can bring to the duke to help free the innocent rabbi?"

She arched a brow and pulled back somewhat, asking, "Is this the usual way you conduct a Shabbat conversation?" Her tone was more of amusement than societal rebuke.

I chastised myself for immediately jumping into the topic of the murder. I knew societal conventions as well as anyone, yet instead of first asking after her family and herself, I had abruptly launched into the pressing matter at hand. I had been taught better, but I was so concentrated on the rabbi's situation that I skipped over those appropriate and expected niceties.

I felt my cheeks redden with my embarrassment and then dared to look her straight in the eyes. "Your forbearance, dear Signora. Please forgive my clumsy lack of courtesy—this matter presses on me so deeply even now, on Shabbat."

She nodded slightly. "Indeed. I can see and understand that it disturbs you so much, and I agree it presents a danger to our community. Yet why would you think I might know any more of this matter than do you?" Her smooth brow wrinkled with apparent consternation. It troubled me so to trouble her. Nonetheless, I followed my instincts and pushed ahead.

"With your wide acquaintance, perhaps you have heard some news, some rumor, that is not generally known."

"And do you think I, or I should say my husband, would keep such information from the duke?" Her voice was low-pitched, melodious. "Rafael Lopes Dias is not the only Jew who has the duke's ear."

I tried to swallow back the heat I was sure colored my cheeks. "Of course I believe your husband would provide any helpful information that came his way to the duke. However, perhaps you have heard some news recently, in the past few hours and, what with it being Shabbat, your husband has not yet had the chance to—"

"And you want to be the one to take such news to the duke," she finished for me.

"I would at least want to know if such news is forthcoming soon. Some relief, some promise that the grimness of the situation will soon be soothed. It may not be generally known already, but the rabbi was attacked and seriously injured in his cell. This does not bode well for his safety there."

A spark briefly flared in her eyes before she tamped down this show of emotion. "No, I did not know this. I agree. It does not bode well. When did this attack take place?"

After I told her it was last night, her brows rose and fell. "You already know this information despite it being Shabbat. How is that possible?"

My cheeks heated further with my uneasiness at having to reveal what we had done. Nevertheless, I told her the full story.

She shook her head. "I am taken aback by what you say."

Tempted as I was to ask whether she was more troubled by the attack or by my actions, I did not. "You can see that the need to free the rabbi has grown more urgent."

"Indeed. I am most interested that you have become so caught up in this situation. I of course understand your desire to have the rabbi's injuries tended to, but would it not have been more appropriate for a male physician to have done that? Further, are not these political matters in the domain of our menfolk?"

"Are justice and truth only in the domain of our menfolk? Are these not also the concerns of Jewish women?"

She favored me with a small, tight smile. For a moment, she looked weary. Then she pulled herself to her full height and put her hand on my arm. "Such fire and strength in your words. A sure sense of right and wrong." She shook her head. "It would be a much better thing for the whole Jewish community if it could be proven that the Egyptian rabbi had not committed this crime. Especially if a Gentile had. However, much as we hate it, the evidence appears to point to our community, specifically, the rabbi. One thing is sure. The sooner the matter is resolved, the better it will be for our community." There she had summed up the majority opinion of Salerno's Jews.

"Come to my home for Shabbat luncheon," she continued. "We can share our thoughts, and maybe better understand each other."

Nina would not be happy at the last-minute change in our routine, but I was sure she would understand after I explained the importance of this unexpected invitation. "Thank you. I shall need to let my servant know. She worries so."

Leah Sara nodded. "Sounds like an excellent servant. Of course, do what you need to and then come to my house as soon as you can."

࿇

When I arrived home, the table was set, though luckily, Nina had not yet put any food out. "I am going to have Shabbat luncheon at the home of another magistra, Leah Sara Garcia, so we can talk about the rabbi's case."

A flurry of emotions crossed Nina's kindly face. "I did not know you were acquainted with her."

"Not a strong acquaintance, but I spoke with her after services."

Nina nodded. "She is an important woman."

"Yes. That is one reason why I especially want to talk to her." I clasped Nina's hand. "Thank you for understanding."

"You caught me in time. We can have our luncheon dish for dinner."

"No," I pressed her, "please go ahead and enjoy it now."

She sniffed. "I will make do. You will tell me anything you learn?"

"Of course."

I did not change or refresh my costume, as I did not want to keep Leah Sara waiting. I walked the short distance to the home she shared with her family. In my haste and carelessness, I had neglected to ask who might be joining us. If we would sit down to a large festive meal, it might be a challenge to talk of anything significant.

To my relief, a servant ushered me to a large table with only Leah Sara seated. "My husband had to travel down to Palermo for business and stay there over Shabbat," she informed me, no doubt in response to my surprise at seeing her alone. "As for my children—each has made plans today that do not include me." She smiled. "Such a Shabbat is rare. Please sit."

"Thank you so much for your invitation," I said, settling in.

"I appreciate the opportunity to have some time with another woman who studied as I did, especially with my Abraham out of town. You know, much as a big, busy family such as mine is a wonder and blessing, a bit of time away from them is a rare delight."

No, I did not know, never having experienced the family life she described except for a very brief time in Barcelona. In any case, I smiled with relief that she would generously give of her treasured time to me.

"The topic for our conversation is grave. This hardly seems the kind of delightful respite you might hope for," I pointed out.

"I agree. But first, after services, I have worked up an appetite and I imagine you have also."

"Normally, that would be true. I have become so caught up in this situation, however, with concern for Rabbi Isaac ben Shmuel, I have had little appetite lately."

"We are all concerned for the Egyptian rabbi and the accusation that a Jew has killed a crusader." Her smile was rueful. "How are you and your Rafael faring in solving the case?"

"He is not *my* Rafael," I protested.

She shrugged. "He is everyone's Rafael. We all care, and care for him. However, I must admit I am as curious as everyone else as to the exact nature of your relationship with him."

I chose to ignore this last bit in order to focus on the true matter at hand. "Then you believe, as do I, in the rabbi's innocence?"

Before Leah Sara could respond, her servant came in with a

beautiful challah and wine. My hostess and I recited the blessings for both. Then another servant brought small dishes of olives and almonds, along with the main course—eggplant stuffed with lamb.

The food looked and smelled delicious, rousing my dormant appetite. As we served ourselves from the platter, I could smell cinnamon, lavender, mint, cloves, and coriander along with the rich aroma of the lamb. What a feast!

"Your cook has done a splendid job."

"She is a treasure." We both savored our food in silence for a few moments. Then, with the first hunger pangs abated, we resumed our conversation.

"I did notice that you sidestepped my question about you and Rafael."

I swallowed hard. "I would prefer to focus on the substance of today's most pressing matter—the case of the rabbi."

"I understand. But allow me this bit of Shabbat indulgence. Surely a few minutes of that conversation will not delay things too much for the other."

I sighed and allowed myself to ease into my role as a guest at this table.

"I have heard that you collaborate with Rafael on translations into Hebrew," Leah Sara went on. "I admire you for this. It is quite a feat to combine strong language skills with the practice of medicine."

"I was fortunate that my early education left me fluent in several tongues. Being a physician is one of the reasons I want to work on the medical translations, to help make sure the most recent information is available in Hebrew. It is a way to ensure that we develop a vocabulary of science for the Hebrew language."

She nodded. "My daughter-in-law's family came from Andalusia, in Spain, you know? There they have a kind of love poem, called the *zajal*. This verse form is Arabic and is especially famous for the way in which it mixes the different languages, ending in a couplet either in Hebrew or in Andalusian Spanish. Her family has impressed us with these poems."

"Yes, I have some familiarity with these. They can be quite beautiful. Of course, scientific and medical translations are much different."

"Of course. However, I believe even scientific and medical translations can arouse passion and strong feelings in much the same way poetry can—can they not?"

I nodded vigorously. "First of all, there is the matter of choosing what will be translated into Hebrew. With so many works being written in Arabic and Latin, how does one choose to translate one and not another? Might not such a question arouse strong opinions?"

"Yes. Even when choosing what to translate of a certain author's work. Such as the Rambam, who wrote so much."

I smiled in happy surprise since Rafael and I had recently had such a discussion. "Exactly. I have had several such discussions recently."

"Have you? Have you read widely of the Rambam's work to consider for translation?"

I nodded again. "There is so much to admire in his work, to want to have it translated into Hebrew. Though I must admit I have been disappointed in his treatment of women."

"As have I."

More and more surprises. Until now, I had not really thought others might agree about a disappointment in the Rambam's treatment of women.

Still, fascinating as this topic was, at this time it was a distraction from helping advance our finding the solution to the case. "I would love to talk about this with you much more, and perhaps we can do this at a future time. But I am concerned this topic is diverting us from the primary matter at hand, the crusader's murder."

Her eyes pierced mine. "Is it?"

"What do you mean?"

"Do you think the matter of Rambam's treatment of women is without connection to what has happened to his colleague?"

I shook my head. "I am sorry, I am not following."

At that moment, I remembered the rabbi's wife had left him for a Christian man. Was there any connection between what the Rambam wrote and how the rabbi treated his wife, provoking her to leave him?

"I do not mean to imply that I know more than I know," Leah Sara said. "But think about it. I can tell, you are quite passionate about how the Rambam's work treated women. You are not the only one. The question is, are such feelings and the passions they might provoke strong enough to motivate murder?"

Her words confused and intrigued me. What was she saying? I needed to respond and fell back on what I considered a fundamental truth. "No. Women do not murder."

She looked at me with some surprise. "Really? Are you quite sure?"

Did she just say what I thought I heard her say?

My face must have shown my confusion and distress. Could this woman of stature in our society—the embodiment of the Bible's *a woman prized above rubies*—possibly have insinuated that a *woman* might be guilty of such a crime?

"I must admit that such a possibility has not occurred to me. Signora, please be even more direct. What, exactly, are you telling me?"

In a calm, small voice, she said, "I have merely tried to open up some possibilities." She sat back in her chair and favored me with a sour smile. "Our history, both ancient and more recent, has no shortage of killings and murders, both of the accidental and of the purposeful type. Committed by men and, yes, though not so often, even by women."

I could not disagree.

"Do you believe the death of the crusader was accidental or purposeful?" She scrutinized me with attention.

I had not considered the matter from that perspective. I took a moment to think while she appeared to wait patiently. At last I said, "I do not see how a stabbing such as he sustained could be accidental."

She nodded. "Yet what if the stabbing were an accident in the sense that what was intended for one man mistakenly was perpetrated on another?"

"A mistake in identity?" I still could not form a picture of what she meant.

"Something akin to that. Unfortunate, but an error all the same."

I shrugged in confusion rather than nonchalance. "I am not learned in the ways of the law. However, it would seem that murder is murder, no matter if the victim is the intended target or not. In fact, it is even worse if a person's life ends because of such a mistake."

She folded her hands together on the table. "Death is death. Predestined or random. Do you not think so?"

"Is this what you think? That the crusader was in the wrong place at the wrong time? Who, then, was the target? The murder happened, after all, in a Frankish tavern frequented by crusaders." A thought struck me. "Do you think the actual target was the rabbi, perhaps due to his hateful sermon? Did someone follow him to that unlikely place?"

"More good questions of possibilities."

I sighed in exasperation. "I am not sure where your words are leading. Myself, I would consider the possibility of any such error incredible."

"Would you really?" She thought for a moment. "I am not sure I agree, but my opinion on this topic does not matter because I am not involved in the way you are. Since you are trying to solve this matter, I would encourage you to keep your mind open."

"It is interesting that you say these words, since I am usually the one encouraging others to do the very same. Until now, I would have considered myself among the most open-minded and yet you are showing me a different perspective. I feel as I did when I arrived in a new, unfamiliar land. Not the most comfortable of feelings."

She smiled and patted my hand. "It is counter to my role as hostess to cause discomfort."

I nodded my thanks for her gesture.

She continued, "I expect your education and experience serve you well, whatever new situation you find yourself in."

If only. Just then a servant brought fragrant mint tea and lovely pastries. After such a lavish midday feast, I would not be very hungry for my evening meal, which was to the good, considering how much work I faced once the sun set on our Sabbath.

My mind would not stop working on the ideas Leah Sara had opened. "Do you think we should be questioning *women* as we try to solve this case?" I could not keep a tone of disbelief from my voice. It would probably fall to me rather than Rafael to question any females whom we suspected.

Yes, women have been known to murder, with poison being their— our—weapon of choice. As a physician, I understood how effective poison could be. I had to be meticulous in balancing the dosage requirements for patients, to make sure they took the right amount of prescribed medications. Too little would be ineffective. Too much could injure or kill. A poisoner would have to know what to use—and how much would do the job. And women could do this at least as well as men.

But a woman stabbing a man? Difficult to imagine. First, for the reason that men were usually bigger and stronger than women. And even small men tended to be much stronger. I could not picture a woman wielding a weapon suitable for stabbing with sufficient force to accomplish the deed, and I said so.

"Under normal conditions, I would agree," she said. "However, there are strong women. And those driven beyond endurance are capable of acts we would not expect."

After a long pause, with both of us seemingly lost in thought, she looked at me and smiled. "Well, much as I have enjoyed the chance to talk to you, my duties summon me elsewhere."

I did not want to overstay my welcome. "Loath as I am to admit to anything good coming from our current enigma, I am glad it has led me to the opportunity to speak with you."

She nodded graciously. "The same for me. I have been remiss in not making the effort to make your acquaintance, and that is my loss. Now, however, I view you as a friend, one to share with my circle of women. I hope you will consider joining us—I think you will find us congenial."

"Though not murderers." I said it lightly, and then hoped I had not caused offense.

Instead of being offended, her expression turned bemused and then, almost as quickly, became rather guarded, which brought more questions to mind. Since it was clearly time for me to leave, I would have to keep any such questions for another time.

"I am so happy I accepted your invitation and look forward to meeting on more fortunate occasions. In the meanwhile, before I take my leave, perhaps you can tell me any last thoughts you might have as to where I might direct my search for answers."

She smiled slightly. "I account our conversation a success because it has introduced new possibilities to you."

"Let us say, I feel my mind is open."

Leah Sara squeezed my hand. "Good. My dear, as to your parting question, I think you might be less happy with my advice. Devastating as it would be for you, you might come to realize the best person has been taken into custody."

I nearly staggered back as her words struck me. "In my belief, that is not the case. The *best* person, the *only* person in this situation, is the guilty one. I thought you agreed about that."

Her brow rose. "I believe in what is real, what we see, hear, and touch. The Egyptian rabbi, a stranger to our community who has created discord, was apprehended by the guards at the scene of the crime. One body on the ground and a bloody knife in his hand."

"All true, but the rabbi was in shock. A murder had been committed before his eyes while he was in an alien setting. From your education, you must understand what that means. He told me he picked up the knife while in a state of confusion and shock. I am surprised and distressed to hear you express the same argument the duke has advanced. Sometimes, we cannot believe all our eyes tell us to be the truth."

There goes my attempt at gracious leave-taking. "Furthermore, the fact that he is an unwelcome stranger who some are willing to sacrifice has too many frightful reflections in our Jewish past for me to consider it."

Leah Sara held out her hand, which I took with less warmth than I would have earlier. "Try to see these matters in perspective," she said, her tone turned cooler.

What happened to my friendly hostess? "Thank you for your hospitality." I said the words with what grace I could muster and left.

Eight

One of my favorite parts of Shabbat was its gift of peace and serenity in the maelstrom of life, and I would often indulge in reading for pleasure in the afternoon. However, once back at home after all the events of the past several days, restlessness and disturbing thoughts kept me from staying in any one place.

After sundown, Rafael and I would meet with Reuben and Benjamin ben Joseph. Because I did not want to succumb to the despair that I had reached an impassable wall, I clung to the hope they could provide some fresh ideas.

In search of peace, I went into my herb garden. My fingers itched to dig into the ground, to pull some of the weeds our gardener had not gotten to, but even this amount of work would be improper for Shabbat. So I sat on my bench, under a lemon tree, which was heavily laden with luxuriantly ripe fruit, its sweet, distinctive citrus smell mixing with other garden fragrances. What could be more beautiful than the scent of lemon mingling with lavender and thyme? Nature was conspiring to calm me, but still I could not let myself surrender to its charms. Instead, my mind kept harking back to the ideas to which Leah Sara Garcia had introduced me. Could a woman somehow have been involved in the murder? A savage death by stabbing brought up all the worst ugliness in our civilization, so contrary to the image of women as nurturers.

Oh, Leah Sara Garcia, what have you done? Why have you opened my mind to look in such distressing places? I cannot bear to linger on the possibilities you have introduced.

I gave myself up to the scents of lavender and thyme, the sweet tang of lemon, and let my troubled thoughts subside for the briefest of Shabbat intervals.

❧

That evening, after the *Havdalah* ritual to end Shabbat, Rafael and I had arranged to meet with the ben Joseph brothers. The two of us were about to set off with Manuel driving his carriage when a breathless messenger arrived from the hospital.

"Magistra," he said, "you have been summoned for an emergency. A young woman brought in, near death. From the da Costa family. The patient will not allow any man near her, so the family sends for you."

Dear God, what now? The servant joined Rafael and me in his wagon, which Manuel drove.

"You know the da Costa family?" Rafael asked. "They are up with the Mendozas and the Garcias, leaders of the Jewish community." *Not my usual patients. Still, if the girl will not let any man near her, her usual physician cannot help.*

As we rushed along, Rafael conferred with the servant, then told me, "There was at least one crusader involved in what happened. A young girl was badly hurt—maybe accidentally."

"Hard to believe it was accidental," I muttered, "but we shall see." My mind grappled with possibilities. Young Jewish girls, especially from the most prominent families, were strictly supervised and chaperoned, so it was difficult to imagine one being hurt in an accident. Of course, given the precariousness of life, anything could happen at any time to anyone. A fire whilst cooking. A mishap with a horse or carriage. In this case, though, a crusader was involved.

I shivered as the ugly possibilities ran through my mind.

Swift as the horses were, the trip felt too long. When we arrived at the hospital, another servant of the da Costa family, ashen-faced, eyes wide with fear, awaited us at the entrance. Rafael and I followed her along the familiar hallway.

"Who is with the girl now?" I asked, while being led at a fast pace to the chamber where she lay.

The servant shook her head. "Only my lady, her mother, who will not leave her side. The girl's father wants to be there, too, but she begins to cry piteously if he comes near to her."

That sounded ominous. "What is the patient's name?"

"Shoshana."

Given what we knew, I told Raphael not to come into the room with me. The scene I encountered once I entered was beyond my worst fears. Obviously badly bruised, the patient was a young woman of maybe sixteen years. She was so scared that even I frightened her, despite the crooning reassurances of her mother and my most gentle approach.

"You are the Jewish healer?" the mother asked above the crying of her daughter.

"Yes, I am Magistra Rebecca. May I examine her?" I asked.

Her mother nodded. I spoke softly to Shoshana before starting the examination, but she began to whimper and then cowered in agony when I tried to touch her. There was no mistaking the terror in her eyes. The innocence of this young woman had been shredded as savagely as her clothing, which lay torn and tattered at the foot of the bed. She was now garbed in the simplest of shifts—with at least the small mercy of being fresh, clean, and whole.

The mother wrung her hands but made a visible effort to calm herself. "Shoshana was going to her friend's house to enjoy the Shabbat
afternoon together. With her *duenna*, her chaperone, of course. Those
horrible men followed them—" She choked and could not continue.

"What men?"

"Knights from the Crusade," the mother whispered, her face contorted with pain.

I shivered at the mention of these men and glanced at my patient.
Her eyes were closed now, and I could not tell if she was listening to
our conversation or perhaps reliving what had happened to her.

"What did the crusaders do to your daughter?" I whispered back.

Signora da Costa shook her head. "They accosted her and grabbed
her. When the *duenna* tried to stop them, they . . . they shoved her
and hit her. They left her crumpled on the ground and unconscious.
A neighbor's servant stumbled on her and took her to their house.
We were out for the day, so we did not learn of any of this until this
evening. It appears the crusaders took my daughter somewhere for
hours—" She could not finish as she broke down in tears.

Clearly, the girl had been raped. My heart went out to her at the
thought of this horror. I put a comforting hand on the mother's arm.
Hard as it must have been for her to talk, I needed to try to understand if I was to find a way to help the victim.

"How did she come to be in the hospital?"

The signora visibly struggled to gather herself and respond. "When
she was late to her friend's house, the girl went with her brother to look
for Shoshana. By the time they found her . . . she was so badly hurt,
they were scared. They ran to the hospital for help. That is why she is
here. Then they came and told us." She wrung her hands repeatedly.

The woman gulped and put her hand to her throat. "They *attacked*
an innocent young girl. Worse than the lowest of beasts."

I knelt next to the girl's bed and bent my head close so I could whisper. "Shoshana, little rose, I am a physician. My name is Rebecca. I am here to help you. Please let me do so."

She whimpered and shook her head, her cheeks bruised, her upper lip swollen, and a cut above her right eye. "No one can do anything. My life is finished."

I put a reassuring hand on the side of her head, on her tangled black curls. "You have been hurt by evil men, but we cannot let what they did finish you or end your dreams. We will not let them have such an unmerited victory. You deserve to go ahead with your life as you and your loved ones wish. That will be the best way to show that they have not won."

When she heard my words, she began to weep, harsh wracking sounds. Signora da Costa put her hands over her face as if to banish from her sight the ugliness before her.

"It hurts so much," Shoshana moaned.

"Tell me what hurts. Let us start to heal you, so you can have your life back."

She shook her head again. "My betrothed. My Yonatan. No, no longer mine. Now he will not want to marry me. I have been tainted. No longer a maiden for him." She choked on the last.

Her soft-spoken words poured over me and burned like lava from a volcano. *I hope the rejection she fears does not happen. I hope her Yonatan will still want her, despite her having been raped by crusaders. I pray that his family agrees. I hope the rape does not leave her pregnant or with untreatable injuries.* One thing at a time. First I would examine her to see the extent of those injuries.

"I understand your pain and despair." *As if anyone really can.* I wished I could comfort her and encourage her to believe her young man would be there for her, but I did not want to mislead her. "The greatest concern now, though, is to make sure you do not have any wound that is untreated. Then you can regain your strength soon. *Then* you will see to other matters. You are not alone."

Her gaze met mine. Her eyes now began to focus, and they showed an intelligent young woman who was grasping my meaning. Was her young man truly worthy of her? I hoped I could help her heal sufficiently in both body and mind so she could resume her life, no matter what.

Examining her upper body yielded cuts and bruises, but no broken bones. I could easily leave her servants directions for poultices and healing drinks and foods.

Then, when I examined her lower body, I bit my lip. She had been violated by the penetration of her reproductive organ and her anus. She was still bleeding from both, so my first task was to stanch the flow of blood and examine her to see what sort of treatment would be required. Despite the violence Shoshana had endured, I could help heal her—physically—with poultices and balms and any needed stitching.

Emotionally, it would take much more to help restore the proper balance of her humors.

"Can you tell me what happened?" I asked when I had managed to clean her up and applied a healing balm made from comfrey root that stopped the spill of blood. I thought we would not need stitches. The servant had gone to start brewing a comforting tea of valerian.

She swallowed hard. "Consuela, my *duenna*, and I were going to my friend's house for a Shabbat tea. She and I are planning a dress for a party for our families—mine and that of my betrothed. I want . . . I wanted to look so beautiful, so special," she sobbed. Her mother turned away to hide her own tears.

"Two crusaders followed my *duenna* and me." She hiccupped. "But we were just walking on the street. So I did not pay them any mind. That is what we were told, to ignore them and they will go away. Only they did not." Overcome with tears and a shortness of breath, she could not continue speaking. I gently massaged her shoulders and murmured softly.

When she regained her breath, she spoke again. "One ordered me to go with them. Consuela told them to leave us alone." Shoshana frowned as more tears rolled down her cheeks. "One picked her up like she was nothing and dropped her to the ground and kicked her in the head. She is little. She . . . lost her senses and could do nothing more for me." She broke off speaking and sobbed. "It is very difficult. I hope Consuela will be all right and can face down the shame. She is the most dignified of women."

How remarkable that a young girl, in the midst of her suffering, thought of the other woman. "Painful as it is to say the words, it is good for you to tell what happened," I said, "but you can stop now if it is too difficult to go on."

She sniffled and sighed. "And then they took me, like I was a thing for sale in a shop. One picked me up, grabbing me with his filthy hands, and they ran with me, laughing. And then in an alley behind some shops, they . . . tossed me down on the ground and fell on me like wild beasts." She shuddered, revulsion contorting her lovely, but now tear-stained and swollen, features.

I put a hand on her arm in a vain attempt to bring comfort. She took a deep, tremulous breath, then continued. "They *attacked* me and laughed at my shame as if this were an amusement. I screamed, I ordered them to stop. Then I begged them to stop. They told me to shut up or they would crush me the way they had done with Consuela. I was so scared."

"Of course you were. Anyone would have been." I patted her arm, a gesture meant to comfort but which I feared to be futile.

"It was not anyone. It was me. Oh, *Dios mio*. It would have been better if they had killed me. Then I would not bring such dishonor on my family."

Her mother gasped at such words, and I prayed she did not wish her daughter had died.

I cursed the traditions all girls and women are taught that would make us blame ourselves for being the victim of two powerful crusaders intent on doing evil. "My dear one, you are brave and strong. You have survived this awful day to live and flourish. The worst now is over."

"Is it? Truly?" She looked at me with disbelieving eyes that had suddenly grown old.

I hoped and prayed my words would turn out to be prophetic. Let her betrothed be a true gentleman who would accept his bride after the crusaders' evil. Let Yonatan be extraordinary among the men of his society. And the same for his family. I tried to hold onto the hope that such would be the case, although this required more optimism than I could truly believe in at that moment.

I stayed with Shoshana while she drank the valerian tea and until she at last fell into an uneasy sleep. Then I turned to her mother and the servant who would be her primary caregiver.

"How could this have happened?" her mother kept asking, over and over. "My poor daughter—how can she have her life now?"

My first impulse was to reprove her for sustaining Shoshana's darkest fears, but how could I fault this woman for being ordinary and in touch with reality?

"You must not allow even the merest intimation of such discouragement to touch your daughter. Your job now, as her loving mother, is to help her have a full, happy life. This means you must not think of her as ruined. She did nothing to bring this calamity upon herself and your family, and she should not be punished. Were there any true justice, the men who did this would be hunted down as the criminals they are, made to feel the agony they caused, and condemned to a dishonorable death."

"If only that would happen," the mother moaned.

Looking back at her daughter with great sadness, she went on, "I wished she had not been brought to this hospital. When can we take her home, to her own bed?"

"It would be best for her to rest here until she begins to regain her strength. At least until we make sure she bleeds no more and that the wounds heal cleanly."

"I think it was a mistake for them to bring her here—" the mother started to insist again as we walked to the door where the girl's father and Rafael awaited us.

"If I could get my hands on those crusaders from hell," the father muttered, his eyes brimming with malice.

"You would do what? Bring down more retribution and possibly a pogrom on the Jewish community in Salerno?" Rafael shook his head. "I understand your reaction. But we Jews have to be especially careful when we are dealing with Gentiles. We have all suffered far too much violence already."

The father's initial anger ceded to heartbreaking pain. "I must do something," he rasped, "or I will go out of my senses with the agony."

Rafael touched the man's shoulder and nodded. "I understand your anger and desire for action. However, your attention must lie with your daughter, not with the crusaders. You must help her proceed with her life. Whether as the bride of a devoted groom or not."

As much as I agreed with Rafael's sentiments, I winced at the starkness of his words, which must have hurt the parents when the wounds were so fresh and the experience so acute. Nothing about this family's reality would be easy to hear. Or to bear.

"I only pray Yonatan does not reject her," Shoshana's father said.

The mother went on, "He is the eldest son of a leading business family here in Salerno. He could have any bride, and he chose her. The two young people know and care for each other. When I remember how excited Shoshana was that Yonatan chose her . . ." she trailed off as her hand clutched to her throat and her tears cut off further words.

"There is no sense mourning the loss of the betrothal until you know that is actually the case," I pointed out.

"If only we can keep this episode quiet. If we can prevent Yonatan's family from hearing what happened," the father said.

For a moment, a glimmer of hope lit the mother's face. As good as hope was for the bereaved, I did not expect they would succeed in keeping the episode silent. And if they somehow could, Shoshana would have to bear a terrible burden trying to start and sustain a new life with a lie.

"What is important now is to help your daughter and your family heal from this shocking crime," I urged, hoping but doubting that they understood. "Please know that you can call on me if ever there is a way for me to help."

The father glared at me. "From now on, we will consult with our usual family physician for our daughter. Your work with us is at an end. Of course you will honor our decision and keep quiet about what happened to our Shoshana."

My words and efforts mean nothing to him.

The signor gave his wife several coins with which to pay me. Though the abrupt dismissal hurt, my feelings were not of importance now. As graciously as I could, I thanked them. "Perhaps you can tell me who your physician is. That way I can speak with him, tell him what I have found."

He folded his arms before him and shook his head. "That will not be necessary. We thank you for helping us at this time of emergency. We will tell our physician what you have done for Shoshana and what you have told us. We are confident that he will be able to deal with the rest."

Clearly, I had overstayed their willingness to accept help from me, now that the first emergency was dealt with. Fighting back discouragement and fear for Shoshana's immediate future, I signaled to Rafael that we should go. He shook his head.

"Signor da Costa, with all due respect, for your daughter's sake and the sake of your whole family, you must not dismiss the magistra without giving weight to her words."

The older man regarded Rafael coldly. "I will thank you to realize that I am the best judge of how to guide my family. Of how to contain the misfortune that has befallen us."

"On the contrary. When a crisis hits, it is often most difficult for those closest to the victim to think clearly and choose the wisest path for their loved ones. Unjust as it is for your daughter, what happened to her cannot be hidden from her intended. There could be a much greater scandal if you were to try to pretend she was as before only to have the unsuspecting groom come to realize the truth. If a child were born out of season, for instance."

Signor da Costa rose to his full height. Tight-lipped he muttered, "You both must go now." He appeared to be at the edge of losing control of his temper.

"Let us go," I said in a calm, measured voice at odds with my feeling of loss and with my wish to urge the da Costas to act differently in their daughter's interest. Right now, I knew, any action other than leaving would only make a horrible situation worse. "You may call on me as you might need," I added and nodded to Rafael.

Lips clenched, Rafael followed me out. Once we were away from Signor da Costa, Rafael said, "I am sorry to say that this behavior is not unexpected. Most especially the efforts given to keeping what has happened a secret."

"Then this type of reaction must influence how we go forward," I said.

"True, though that does make our roles even harder." Rafael patted my arm over my dismissal by Shoshana's father, a gesture I appreciated, though comfort eluded me. "I will send word to the duke of this crime. The danger to our citizens has escalated when a young girl and her *duenna* are not safe in the street in daytime."

"Her father is insistent that we try to cover up the crime." My voice sounded as disheartened as I felt.

"As if that would be possible," Rafael muttered. "Very well, I will not identify the girl or her family. And now, Rebecca, I am taking you home, where you must promise me that you will get some rest."

"I think that will be as impossible for me this night as it will be for you," I said. "In any case, it is far too late for us to talk with the ben Josephs as planned." *Another delay. Yet, the miserable crusaders are free to go where they will, to rape and to ruin lives. And there is good reason to fear they will cause even more mayhem among us.*

"Try not to lose hope," Rafael said. "There is always tomorrow."

"Tomorrow," I sighed, as he helped me into his wagon. "With so much to do tomorrow, it is good that we had a Shabbat today." The bit of respite we had had seemed far distant in the past.

Rafael laughed. "Good that you have not lost your sense of humor. That, a bit of hope, and the rabbi's actual innocence might see us through."

"It is good you can be an optimist in this situation."

❧

Tonight's experience shook me. Poor Shoshana's horrifying ordeal catapulted me back to my own experience in England, as the kidnapped captive of the Knight Templar Brian de Bois-Guilbert. Though he claimed he loved me, I was never free of the fear that he would assault me in the name of whatever emotion he labeled as love. The threat of the underlying violence that animated this supposedly chaste priest-warrior had loomed over me without cease in the days when I was his prisoner. His so-called love nearly cost me my life. Time did not dim the fearful memories.

I may exhort Shoshana to be brave, but had I been so violated, would I have been brave? I was not put to the test that way, for which I thank God every day, and I must have compassion for what the victims endure and need to survive.

Such events only underscored the true powerlessness of female physicians, who, like me, hoped we could save the world—or at least bring healing to those who suffered the injuries that the powerful inflicted on the weak.

Even though Signor da Costa had clearly and harshly dismissed me from his daughter's case, I still intended to follow through and see how she progressed. I would go back to the hospital tomorrow after Rafael and I saw Reuben and Benjamin ben Joseph. I could only hope the da Costas were wise enough not to move Shoshana immediately. With their determination to keep things secret, however, I doubted they would listen to my advice.

As I had feared, sleep neither came easily nor lingered to provide much rest.

❧

As I awoke on Sunday morning, I had little appetite for a first meal. Of course, Nina had other ideas. She had gone to great effort to make sure I broke my morning fast with foods I usually found difficult to resist—sliced oranges, soft cheese, and her wonderful little bread rolls. Mint tea flavored with lemon and honey completed the menu.

"You must eat to keep up your strength," she scolded when I hesitated to dig in quite as enthusiastically as she would have me do.

I was still at the table when Rafael arrived. Of course Nina insisted that he too must eat. Thus it was mid-morning by the time we set off to see Reuben and Benjamin ben Joseph.

En route, Rafael asked if I had heard any more about Shoshana da Costa, and I told him no, though I would check on her later.

"Cursed crusaders," he grumbled as we made our way through the streets crowded with Sunday churchgoers and others intent on enjoying the beautiful day. "First, they sacked Constantinople, a Christian city that gave them no cause for attack, and then they wander wherever they want and cause more trouble. Manuel complains to me that the Christians are supposed to regard them as heroes, but he and his fellows have seen too much evil committed whilst they are supposed to do good."

"So it is true, what I have heard—that the crusaders destroyed Constantinople."

With a disgusted look, he nodded. "While not as unhappy with the crusaders as we Jews, Salerno's Christians also have little love for the unholy warriors. The leaders of Constantinople made bad agreements, and then the crusaders were not paid what they expected. Instead of trying to solve the problem and get their pay, they sacked the city. To my way of thinking, it has given them an unholy taste for having their way regardless of whom they hurt."

"An even greater unholy taste." I shivered as the possibilities of such attitudes and behaviors came to mind. Shoshana was an example. What if more young girls were attacked? What other crimes did the crusaders feel entitled to commit with impunity?

"I wonder if the unhappiness of the Christians could be useful for us," I said.

Rafael eyed me. "You mean in the sense that the enemy of my enemy is my friend?"

"Yes, I suppose that is what I mean. Surely Duke Henry and his guards will step in now to safeguard us," I asserted.

Rafael shook his head. "You mean the same duke and guards who are so busy safeguarding Salerno from the danger posed by an Egyptian rabbi who looks as if a strong wind would knock him to his knees? Our duke seems determined to stick with his ideas, and he will not let truth alter his course of action."

"We cannot give up. There must be something else we can do to safeguard the Jewish community while we find the murderer. And it is not only our community at risk. As the case of Constantinople shows, these crusaders will attack anyone, even those of their own faith."

His mouth in a grim line, Rafael nodded in agreement.

The ben Joseph brothers occupied homes in a row of buildings that belonged to their family and included their library. They were only a few doors down from the Mendozas' residences in the wealthiest Jewish section of our city. At the home of Reuben, the oldest in the family of five siblings, a male servant answered, ushering us into a sitting room to wait. Before the servant left, he invited us to sit on finely crafted wooden chairs with golden silk cushions. From my vantage point, I could view the highly polished tables, exquisitely carved of dark wood, and the gleaming statues of marble that punctuated the room. I especially admired a tapestry of a scene from the Bible—Adam and Eve in the Garden of Eden—hanging upon the wall opposite us, so intricately created, it must have taken a decade to construct.

Before the snake, obviously. I sighed. There were many snakes threatening the Garden of Eden that had once been Salerno.

"Reuben ben Joseph has had many dealings with the Egyptian court over the years," Rafael said. "There could have been communication between the brothers and the Rambam that involved our rabbi. I seem to remember that they actually voyaged to that court, so their experience might be firsthand."

"Interesting. I did not know there was so much intercourse between these places."

Rafael nodded. "Yes, in spite of difficulties in travel. I am sure you must know of such from your father's experiences."

"All too well," I agreed. "Not to mention my own problems whenever I must undertake any journey. Land or sea."

He gazed at me in some bemusement. "This is something I did not know about you. Have you been on many voyages?"

I was saved from having to delve into my earlier life as Reuben did us the courtesy of arriving promptly.

"We shall continue this conversation later," Rafael whispered before turning his attention to Reuben.

Our host was far more welcoming than what we had experienced at either of the Mendoza homes. "I have sent a servant to fetch my brother since the two of us share in the work of the library. He should be able to join us soon. In the meantime, my servant will bring refreshments."

Since Rafael and I were still full from Nina's breakfast, we declined the kind offer. While we waited for Benjamin, we exchanged small talk, which, however, soon took on the ominous tone that most conversations seemed to these days.

"I am worried about the crusaders. More of them arrive each day, supposedly on their way home, but too many seem in no hurry to leave," Reuben said.

I told him of the attack of the young girl whom, of course, I did not identify. Reuben's expression clouded over with anger, shock, and sadness, mirroring my feelings.

"I am very distressed. I too have a young daughter. I do not know what I would do if—"

At that moment, his brother, Benjamin, a larger, more optimistic-looking man, arrived. "Good morning. Can I believe my ears, that there is any situation in which my older brother does not know what he would do?"

This was meant, no doubt, to be an amusing opening. Of course, in this case, the words had a different effect.

"This is not a time for levity," Reuben admonished his younger sibling. He then informed him of the latest outrage perpetrated by the crusaders.

Suddenly quite pale, Benjamin sat down heavily beside his brother. "I cannot overstate how much I am aggrieved that the situation has reached such ugly proportions. Clearly, we have to do something. Take some action." He looked straight at Rafael as he added, "If the duke refuses to do his duty, the men of Salerno must."

Rafael shook his head. "The duke has the backing of Palermo and the pope."

Benjamin breathed deeply. "You are right, of course." He punched his right fist into his left hand.

Reuben shook his head and said, "We have learned from other places where they have been that the crusaders pay no attention to local laws. They claim special status, protected by the pope in Rome as well as by the nobility and kings."

Rafael spoke up. "It is one of the few instances when Duke Henry and the pope in Rome actually agree on something—all ways to overlook the nastiness they do to us Jews."

Though I preferred to believe in the goodwill of my Christian neighbors, this sometimes proved a challenge. "I have heard rumblings that, even if the crusader was killed by one of his peers, the duke will choose to convict the Egyptian rabbi so as not to subject one of the holy warriors to our system of justice." I looked from one brother to the other. "Do you agree that this could happen?"

Both men nodded. Reuben said, "The rabbi is seen as an easily disposed pawn. After all, who is going to protest if a Jew is hanged for the murder of a crusader? But hanging a crusader, no matter what he has done—that is unheard of and would, no doubt, ignite their wrath."

My stomach clenched hard at the truth of this prospect. "Still, someone else is guilty of this crime and remains free."

"I understand there are no suspects other than the rabbi," Reuben said.

"True," Rafael said. "However," and his glance included me, "the magistra and I are attempting to investigate further to really understand what the Egyptian rabbi was doing and with whom he has had contact. Unfortunately, we are having difficulty getting cooperation in that effort, especially because it appears he has no supporters."

Benjamin and Reuben both agreed. Then Benjamin said, "Rabbi Isaac ben Shmuel has never been the easiest person to get along with, but being disliked is not a death sentence. If it were, our population would be a lot smaller."

Reuben and Rafael smiled ruefully at this attempt at humor. I saw nothing funny in the truth of his statement.

"We have been hoping you might be able to shed some light. Did the rabbi make use of your library?" I asked, attempting to move the conversation forward.

Reuben nodded. "Yes. You see, I had met with him briefly in Egypt. Afterward, we had some correspondence with him. Because of that, he came to us as soon as he arrived in Salerno and had found a place to stay."

"What sorts of documents was he especially interested in?"

"Back in Egypt, he spoke to us regarding texts the Rambam requested. But after the rabbi arrived here, he wanted different types of texts. On the matters of marriage and purity of women. Also the fraternization of Jews and Gentiles, apostasy, and conversion. He read them here, in our study room."

I realized these topics could all relate to his wife leaving him for a Christian. "Did he ever discuss any of these matters with you?"

"No. He was not an especially friendly or social type, which is fine. Many scholars and rabbis prefer their privacy. Besides, he was displeased with what he called the loose atmosphere of Salerno. The way women mix freely with men at the medical school. The way Jews and Gentiles mix," Benjamin said. "As he made clear in that sermon."

No surprises. What are we missing?

"I sought to consult with the rabbi for a translation of work from the Rambam," Rafael offered. "He objected immediately to my choice of which of the writings to translate into Hebrew, and so we quarreled. But his greater quarrel with me was that I include the magistra in my medical translation work."

The other two men nodded in apparent agreement. "That sounds very much like the man we came to know a bit," Reuben said.

Rafael sat back in his chair and crossed his legs. "Not so unusual. Translations often lead to disagreements and arguments, sometimes very heated. This can actually be helpful, when they spur thought and creativity."

Benjamin agreed. "Of course. I have never seen a talented translator back down from a controversy about the work. They are usually open to examining writing from several points of view before they settle on the best choice of what and how to proceed."

"Gentlemen," I interrupted, as it seemed that Rafael and the brothers were about to embark on a long discussion of the finer points of translation, "I truly thank you for including me in this conversation. However, it does not appear to be related to the topic that brought us here."

The brothers appeared a bit surprised at my interruption, but Rafael nodded. "As you can see, gentlemen, the magistra is quite determined to keep us on track. For which I thank her."

"One other thing we wanted to ask," I said. "Do you know of an apprentice named Moshe ben Shlomo?" They knew little about him— far less than we did. As we parted from the ben Josephs, they agreed to contact Rafael and me if they thought of anything else.

Another dead end in our search. Surely, something would have to change soon or the next dead end would be Rabbi Isaac ben Shmuel's life.

When we were outside once again, Rafael asked, "Why did you ask about Moshe ben Shlomo?"

I shook my head. "I cannot say exactly. There is something about the young man that I cannot shake. Some sense that there is more that he can tell us."

"Perhaps we should go have another talk with him."

"Since he showed himself most unwilling to speak frankly with me present, perhaps you should do that without me."

"I shall."

Then Rafael looked into my eyes with some emotion I could not discern. "Tell me more of your difficulties with voyages."

I felt my cheeks redden. "With everything going on, I cannot believe that is what you choose to focus on."

He smiled. "Now I know this is *definitely* a topic to discuss."

"Only *after* we have solved the murder and the rabbi is free."

"As you wish," he agreed. "I shall not forget."

I hoped he would, but, in my experience, he never did forget things he said he would not.

Nine

Monday morning, taking a basket of provisions prepared by Nina, Rafael and I went to the castle. There, a messenger from the duke arrived to summon Rafael.

"How did you know to find me here?" Rafael asked.

"I went to your house where your servant informed me I could have saved myself the trip. Come with me at once. Duke Henry must not be kept waiting."

Rafael turned to me. "I must go."

I nodded my agreement. Maybe it was something to do with the Egyptian rabbi's innocence. "Do not worry. I will take the food to the rabbi myself. As soon as you can complete your business with the duke, you can join us."

"There is no telling how long I will be. If it appears that the conversation with the duke will be long, I shall request a messenger be sent to let you know so you can leave. If not, I shall be along directly."

Now, alone and nervous at my surroundings, I arrived at Rabbi Isaac ben Shmuel's cell to find him even more subdued than before, despite the items in the basket, which he fell upon with some appetite. I did not attempt to start a conversation with him while he was replenishing his strength with the food. Much to my relief, Rafael arrived before too long. From the worried expression on his face, though, I knew that my relief was to be short-lived.

"What is it?" I asked in our Salernitan language, to keep this from the rabbi.

He shook his head. "I shall tell you both at once."

With Rafael there, the rabbi appeared to revive a bit, though this may have been an effect of his appeasing his hunger.

"Why did the duke summon you?" I asked in Salernitan, unable to wait a moment longer.

He took a deep breath before responding in Arabic. "I am sorry to say I have bad news. Duke Henry is preparing to send the rabbi to the king's court in Palermo at the earliest possible time, within the next few days."

The effect of his words was immediate. Rafael stepped closer to the shriveled man, crouched on the floor where he had dropped the remains of his meal.

"Once there, Rabbi, you will be subject to the king's justice. That means a very fast, unfair trial . . . and almost certainly execution." He spoke the last words quickly, his voice and face grim.

How can this be? I dreaded the despair I was sure I would see on the rabbi's face, but instead, his expression was one almost of indifference.

"What are you saying?" A surge of anger mingled with the fear roiling within me. "Can the duke act in this manner without making any attempt to locate the actual murderer?"

"Does this really come as such a surprise?" Rafael asked in a low voice, at last tearing his gaze from the rabbi and looking at me.

"You are right—this is what we have been dreading. But why now?" I tried to keep my voice steady. "And how much time do we have left to find the murderer?"

"As to why, for all the reasons we have been dreading. As to when," he sighed, "it appears it will happen within the next three days.

"Aside from the horde of crusaders," Rafael asked, "are there any even slightly possible suspects?"

"Alas not," I said. Then I recalled, "However, Leah Sara Garcia raised the strange possibility that a woman may have committed the murder."

The rabbi watched and listened with detachment, as if nothing we said had anything to do with him. Was this from depression or from extreme denial of the truth?

"Leah Sara Garcia? She is definitely a woman of great talents. Her ideas are worthy of attention." Rafael rubbed his forehead and considered. "That certainly is a strange possibility. Of course, it is not hard to see that our forward-looking Salernitan women would not be so pleased at the arrival of such a fierce traditionalist. I recall there were several unhappy women, even at the home of our own rabbi, who was hosting the visitor. And the Mendozas were not among his admirers. Leah Sara Garcia is part of that family. However, I find it very hard to believe that a woman would commit such a grisly crime."

"I agree. But I cannot completely dismiss this idea," I admitted. "The rabbi did say that the killer wore a cloak that disguised his identity. A woman could have worn such a garment. Let us hold onto the remote possibility as we try to come up with some ideas."

Rafael nodded. "Rabbi, would you know anything about a woman possibly being involved?"

The rabbi snorted and shook his head.

"Another piece of the puzzle seems to be your apprentice, Moshe ben Shlomo. I have questions to ask that elusive man," I pointed out.

"Yes, there is a slim hope he might know something. Since he often works for the Mendozas, perhaps they can tell us where to find him."

I regarded the silent rabbi. "Getting him to talk might help. Yet that does not appear likely." I looked at Rafael. "What do you say? Shall we try the Mendozas next?"

"With our deadline looming, I am at a loss as to where else to go with our investigation."

As we were leaving, I addressed some last words to the rabbi. "Do not lose hope. Have faith that God will guide us to make sure justice is done."

He remained impassive, only murmuring in a raspy voice, "*Baruch Dayan HaEmet*"—Blessed is the One true Judge—a blessing most usually said when one hears of a recent death.

Unwelcome tears formed, and I sniffed them back. I absolutely could not let Rafael see me weep, not then, when our emotions were so prone to fall out of balance, when we needed to keep our thoughts and our humors on an even level. We bade farewell to the now silent rabbi and went off to try yet again to save him.

※

Once out of the dungeon, I needed a moment to recoup my spirit. As even-tempered as he was and as usually unshakeable, Rafael also seemed to need time to collect himself. We found a bench near the castle and sat for a few minutes. Despite our perilous situation and although neither of us even spoke, I found comfort being with this man, my longtime friend.

After several minutes of silent seated contemplation, we arose and walked down the hill from Duke Henry's castle, through Salerno's streets to the large home of Natan Mendoza. With people carrying on as usual, we could almost pretend that life was back to normal. Until the next outrage. I wished I could believe there would not be one.

A servant admitted us and instructed us to wait while he went to see if Signor Mendoza was at home to visitors. As the wait grew long and rather awkward, my nerves began to fray. Was this really the best way to use our limited time? I was on the verge of suggesting that we go elsewhere when a red-faced Natan Mendoza came striding into the hall.

"Why have you come here today?" he asked without pretense of courtesy. "I have no business with you that requires you to come to my home to disrupt my family's midday meal."

This was indeed a discourtesy on our part. I began to apologize, but Rafael interrupted. "We have recently learned that, if the true murderer is not identified immediately, the Egyptian rabbi is to be transported within two days to face the regent's justice in Palermo. More like the regent's *injustice*. News such as this impels us to forsake the usual politeness for a greater end."

Our reluctant host nodded and sighed. "I did not know this." He turned to the servant who had followed him in. "Tell the family to proceed with the repast. I will talk with these people and return to the table shortly."

Natan showed us into a small study and directed us to sit in the chairs surrounding a wooden table.

"I am sorry we have interrupted your meal," I said.

Natan shrugged. "As I am sure you know, Magistra, Lopes Dias and I have had disagreements in the past. However, at times like these, when Jews are at risk, we are called upon to support each other and look to the safety and well-being of all."

Rafael nodded in agreement.

Natan ran a hand over his chin. "I know you both are privy to the horrible crime that happened on Saturday to one of our girls at the hands of crusader scum." He pursed his lips. "Her family has moved her from the hospital to their home, where she should have been taken first."

So much for confidentiality. I should have realized poor Shoshana's plight would not long remain secret.

"This girl was not the first to suffer such an assault," Natan continued. "It seems the crusader rabble have developed a taste for our women."

"More like they have developed a taste for victimizing those they can easily overpower," I interjected. "Young women from every group are targets."

Natan grunted. "We Jewish men have no recourse when our women are so attacked."

"In these times," Rafael said, "even those who are usually understood to be strong may be at great risk. From what my servant, a Christian, has told me and I have heard from others, when it comes to defending their women from the crusaders, it is not clear that Christian men here in Salerno have recourse either."

Natan nodded and rubbed his chin again. "I can see this might be the case. Duke Henry appears to believe he is obligated to 'protect' the crusaders while they are on our soil, because of the political situation. Of course, I suspect that obligation would be sorely tried if a woman attached to the court were attacked, which I believe has not happened. In that respect, the crusaders do have some common sense. As you said, they attack those *outside* the sphere of power."

"I agree that they seem to know how far they can push the authorities," I said. *They are definitely wily, making them even more dangerous.*

"Yes. If the crusader was killed by another crusader, the rabbi's fate is sealed. The duke will not extend a finger to punish one of them." He frowned.

"Solving the murder is like a great puzzle with the important pieces missing," I lamented. "Rabbi ben Shmuel has been mostly silent since his arrest, especially as to why he was even with the crusader."

Natan regarded us both. "Would you be able to accept that he might indeed be guilty of what he is accused of? Sometimes the simplest explanation is the true one."

We had been asked that before. Both Rafael and I shook our heads, and then he spoke. "The rabbi knows more than he is telling, and he seems to prefer taking his secrets with him to the grave. And yet, at the same time, he swears he did not kill the crusader."

Natan had listened intently. Now, he let out a breath. "Guilty or innocent, he might indeed end up being executed for this crime. The question for us Jewish Salernitans is, will his execution be enough to calm the waters?"

"That would appear to be the duke's position and his hope," I said. "Yet, even if we were to accept the injustice, it is unlikely that the rabbi's execution will stop the crusaders' crimes, which, of course, were being committed even before the murder of the crusader. Thus, it will be an injustice without purpose. If only the duke could be persuaded to make a greater effort to keep us Jews safe and guard the peace. To make *any* real effort in fact."

Natan shook his head. "In this, our duke is unlike our previous rulers under the Normans. They extended their protection to all Salernitans. This Duke Henry—" he shook his head. "The risk of attack by crusaders is too great to allow our girls and women even the small measure of freedom they had known before. Magistra," he added, holding my gaze, "you must take note of this too, and guard yourself."

Rafael frowned. I, for one, was almost touched by Natan's concern for my safety. At the same time, though, a prickling of fear and negativity skated down my spine. Danger had played a large role in my

life during my younger days, in England. I dreaded the thought of
this again in Salerno.

"I will make sure that the magistra is safe," Rafael said.

His words, said with grim determination, touched me. Yet even
more injustice, unfairness, and insecurity—my heart wept at the
harsh reality before us, and at what women had to endure—both
those already victimized and those who had managed to evade harm.
Living with mortal fear wore at people's souls. Even as a young girl,
I had always appreciated freedom. I gave my beloved papa plenty of
reason to regret his leniency with me at a time when my peers were
strictly guarded and regulated. Now, as an adult and a physician, I
again enjoyed more freedom of movement than most other Jewish
women. Of course, I took care to be safe, to have an escort when that
was deemed wise—though I chafed at even this restriction. However,
in the current climate, it was doubtful any female could be confident
about her safety. I very much appreciated Rafael's pledge.

Natan went on, "My brother and I have joined with others to
discuss this topic. So far, the duke pretends to listen but does little.
Sending the rabbi to Palermo only confirms his stance."

Rafael acknowledged Natan's words with a cursory nod, and then
he came to the reason for our visit. "As you know, the magistra and I
have had no success in finding the true murderer. With the Egyptian
rabbi's imminent transport and then execution, time has become
even more precious. So we ask: Have you or your brother come up
with any ideas? We can talk freely now, out of the duke's presence."

Natan shook his head grimly. "There is no way. Alas, it is not the
first time our people suffer to have a martyr, one put to death unjustly,
and I fear it will not be the last."

I clenched my fists with frustration. I still could not accept this
unjust death sentence.

"By the way," Rafael asked, "do you know where we might find the young apprentice, Moshe ben Shlomo?"

Natan made a face as if he was choking on a chicken bone. "Why do you ask?"

"We have several questions for him about the current situation. I have not been able to locate him, and I remember that you were the one to introduce him to me."

Natan frowned. "He came to me and offered translation services. I assumed you would be the natural one to evaluate his ability in Hebrew. Now that has finished. I believe he departed several days ago on one of our ships bearing goods to Egypt."

Rather a sudden departure! We shall never have another chance to question the young man. "Are you sure of this, sir? Is there any way to check?"

"As I often do when Baruch is especially busy, I happened to review records for that shipment two days ago and saw several passengers had been logged. He was one. People like him, the poor and the rootless, often catch such a ride. It is less expensive than other modes of travel."

Rafael and I thanked Natan Mendoza, who had been more forthcoming than I had expected, and left.

❧

"Strange about Moshe ben Shlomo. And now we cannot question him," I said as we arrived at my home. Rafael came in with me.

"I agree. Losing the chance to talk to him is not good. His departure puzzles me especially because he and I had made plans to work together, so it appears to me that it came about suddenly."

Exactly my thoughts. "I wonder if there is any way to contact him in Egypt?"

"We can try, though I expect that we will not be able to make any such contact in a timely fashion. We would do better first to see if there is any way to come up with other suspects." He sighed and pursed his lips.

Just then Nina summoned us to partake of a meal. From the look on her face, it appeared she had more to provide us with than the meal. "First, you eat. Then I shall tell you what I have learned."

"Nina, if you know something that will help, tell me now. That will be best for my appetite."

She shook her head. "This talk will keep. My soup will not. And, believe me, what I have to say would ruin anyone's appetite. Better you should eat for strength first."

There was no sense arguing with Nina, who could teach mules a thing or two about stubbornness.

As usual, her soup was wonderful—based on a vegetable broth, no doubt because the meal would include dairy. This, as did all our meals, conformed to our traditions and commandments of not partaking of meat and dairy in one sitting. A hearty concoction of carrots, onions, mushrooms, and garlic, the soup was paired superbly with delicious warm rolls and fragrant cheese. A lemon cake afterward. Concerned as I was by our efforts to save the rabbi, I still savored what I ate.

Only after the meal—with all the appropriate blessings and graces—did Nina report what she had heard. "Everyone was shopping and talking. People are afraid there is going to be even more trouble, and they want to make sure they have supplies. What the Mendozas' servants said was especially interesting, along with the da Costas'."

I gripped her arm. "What about the da Costas?" Because of patient confidentiality, I had not told her about Shoshana.

Nina's eyes filled with angry tears. "Everyone was talking of the crusaders' cruel attack on their girl."

I gasped. Her secret had been so widely exposed. "What else?"

"Other girls have also been attacked. The men talk of confronting the crusaders, to get them out of Salerno."

I did not think it was possible to be even more worried, but Nina's words had that effect. Our men were not fighters, and certainly not of the caliber of the crusaders. If there were any sort of confrontation between the two groups, our men would be injured—or killed—far more than the enemy. And if any of our men could stand against the crusaders, the duke and his guard would surely punish the Jews.

I groaned. "I hope someone can talk sense into our men before they commit such an act of . . . of suicidal folly."

Rafael rose. "This cannot happen. I must go at once and talk with those who will see reason."

He started to go, but Nina stopped him. "Before you leave us, you must know the situation is even more complicated." She took a deep breath. "Hard as it is to believe, it seems the Egyptian rabbi was in contact with crusaders—not only here, but also in Egypt."

I could not believe my ears. "What do you mean?" *Can this possibly be correct?*

"You know the rabbi was part of the group around the Rambam of blessed memory, in Egypt. And the Rambam was the court physician to the sultan, a descendant of the famous warrior Saladin."

"Yes. This is all well known," Rafael said, clearly impatient for her to get to the point.

"Well it seems," Nina continued, "that Rabbi Isaac ben Shmuel consulted with crusaders to try to find a way to undermine the sultan. He was heard to say that this would free the Rambam from bondage to the unclean despot."

Maybe this bizarre incident casts light on why the rabbi was in the Frankish tavern.

"Obviously, the rabbi did not succeed," I said. "Until his death, the Rambam continued as the court physician to the sultan as well as to the sultan's son." I thought about this. "Actually, considering the rabbi's plotting, it is surprising the Rambam did not banish *him* from the court. Or turn him over to the sultan's guards. After all, how secure can any Jew ever be in such an environment?"

Nina nodded. "It seems the rabbi was a relative of the Rambam's wife, so the Rambam had to put up with him. Also, the rabbi proved so ineffective in his schemes, maybe the Rambam did not take him or his machinations seriously."

"You learned all this today? It is quite astonishing." Rafael looked as surprised as I felt.

Nina blushed slightly. "There is always much talk in the market-place, especially when trouble is afoot. The rabbi's attempts to con-spire with the crusaders were the true reason why he had to leave Egypt after the Rambam's death. Evidently someone who had the ear of an important member of the court knew of his plot. Once the Rambam was no longer alive to protect him . . ."

"That I can understand. The rabbi was fortunate he was not put to death immediately, as would be the practice in many courts. He had good fortune that he could leave, though in light of what has happened since, that good fortune has not lasted." I thought for a moment, trying to connect the new information to what I already knew. "Why, then, would he have made contact with crusaders again here in Salerno? After all his ranting and raving about Jews and Gentiles interacting, he was guilty of even more of the same."

"It seems he considers himself free from the rules others must follow." Rafael shook his head. "A mystery."

"If he comes through this ordeal, perhaps he will explain himself." Now that we knew more of his story, we might have been on a clearer path to understanding the whole chain of events that landed him in his predicament. And how to help him.

Nina continued, "Both the Mendozas and the da Costas seem especially set on organizing to push back against the crusaders. For men to start arming themselves."

I groaned at this prospect. "Natan Mendoza hinted that some may feel this way. Does either family have a special connection with Rabbi Isaac ben Shmuel—something else Natan Mendoza did not mention. Perhaps if we pursue the question that way, we will find answers."

"I am not aware of any such connection, but let us remember how short a time the Egyptian rabbi has been with us," Nina said.

"True." I thought back to what I did know. "Natan Mendoza did not appear to have any difficulty with having the rabbi take the punishment for the crime, whether guilty or not."

"Despite our efforts, the situation is worsening." Rafael ran a hand over his chin. "We need answers pronto."

꙳

When Rafael and I arrived at the dungeon the next morning with another basket for the rabbi, other supplicants were jostling for position to get in to see prisoners. This had not been the case previously, and I asked one of the guards' servants why.

"It is because of the upcoming transport of prisoners to Palermo," he whispered. "Whenever there is a transport, the families of the condemned come to do what they can. It can become chaos, as it is today."

At last, it was our turn to speak to the guard, and we provided the necessary bribe. When we arrived at the rabbi's cell, he was pacing, showing more energy than he had in days, though he did not look well. Easy to understand why anyone would get sick after days confined here, and he might still have aftereffects of the attack. Perhaps today, though, we would get some useful information from him.

We greeted the rabbi as usual, and I laid out the provisions we had brought. Cloaked in his customary stony silence, he watched me as I worked. After saying a blessing, he began to partake of the food.

Rafael directed an icy glare at the man. "Rabbi, you know about the transport tomorrow. Do you have anything more to say that may help us help you?"

"No," the rabbi said before clamping shut his thin lips.

Rafael raised a brow. "Was the crusader you were with one you knew in Egypt?"

"I have no more to say on this matter." The rabbi shrank back into himself. "I am doomed. Leave me alone, leave me to my fate."

Rafael got very close to him. "Because of this crime, the whole Jewish community in Salerno is at risk. What can you tell us to keep your fellow Jews from harm?"

He shrugged his bony shoulders. "I can no longer help anyone."

I curled my hands into frustrated fists. Why was he so stubborn and closemouthed? Did he not care what harm he brought us?

"You were in a Frankish tavern among the lowest of the unclean," Rafael persisted. "Why?"

Something appeared to crack in the rabbi. "Better than the other places those degenerates frequent. Gaming places. Brothels. Churches."

"Yet you do not appear to be a drinker or carouser," Rafael said in a reasonable tone.

The rabbi appeared to bristle. "I am not."

"Were you having an argument with the crusader? Had he done something to you?"

"I was not, and he had not."

"I repeat myself because the question is of the utmost importance. Was he a crusader you had known in Egypt?"

The rabbi sighed. "I do not want to talk any more."

"You swear you did not kill this man?"

"I did not kill him. I will not add the falsehood of saying I killed him to my other sins. Now I am finished with talking."

Rafael and I had finally gotten something from the rabbi, but not enough.

Rafael, whose eyes flashed with anger, a rare emotion for him to display, said, "My good rabbi, is it not a sin to throw away your life?"

"I shall not discuss this with you." He curled himself into a corner of the cell. "You have tried to save me and failed. I have no more to say."

"Despite your silence, I still hope that we will identify the culprit and name him to the duke before the ship sails." Rafael's face and his bearing glowed with confidence.

It behooved me to remain calm, a skill I had tried to perfect as a physician. Still, I could feel the twitch of nerves in my left eye. My mouth had grown dry, in part because of my anger with the rabbi. I took a deep breath as I considered what to say. "I hope we can live up to your faith, Rafael. At this point, I believe we will need a miracle of the type only the Lord can provide."

"I did not include the deity in my statement of belief, although I appreciate that such is part of yours."

Same old Rafael, even at a time like this. "When is the ship scheduled to sail?" I asked. Maybe that would get the rabbi to acknowledge us.

"Tomorrow before noon. That is all we have been told."

The guard arrived right then, and we had to take our leave. Not that the rabbi reacted in any way.

"Before we continue," I told Rafael, "I must look in on a patient to see her progress. I will hurry. I know we must make haste."

He nodded. "While you do that, I will try to learn more about the crusaders. On my own."

"What is your plan?"

"I want to visit the Frankish tavern where the murder happened. Maybe I can find out something more."

"Please be careful. Shall we meet later, at my house?"

He agreed. Since it was morning and full daylight, I decided to risk being unaccompanied, and so we parted. I was closest to the da Costas', so I went there first.

Ten

Aservant ushered me into the hall where Signora da Costa came out and greeted me. "I am glad you are here." She extended her hand to me, which I took, relieved that she welcomed me in spite of what her husband had said when we parted at the hospital.

"How fares Shoshana?" I asked.

She shook her head and tears welled up. "She is so sad, it breaks my heart." Her sigh bore the sorrows of injured motherhood. "Her fiancé's family insisted on breaking the betrothal even though he implored them for permission to continue with their plans to marry."

My heart sank, though I was not surprised. Families could inflict such damage. "I am so sorry. He sounds like a very special young man."

She swiped at her tears as a burst of anger lit her eyes. "The two of them have loved each other since childhood, so when the time came to make a match, it was easy. Now, I am sorry to say, I wish these young people had not been so wise and temperate in their behavior. From the depths of my soul as her mother, I wish she had already given herself to him before the crusader took what she safeguarded for her *bashert*, her fated one." She choked and put a hand to her mouth.

I touched her hand, discouraged that there was so little I could do to provide comfort. "It is a story to break the hardest heart."

"Not the hearts of her fiancé's family. If they in fact have hearts, which I doubt." She sighed. "They said, what if she is carrying the seed of a crusader's bastard?" She looked at me. "Magistra, might she *actually* be with child?"

With all my heart, I hoped not. Surely, God could not be so cruel. "It is too early to be sure. Let us pray that is not the case."

Her eyes narrowed, and she assumed a more calculating expression. "There must be something you could give her if she is carrying a child. Surely you know what could be done to spare this additional agony."

If only the matter were as simple as this good woman assumed. "There are remedies, but often they are more dangerous to the mother than to the unwanted child. Difficult as it is, let us try not to worry yet. Right now, Shoshana needs our care and support the best we can provide them."

"Thank you for coming, though I must tell you that my husband ordered that our family physician should take charge of her care." She shook her head. "You and I know the truth. A man cannot understand what my child needs the way a woman can. I hope we can convince my husband to let you help us."

"Thank you for allowing me. I always want to follow the progress of a patient I treated. Perhaps I can explain this to your husband? It is not that I am trying to take the place of your family physician."

Determination and strength returned to her mien. "Leave my husband to me. Come, I shall take you to Shoshana."

She led me outside to a small walled garden where the sun shone and sweet scents of citrus perfumed the air. The gentle buzz of bees amongst the flowers provided the only sound. Shoshana was seated at a small table set with a silver cup and a dish of miniature pastries and confections. To someone not privy to the circumstances of this beautiful young girl, this scene would surely have seemed idyllic.

Shoshana did not seem to have eaten or drunk any of these treats. She stared out at some point on the horizon and, except for the occasional wringing of her hands, sat still. I tried to find a reason to feel encouraged.

"Shoshana, you have a visitor. The magistra from . . . from the other night." The signora swallowed hard. Her daughter did not react to any of the words her mother said. The signora looked at me with an expression of helplessness.

I approached the girl. A servant brought me a chair to sit next to her, which allowed me to be at the same level as my patient. When I put a gentle hand on her arm and spoke softly, "How are you?" she flinched.

When I repeated my question, she turned to me. Eyes filled with tears, she said, "My life is over. My family should put me in the ground and sit shiva for their lost daughter." She bit her lip as tears began to course down her cheeks.

At least she was able to whisper a few words, though they cost her great effort and expressed such despair. If I was to find any hope for her, I might do so only in that she managed to say something.

However, when I looked into her eyes and saw the extent of her agony, I found it hard to hold on to any positive attitude. Shoshana, so recently healthy and young, should have been able to look forward to many happy years ahead of her. Instead, all she wanted was an end to her life.

"Your family loves you very much, and they do not agree with the words that your pain has driven you to. I care also, very much, dear little rose, as do your dearest loved ones."

She turned and glared. "Not true. Not his parents. Not the ones who count. They have forced us to break our betrothal. My life is over." Two spots of color livened up her pallor. A small spark of emotion that lit her otherwise dull eyes indicated her life force had not been totally destroyed.

"Where there is life, there is reason to hope. Perhaps, in time, he will be able to convince them to change their minds." I prayed I was not leading her astray by raising false hopes. On the other hand, we needed to get her through this crisis, and hope could be the best medicine. Once she regained her health, she would be able to deal more positively with her life and her possibilities.

"Hardly. They have already engaged the matchmaker to find another bride for Yonatan." She sobbed. "He's not *my* Yonatan anymore." She swallowed hard. "His parents threatened to push him out of the family business and give everything to his younger brother if he weds me."

I stroked her arm in a futile attempt at comfort. I hated feeling so helpless. However, my becoming angry at those harsh parents would do nothing to help Shoshana.

Indeed. If only he were not so young, he might have a chance to save her. "Try not to regard the situation at its most hopeless. Things change."

She looked at me as if I had lost my last shred of intelligence. "He has not tried to see me again." Pure heartbreak with each strangled word.

What more could I say? Nothing. At least, not anything that could fix her situation. Still, my silence would do more harm even than useless words. I squeezed her icy hand. "Know that you are loved. Even if you are not hungry or thirsty, partake of the good food and drink those around you provide. Take short walks in your lovely garden. Smell the sweet flowers. Take your rest so you are no longer fatigued. Make one small effort after another to regain your health."

She cried out, a sound to move the hardest heart. If only Yonatan and his family could witness her agony, they would have to find their way to accepting her. Would they not?

"I cannot do what you say, Magistra." Her words were barely above a whisper.

"Try. That is all anyone can ask. If you take these careful steps, your humors will come into balance. Maybe not as quickly as one would wish. In fact, so slowly, maybe you will not even feel your progress. Then one day, you will wake from your slumbers on a beautiful morning and look around with a bit of delight. An appetite, even tiny, for the day to come."

At least she stopped wringing her hands and looked more thoughtful. As I was leaving, I spoke a few words to the signora and encouraged her to be patient in her efforts to help Shoshana. A frowning Signor da Costa joined us at that moment.

"Why are you here, Magistra? I told you the family physician will see to our daughter. You are not to come to our house again."

"I shall speak with your physician and let him know what I have observed and done. Amongst physicians, shared communication is valued as helpful to our patients."

The signora bowed her head slightly. A servant saw me out.

&

As arranged, Rafael and I met at my home for a quick midday meal of bread and cheese provided by Nina. I needed to go quickly to the hospital, where I had several patients to see. As Rafael escorted me there, I asked, "What did you learn in the tavern?"

He snorted. "Not exactly news—that these crusaders are a rough bunch. After the sack of Constantinople, they still were not satisfied. They wanted to continue on to Jerusalem, but without leaders and money, they disbanded. Slowly, they are making their way back to their own Frankish kingdom which, I tell you, must be a sinkhole of uncivilized living."

"Far too slowly," I started.

"Yes. And the crusaders have a view of the tenor of Salerno's society that is, ironically, similar to that of the rabbi. Like him, they do not understand the way we live together. Christians, Jews, Moslems. When the crusaders came here because it is a convenient seaport on their way home, they assumed Salerno to be like other places, that is, totally intolerant. Where Jews and Moslems can be attacked by Christians with impunity." His voice broke.

"Do they now know otherwise?" I asked.

"Clearly not. And, what is worse, it appears that Salerno may be changing so that that view is becoming more accurate."

As we had arrived at the hospital, I bade him farewell. I spent a moment clearing my mind so I could focus on my patients.

The first patient was a woman who suffered from terrible stomach pains and vomiting. After examination and questioning several days before, I had discovered her pain came only when she ate a bit of the butter or cheese she so much loved. For her, I had recommended a strict regimen with no dairy. Thus, she was now on the mend from the attack that had brought her to the hospital.

The second patient was an old man who had fallen and broken his left femur. Though he appeared to be healing, we had not yet been able to determine the reason for the dizziness that caused his fall. I made sure he was comfortable and his physical wounds were healing. I wrote a note to myself to speak with members of his family to try to clarify his situation. I had several ideas, although until we managed to find root causes, it would be difficult to treat him effectively.

When I came out, I saw Rafael stopped at the stand of one of the street vendors who sold kosher food, buying a bread loaf filled with a hot lentil mixture. The cheese and bread we shared earlier had been a bit meager.

The elderly woman who handed him the food favored us with a toothless smile. "Much nicer to serve decent folk like you and not those awful crusaders. Crude, ignorant gangs who think they own the world." She made a face. "Salerno is not what it used to be."

"What do they do?" Rafael asked.

She rolled her eyes. "What do they not do? Never want to pay the little I ask. One tries to distract me, telling me he wants to . . . well, words I will not repeat. Things married people do in beds." She colored. "Nasty married people."

"That is terribly rude."

"Oh, yes. While one flusters me, the others try to steal what they can. Food. Coin." She shook her head. "Makes it hard for simple folk to make an honest living."

"I am sorry. Like you, I hope they are soon gone."

"Amen to that. Enjoy your food, sir."

Rafael insisted the poor thing take an extra coin for her fare, then we sat on a bench and we bit into warm crispiness.

"Were you able to learn anything more about the encampment?" I asked between bites.

He shrugged. "Yes, though what I found out is strange and unsettling. First off, I learned that the crusaders are not quite as much the leaderless horde as I thought."

"Truly?"

"There are two nobles who have taken on the role as leaders of the so-called soldiers for Christ, at least for now. I was able to speak with one of them, Sir Thomas Dulac, a knight who appears to own no actual land. He knew Rabbi Isaac ben Shmuel and had actually talked with him back when he was at the sultan's court."

"What did he have to say?"

"This is where the whole thing becomes even stranger. He confirmed the story that Nina told us, about the rabbi conspiring with crusaders against the sultan."

"How peculiar. I find it difficult to accept this bizarre story as true, but it appears I must."

"And listen to this. According to Sir Thomas, the rabbi asked him and others how the crusaders regarded apostates who leave their religion—what should be done to apostates and to women who disobey their husbands."

"What?" Again, shock hit me. "Why would he ask such a question of the very people he despised? Surely, he could have consulted the Rambam and other Jewish authorities."

Rafael agreed. "I asked Sir Thomas to repeat his words so I could be certain I had heard correctly. He did and I had."

I blinked several times. "This is critical information. Tell me, what did this knight say were the reactions of the crusaders?"

"As I think you would expect, they all regarded the rabbi as a joke."

"Dear God." I swallowed hard. "What could the rabbi have been thinking—to discuss such subjects with these men? Did he really think they would give him an accurate picture of how his formerly Jewish wife and children would fare with a Christian husband? I *have* heard some crusaders were so disgusted with what they saw on Crusade as to question their own faith. A few even renounced Christianity for the Moslem faith. Who knows? Perhaps a few might even have turned to Judaism?"

"After what such men did on Crusades, nothing would surprise me." He shook his head. "We definitely must get the rabbi to talk before he gets on the ship to Palermo. But I have yet *more* information. It turns out this Thomas Dulac has been in contact with our duke on the current situation. He claims the crusaders' lawlessness here is in response to the murder."

I shook my head. "They were lawless criminals here even before the murder."

"True. But the crimes have since increased. And, according to Dulac, if the murder is not soon expiated, there will be a pogrom against the Jews. Because the crusaders suffered no consequences after sacking the Christian city of Constantinople, they certainly have no fear of what would happen if they attacked Salerno's Jews. The duke wants to keep Salerno peaceful. Clearly, this is part of his motivation to have the rabbi shipped out to Palermo with great haste."

$\mathscr{E}$leven

With the sudden frightening news of a looming pogrom, our need to deal with the situation became even more desperate. Because my previous conversation with Leah Sara Garcia did not finish satisfactorily, I had arranged another meeting with her. Rafael escorted me to her house. He was about to leave me at her door, when my most flustered-looking hostess rushed out. She frowned, appearing not to have remembered our appointment.

"Leah Sara, is something wrong?" I asked.

"Excuse me. We shall have to meet at another time."

"What has happened? Please tell me. Perhaps Rafael and I can help."

She paused. "Yes—that may be a good idea. I have been called to the home of my sister's brother-in-law, Baruch Mendoza. Their usual physician is not available, and the family has asked for my help for a crisis. They think my medical training might come into play. Of course, it has been many years since I have practiced seriously. But you, Rebecca, are much more capable. Will you come with me so we can see what needs to be done?"

"Of course." We covered the distance to Baruch Mendoza's home quite quickly. Just as a servant opened the front door to us, we heard an outcry from within. Natan Mendoza, looking frantic and terrified, rushed into the hall. "Baruch has collapsed in the library. Help is needed."

"Natan, I am here," Leah Sara said. "And I have brought expert help."

He scowled when he caught sight of Rafael and me, and I feared he would send us away. Instead, because it appeared the need he faced was overwhelming, he nodded.

Natan led us into the house, saying, "Baruch complained he felt ill and was coughing terribly. But now, he fell to the floor, and I cannot rouse him. I have been told our regular physician is not available. Can you do something to help him or at least make him more comfortable?"

Leah Sara nodded. "Rebecca will know better than I."

Even before I saw Baruch Mendoza, I heard his harsh cough. My mind whirled with possibilities. I knew him to be a man of more than fifty years, someone of immoderate habits of food and drink, and unbalanced humors. If I had been his physician, I would have striven first to have him moderate his behaviors and then to balance his humors. Arturo de los Reyes Blancos, also physician to the duke, had that esteemed appointment, but apparently had either not tried or not succeeded in such a course.

We reached the library where Baruch Mendoza lay covered with a thin blanket, stretched out on the rug, a pillow beneath his head. His wife, Raquela Susanna, eyes filled with tears, knelt beside him, his hand in hers. She appeared utterly bereft. A servant crouched next to Signor Mendoza on the other side.

"Perhaps you can help Raquela Susanna, while I minister to her husband," I said softly to Leah Sara.

"Of course." She went to the woman and convinced her to move from her husband's side.

I focused on the patient. He looked pale, and his eyes remained shut as he took rapid, shallow breaths. I knelt beside him and took his wrist—ignoring the gasp from Natan—as I felt for Baruch's pulse, which was rapid and thready. I looked up at the now-frowning younger Mendoza brother.

"Were you with him when he collapsed?"

Natan nodded.

"Had he been complaining of any discomfort before he collapsed?"

"He has been coughing a lot these past few days. We thought maybe he had a catarrh. He said his cough has been keeping him awake nights, so he is tired. He has also not come to meals with his usual good appetite."

The loss of appetite could, of course, be related to the stress we all lived with. Likewise for the lack of sleep. The cough indicated a different cause. And Signor Mendoza did not appear to have the nasal congestion typical of catarrh sufferers.

"Has his regular physician seen him regarding these symptoms?" Rafael asked into the silence while I lifted Baruch's eyelids and peered at his pupils.

"Yes, though my brother is not one to summon a physician with any ache or pain. He believes a man should be strong, eat and drink the best of foods and beverages, and look to God for matters of life and health."

I put my ear to Baruch's chest, eliciting another gasp from Natan, and listened to the supine man's heart. The irregular beat was not encouraging. I also listened to the lungs, which were congested. This was not a healthy man. I would need to examine him more closely to get a clearer idea of what was afflicting my unexpected patient. Or I would need to confer with Magister de los Reyes Blancos, who, I suspected, would not welcome me as a colleague. But right now I needed to address the patient's immediate state.

Taking sal ammoniac from my satchel, I placed it beneath his nostrils. He stirred but did not fully rouse. Just then, a servant came in.

"Magister de los Reyes Blancos is still not able to come tonight. His servant asked if we could take Signor Mendoza to the hospital."

Natan shook his head. "My brother would be most distressed to find himself there," he said to Rafael. Then he turned back to me and somewhat reluctantly asked, "Magistra, what can you do for him here in our house now?"

"Let me try again to rouse him. I want to ask him what sensations he felt before he became unconscious. And then we can also get him to his bed, where he will be more comfortable."

Natan nodded. When I put the sal ammoniac under his nose a second time, Signor Baruch responded by moving his head slightly from side to side. Then his eyelids fluttered open.

"What happened?" His voice did not sound anything like his firm and steady usual self. Evidently he must have then spotted me because he added, "Why are *you* here?"

"I have been called to help you," I murmured. "Your brother Natan can explain."

I indicated that Natan should kneel down alongside me and noted that he did not move into that position with ease. Perhaps he should also look to *his* health.

"Baruch, my brother, you collapsed. Our physician is not available, and we have sought aid from the magistra and Leah Sara Garcia." He squeezed the patient's shoulder.

"Women?" The stricken man managed to demonstrate his distaste, showing he still had some of his usual habits of mind. Despite my unhappiness with his opinion, this was a good sign.

"Yes, a woman. You know how things are here in Salerno," Natan said. "Besides which, you scared us when you collapsed."

The patient grunted. Natan nodded for me to proceed.

"Signor Mendoza," I said in my most no-nonsense voice, "when you are ready, we would like to help you stand so we can escort you to your own bed. You will be most comfortable there while you recover."

He grunted again and seemed to rally.

"Before I let these gentlemen help you up," I continued, "perhaps you can tell us what happened. How did you feel right before you fell? Did you have a pain in your body or head?"

"I do not remember. One minute, I am talking to my brother, and the next, I find myself stretched out on the floor with people around me." He went into a spasm of coughing, a loose, rattling sound.

"How long have you been coughing like that?" I asked.

He shrugged. "Damn cough has been keeping me up at night. Nothing the physician has given me for it has helped."

He let the men help him to sit up. That simple motion appeared to require a lot of his energy, since he needed to pause and rest. I offered him a draught of elderberry in honey, which I kept in my satchel for patients with coughs. His willingness to take the remedy without an argument was a further indication of his fatigue.

The spoonful provided some relief, and I handed the bottle to a servant with instructions for the use of the remedy.

In a short time, Baruch signaled that we could help him to his feet. His brother on one side and Rafael on the other, they walked him to his bedroom. At this point, my friend left the older Mendoza to the ministrations of Natan and his servants to settle him in his bed. In a few minutes, Natan opened the door and ushered us inside the room where Baruch was now propped up on pillows in his large bed. I offered to examine him again, and he waved me away.

"Thank you for your help thus far. Now I can wait for my regular medico." His mouth formed a hard line.

"Very well. Here is what I have found so it can be conveyed to Magister de los Reyes Blancos."

Natan stood at attention alongside Baruch.

"Signor Mendoza, your heart is greatly burdened and weakened. Your lungs sound so congested as to be a concern. Please tell the magister he can confer with me if he so desires."

Baruch did not acknowledge my words, but Natan nodded, looking a little afraid, as if he had not known his brother was in such poor health. Not exactly gratitude, yet at least an acknowledgment of my help.

With Baruch settled, the servants showed Rafael and me to the door. Leah Sara, who had been silent during most of the process with the patient, said she would remain in the house and that she and I would have to talk at another time. This postponement frustrated me, but I did not see any way to arrange otherwise.

I wondered if this episode signaled a new development. Though the whole clan appeared adept at keeping secrets, one as big as Baruch's health problems could not remain unknown forever.

The wind had grown stronger while we were in the Mendoza home. With the hope, however irrational, that a storm would delay the departure of the ship scheduled to transport the rabbi, I said, "Maybe there will still be time for us to solve the case and save the rabbi."

We were able to pay an evening visit to the dungeon—allowed because of the transport scheduled for the morning. I braced myself for this last meeting with the rabbi. Manuel and Nina had selected the items for the rabbi's travel satchel with care, as if for his last meals and final moments in our world—which it well might be.

"This looks to be your last time here," the guard boomed in false heartiness. "Your man is off to the hangman come morning. Pity that. I appreciate your presents."

I bit back a protest, as did Rafael.

To my surprise and relief, the rabbi was in a better mood than I had ever seen him before. Though he was neither warm nor friendly, at least he did not look on the verge of ordering my exile to a primitive desert.

"It is good you are able to come tonight," he said. "The ship to Palermo is first thing in the morning, so I shall be leaving this cursed place."

He spoke as if he were going on a pleasure trip, not to his execution. Before I could say anything, he added, "This allows me to thank you for the food you have provided me."

"You have given up," I muttered.

His brows beetled. "I am facing reality. I do not want to die, but I must surrender to my fate. I did not commit the crime of which I am accused, so my execution will be a transgression against justice. Not the first nor, almost certainly, the last. So, I accept the role of holy martyr. As I have nothing more to live for, I do not fight against it."

Rafael and I regarded each other with chagrin.

"Rabbi," I said, "we have put forth great effort on your behalf. You cannot simply give up without making any effort to help us save you."

"It is my fate. The morning fast approaches. Once I am on that ship—" he trailed off and shook his head.

How can he be so cavalier about his life and death? "We are praying for a huge storm, one that will prevent any departure by sea tomorrow morning. From the look of the sky, our prayers may not be in vain. I suggest you pray also." My gaze moved between the rabbi and Rafael.

The rabbi shook his head. "I do not pray for such things. I am in God's hands." He bade us farewell. There was nothing else to do now except leave the man in peace. For the first time, we called for the guard to release us before our time was up.

Once outside the castle, I sniffed the air. Though I was hardly in a league with the true weather prognosticators—those who could predict a coming storm from just the feeling in their joints—I sensed the changing atmosphere. The hoped-for coming storm swirled air around me in a wind heavy with the promise of drenching rain and more.

Come thunder, come lightning. I could not let the Egyptian rabbi be lost. Despite himself.

❦

By dawn Wednesday the tempest was upon us—thanks be to God. A fierce, wind-driven rain pelted our house while it shook slightly with the rumble of thunder and flashes of lightning. Of course there was no guarantee the storm would prevent the sailors from leaving, but we understood the usual practice was for early departure, just after dawn. And the duke's ships never departed later than midday.

The night before, Leah Sara Garcia had sent a servant with an invitation to have our postponed meeting this morning. So, between the storm and the prospect of the meeting, I was in a somewhat more positive mood as I rose from my bed, said my morning prayers, performed my toilette, and dressed. Nina, who slept even less than I, had made a frumenty for breakfast—the hearty food she deemed necessary for me to get through the fraught day ahead.

Sated with frumenty and tea and dressed well to protect myself from the still-raging storm, I set off to Leah Sara's home for the meeting. *Today I hope to have some more answers that will save the rabbi—may they arrive in time!*

Despite the early hour, Leah Sara Garcia was up and about. We sat in her parlor with a teapot and a platter of pastries between us. Already sated, I turned down the pastries but was happy to sip tea with my hostess. "There is so much going on, I scarcely know what to attend to first," she admitted. "Raquela Susanna sent word that Baruch's condition has not changed significantly." She squeezed my hand. "We all owe you our gratitude for your help yesterday."

"I only wish I could do more." Nice as it was to hear such compliments, it was time to get serious. "Despite your warmth and welcome, I cannot help believing there is more you can tell me to help the rabbi."

She regarded me sharply. "You must understand the need to protect reputations? If it is your loved one who is at risk—it is a difficult decision."

What does she mean? Why speak of reputations at such a time? "I beg to disagree. Truth and justice must outweigh any such considerations."

She sighed. "If only real life were so simple. But you have no close family," she said in an almost inaudible voice. "You cannot truly understand."

I flinched. Quite frankly, I was tired of being reminded of the roles I did not fulfill. Not being a wife or mother made me a pariah to many. But now, Leah Sara claimed this lack of experience also compromised my ability to understand.

"No, maybe I cannot," I admitted, choosing my words carefully, though I really believed I could understand. "Perhaps you can tell me exactly what that means."

She shook her head. "I have learned that you did not have your own mother as a model."

So, I have been more a topic of interest to important Salernitans than I realized. But now is not the time to talk about myself. On the other hand, perhaps this is needed to break through to what Leah Sara knows. I continued on this topic. "That is true. My beloved mother died not long after my birth. I was fortunate to spend time with aunts and other family members who attempted to mother me. They did not replace her, but they helped."

She squeezed my hand. "Wherever she is, your mother must be proud."

"Thank you. I hope so." *I cannot have my head turned by kind words.*

"Alas, you do not know the connection between daughters and mothers. Cannot know how strong and fierce it can be."

I sat back in my chair. "You are correct. And you? You were blessed to be raised by your mother? You have sisters?"

"Only one sister—Malka Freya Mendoza, and I have sons, thanks be to God. I have been blessed. My mother is still alive, still as fierce to protect me as when I was a mere babe."

"Yes, I am aware of that instinct. My father's protectiveness is still part of my life."

"Our menfolk are indeed endowed with this instinct too. With them, I believe it is also being possessive. Like the male of any species, they want to warn off predators. 'What is mine is mine. Do not dare trespass.'"

"There is that."

"Yet with women, it is different. In some ways even stronger. This instinct guides us to be fierce along with being tender. I can go to my mother for comfort. I also know that, if she felt me to be threatened, she would not hesitate to do whatever was needed." She looked me directly in the eyes and added, "Even to kill."

I sat up straighter. "To kill?" I swallowed. "As we said the other day, it is most unusual for a woman to be violent, though not unheard of." *What is she about to expose?*

"If driven hard enough, if desperate, a woman will lash out."

I shivered. I thought about the most desperate times in my own life, when the threat of imminent death loomed large. Given the opportunity, would I have killed the Knight Templar Brian de Bois-Guilbert when he threatened me? I had never before so questioned myself.

To my surprise, I had no easy reply.

$\mathcal{T}$welve

Leah Sara Garcia went on, "I have thought a great deal since we talked. I like you, Rebecca. I sense that we have a special understanding of each other. I have considered telling you the most difficult thing I have ever had to tell anyone."

Her implied confidence pleased me. At the same time, however, I was almost afraid of what she would say next. *Can anything else shock me*? I nodded for her to continue.

She took a deep breath. Though I did not consider her to be of an emotional, highly nerved nature, there was a breach in her calm demeanor, an unbalance in her humors. So agitated was the atmosphere, my own sense of balance faltered. It was as if the storm outside had followed me in.

"The Jewish community here in Salerno has really never taken well to your Rafael. We do not easily accept newcomers."

Her words surprised me. I could not let her statement pass uncorrected. "Again, he is not *my* Rafael. To your point, however, he has been in Salerno for more than twenty years. Since I have been here a far shorter time, I must assume I am even less welcome."

An expression of sympathy briefly softened her face. "I am sure you are aware of the resistance to you. That is probably one reason why you have such an affinity for Rafael Lopes Dias, who is also unmarried. Not that I am prone to gossip, though some of us wonder why you two have chosen not to wed."

I decided to address her personal remark. "He has asked me to marry him, but I have my reasons for turning him down—despite convention, tradition, and demands from my family. And from this community." That was enough of my personal life. "Leah Sara, we are straying from what you said earlier—how you were considering telling me something difficult."

She put a hand on my arm and offered up a tight little smile, almost a grimace. "Like you, I was drawn to study at the faculty of medicine. Since I am a member of one of Salerno's leading Jewish families and because I wed as expected, my studies were tolerated. Especially because I did not go on to practice the profession. I have used my skills and knowledge for the good of my loved ones, my dear family, as you saw the other day. But you . . . Rebecca, you are most unusual."

She shrugged. "However, as you say, we have other matters to speak of today."

Finally. Before she could utter another word, an unearthly moaning reached us, followed by the shuffle of approaching steps, and someone muttering incoherently. *What in heaven?*

Leah Sara sprang up as if scalded by a cauldron of hot soup. "My God," she whispered as she rushed toward the direction from which the sound came.

A clearly deranged woman—face contorted, eyes bulging, red from tears or another source, mouth moving constantly with incoherent words and sound—scurried in followed by two female servants whom she seemed determined to elude. Her wig, worn to fulfill the command that married women cover their hair, was of the highest quality though sadly askew, making her appear drunk. Her robe was also well made and of top quality, yet seemingly too large, adding to her look of imbalance.

Leah Sara sprang up and firmly took hold of the woman, who calmed a bit. Then my hostess glared at the servants, who stood frozen in their places. "What happened? Why is she here?"

The older of the two swallowed hard before speaking. "We cleaned her and dressed her as we do every morning. We were gathering our supplies when she ran out, and we could not catch her." They glanced at each other. "She runs very fast."

"You must have turned your backs on her. Have I not told you often that you must watch her every minute and keep her door locked?"

"Usually our routine works well," the younger servant protested, "but this morning, she seems unusually agitated."

"She is especially sensitive to the weather. No doubt the storm has unsettled her," Leah Sara murmured. "Go now," she told the servants. "I will take care of her."

The same storm that I hope has given the Egyptian rabbi a reprieve. I looked from Leah Sara to the disheveled woman, who remained holding on to my hostess's hands. In my own shock, until this moment I had not recognized who this crazed woman was!

"What has happened?" I cried out. "Why is Malka Freya here in such a state?"

Leah Sara glanced at me and signaled that I should be quiet. Then she released Malka Freya's hands slowly. Malka Freya cowered away, reluctant as an animal that had been beaten.

"Malka Freya, this is the magistra, Rebecca," Leah Sara said.

I smiled at the woman, whose gaze did not meet mine.

"We last met at Shabbat services," I said, "during the Egyptian rabbi's sermon."

That day, though she had fainted, when she had come to, she had spoken sharply to me in full command of herself. Now . . . it was as if this woman, recently a comfortable matron, had shriveled into faltering, bewildered old age—and worse.

She looked at me and spoke quite clearly. "All in vain. She died."

She then repeated these same phrases thrice, in a voice that was now little more than a rasp of pain. After each time, she regarded me as if to seek confirmation. She then commenced to wring her hands with great agitation and took to pacing and repeating the phrases under her breath. She peered at each of us each time she said the word *died*.

"What has happened to cause her to be in this state?" I asked, pity stirring my heart. Clearly the woman's humors were badly out of balance since they pushed her to this crisis stage.

"Why is she here like this?" I whispered, though I doubted that any of my words would penetrate the mist around Malka Freya.

Leah Sara held up a hand, as if to stop my stream of questions. "Rebecca," and she paused before going on in a barely audible voice while looking deeply in my eyes. "Here you have the real murderer. It is she who committed the crime of which the Egyptian rabbi is accused."

At first I could not credit what I heard. And when I did, I felt as if I had been struck to my abdomen and my breath knocked out. My knees buckled, and I barely managed to fall into a chair on my descent. As promised, Leah Sara had indeed managed to shock me, even more than the state of Malka Freya.

When I regained my breath, I stammered out: "She killed the crusader? This poor wretch of a woman?"

Malka Freya must have been hearing more than I thought, because when I said the word *crusader*, her movements, like a hunting dog suddenly sniffing prey, stopped, and her eyes lit up with an unholy fire. After a few moments she shook her head and resumed pacing and wringing her hands. I watched in confused silence as she moved agitatedly around the room while Leah Sara kept a sharp eye on her.

"You see, it is about my niece, Gabriela Mendoza. After she was assaulted by a crusader, she took her own life."

My hand flew to the base of my throat, which I grasped in horror. Another rape victim of the crusaders. Dear God in heaven, how can this be? Leah Sara spoke softly so as not to further disturb Malka Freya, but the woman was so lost in her own world, I did not think she heard.

Leah Sara continued, "Yes. Malka Freya is the bereaved mother. Before I continue, I must try to settle her." As I watched, Leah Sara persuaded the poor woman to sit with a small cloth doll drawn from a pocket in her garment. Once this was accomplished, Leah Sara turned to me. She glanced frequently at the woman cradling the doll.

I struggled to take in all she was saying. "You must tell me the whole story from the beginning—and why you have not told the duke that the Egyptian rabbi is innocent of the charge." *I must remain calm and in full possession of my faculties. I must not give in to my anger and bewilderment.* The futility of Rafael's and my efforts, not to mention the time ill-spent, as well as confusion at Leah Sara's duplicity—how was I to swallow the emotions swirling through me so I did not appear as mad as this deranged woman? I needed to regain control of my senses, to get an idea of how to proceed when I had not a clue.

Leah Sara had resumed something of her usual air of assurance. "My kinsman Natan Mendoza has been conferring with Duke Henry. We have a hope that the 'unholy warriors,' may their days in hell be eternal, will not punish all of Salerno, especially the Jews, if a Jewish killer is promptly dealt with in a public manner."

"But the rabbi is *not* the killer. How can you allow such an injustice to take place when you know the truth?" My voice broke as I flung my hands up in despair. "How can you, as a good Jewish woman, allow such a perversion of justice?"

She nodded her head in the direction of the clearly deranged woman. "And you think justice will be served by putting this poor, suffering creature, my sister, to death?"

What a question! My heart ached at the impossible situation of a bloodthirsty demand for one more killing to counterbalance the one already committed. I sank back in the chair, my hands on my knees to steady their shaking. I trembled at the terrible sadness of this family. "Gabriela was the daughter of Natan Mendoza? He has shown no sign of having to endure such a loss."

Leah Sara gathered herself and resumed speaking. "Natan." She shook her head. "He rules the women in his family with a strict hand. They must follow his dictates. He never shows them any softness or tenderness. My sister suffered from this. As do his daughters."

"It is sad when men are so hard and unbending," I said, "but, alas, not rare."

She nodded. "More than sad. My niece was assaulted by a crusader. At first, my sister tried to care for her daughter in secret, as her husband demanded. Soon, Malka Freya saw the situation as hopeless and gave in to rising despair. After hearing the Egyptian rabbi's sermon—you remember, she fainted in the synagogue—and seeing Gabriela's decline, my sister started to go berserk." Her eyes filled with tears, and she paused.

"Despite all that Malka Freya tried, the night after the rabbi's sermon, Gabriela took her own life." Leah Sara swallowed hard and, for a moment, could not go on.

I put my hand on hers in a futile effort at comfort. She nodded, then continued, "Natan decreed that Gabriela's suicide and burial be kept secret." She sniffed. "He directed Malka Freya to carry on as if nothing had happened. The story to be told was that Gabriela was away with family in Genoa. She actually had been there. The assault happened when she was en route home. Natan said they would tell everyone Gabriela extended her stay."

"Dear Lord," I whispered as lies piled upon horror.

"The night after the secret burial, when Natan was out, Malka Freya covered herself in a cape, grabbed a knife from the kitchen, went to the Frankish tavern, and attacked the first crusader she saw. Natan had hired a young Egyptian student, Moshe ben Shlomo, to watch his house. The student followed Malka Freya. Unfortunately, he was unable to stop the crime. After she had attacked the crusader, ben Shlomo was able to quickly spirit her away."

My mind was spinning with these facts. "Why would she do such a thing?"

Leah Sara's eyes filled with tears. "Who can say for sure? As well as I know my sister, I can only guess. I think she did this awful thing because her mind snapped. Maybe she figured God would point her to the man who hurt her Gabriela. It is, of course, highly unlikely this crusader was actually guilty of the assault—he just happened to be in a tavern when Malka Freya arrived. And, as we know, his death has not stopped other such attacks."

If anything, it may have inspired even more such attacks. "Malka Freya must have been sick and hurt in her thoughts beyond imagining to do such a thing."

"Yes. But as a mother I have an idea how the suicide of one's child could cause such an act, even for someone as gentle and loving as my sister." She swiped at tears, crouched by her sister's side, and touched her shoulder. "That is why I said that you cannot understand the heart of a mother. Or a sister."

"True in the most literal sense. Yet you, Leah Sara, you know the truth, and you also know the Egyptian rabbi stands to be executed for her crime."

"Perhaps that serves to provide some justice for Malka Freya. She hated the rabbi's sermon because she thought he claimed her daughter's rape to be a punishment from God. After she killed the crusader, she might have killed the rabbi too, if Moshe ben Shlomo had not rushed her away."

Leah Sara paused. "And why *was* the rabbi with a crusader in a tavern?"

"I do not know," Rebecca confessed. "And considering his current situation, I do not agree that he was saved, as you say. Seeing a woman commit this horrible crime immediately close to him, he must also have been in shock, for he picked up the bloody knife, and the guard found him holding it." I spoke the words slowly.

She nodded. "I must tell you the rest. Several days later, Moshe ben Shlomo, who was in great debt to the Mendoza family, followed Natan's instructions and attacked the rabbi in his cell."

Shock upon shock upon shock. "Why? Moshe ben Shlomo's attack came close to killing the rabbi."

She held up her hands to stop my questions. "I cannot answer for my brother-in-law. Maybe he thought that if the rabbi died in prison, that would bring a swift end to the matter. The duke and the crusaders would be satisfied that the murderer had been punished—"

I shook my head. "That is the worst reasoning I have ever heard, committing one unjust sin after another."

She sighed. "I cannot say Natan was thinking clearly either. The man had lost his daughter and appeared to have lost his wife. At any rate, the rabbi survived, and then Natan ordered Moshe ben Shlomo back to Egypt. I am not saying this was right. You must understand,

Natan and the rest of the Mendozas put family before any other consideration."

I also loved my family. I wondered, to what limits would such love go?

Knowledge of the truth brought a feeling not of relief but of anxiety. More than anything, I wanted to speak to Rafael. He would help me make sense of a world gone mad. Identifying the true murderer might not be enough to save the rabbi after all. "How extraordinary that she had the strength to commit such an act. The crusader was a soldier, a man used to battle."

"A mother who thinks she has found a way to avenge her child's suffering," Leah Sara offered, "what would she not do in her child's name? You do not know about a mother's heart in this way, but you are a physician."

"Yes, I know people under stress can perform acts of stunning strength." I looked at Malka Freya. "When did she become as she is now?"

Leah Sara made an ugly face. "Following her deed, Moshe ben Shlomo thought best to bring her to me, covered with the blood and filth of the crusader. She, as you might imagine, was incoherent and in shock. Moshe ben Shlomo, in a few words, told me what happened and then disappeared into the night."

Leah Sara's eyes had turned flat and dull as she recited this final series of events.

She went on, "After I cleaned her up, I wanted to return her to her home, but her husband Natan came and demanded that she stay here. Upon hearing these words, it seemed her last nerve and shred of sanity snapped. She unraveled before me. Natan has subsequently refused to see her or talk with her. She has been the way you see her ever since."

Leah Sara bit her lip, and I thought she might start to weep, then she added, "Magistra, my poor sister was not even able to go to her own child's burial. Natan has told everyone that Malka Freya is in Genoa with Gabriela and that they will stay there until the current troubles are resolved. Of course, since everything is a secret, there was not even a proper shiva. Not one drop of comfort."

What a horrible story! Gabriela, Malka Freya. And the other daughters—they had lost their mother too. What of Natan? Surely he had to be touched by the misery around him. After all, he claimed to care greatly for his family. He must surely also be suffering.

"You have studied medicine and healing more recently than I and have more extensive practice," Leah Sara went on. "Is there some way to help my sister? To bring her back toward sanity?"

"Perhaps we can find a way to rebalance her humors," I said, though I wondered if this would be possible. Such disturbances of the spirit and the mind greatly challenged physicians. In any case, I was concerned that it might take a long while for Malka Freya to recover. "I can examine her and consult with colleagues. First, though, we must rescue the rabbi from the fate that looms before him. Leah Sara, he is an innocent man. Surely, the balance of justice must be considered."

"No man is completely innocent," she sniffed.

This was not the time for a philosophical discussion about the word *innocent*. I rose. "I must go to the duke with the truth."

Leah Sara looked on the verge of stopping me, if need be by blocking my exit. "No matter what, you must promise—before you reveal the truth to the duke, you must insist that my sister will not be made to pay for this act more than she already has."

I must have grown pale at her request. How could I ensure this?

She inclined her head. "I have invited you into my home and thus you have learned the truth of the matter. I believe in justice, but not at the expense of my poor deranged sister's life. You must assure me."

I put my head in my hands in an effort at clear thought. "And what would you recommend? How to resolve this?" I sighed.

"All I care about is that my sister be protected."

You do not ask for much, do you? "I will do all I can to protect your sister. As to the rest—we must take action to serve justice."

Malka Freya dropped her doll and resumed pacing. Leah Sara managed to convince her to sit with the doll again, though it did not seem she would remain calm for long.

"You would need a Solomon to come up with a solution, and wise men of that sort are in short supply." Leah Sara's voice sounded weary.

I agreed. "Rafael Lopes Dias is wise. Not quite the caliber of a Solomon, though very much a wise man for our era." I thought for a moment. "Also, I have a patient who is a skilled avvocato, a lawyer who is Gentile. He might be able to provide worthwhile insight."

"Perhaps. Talk to whom you will. However, you must give me your word that you will safeguard my sister's life."

I had sought the truth, and I had found it. Sadly, it raised more questions than it answered. "I agree it would serve no one for your sister to be executed." Would Rafael agree? Would the duke? Did I have the right to make this judgment? What would I need to seek now when truth was no longer the clear objective of my efforts? Could I separate truth and justice? "I will confer with the others. We will come up with a solution."

"I need more than that from you. Much is at stake here, including my family's honor."

A wave of pity rushed over me, mixed with my disappointment in this woman. "How, then, would you recommend I proceed? For I cannot in good conscience simply let an innocent man die." *Perhaps a woman of such great intelligence and experience of life will be able to see what I cannot.*

She thought for a moment. "You can say you have learned the murder was committed by a poor madwoman. Knowing her identity would help no one and hurt many."

Really? She thinks I will be able to guard such a secret? That the duke and anyone I speak with will accept such a statement without further questions? I took her hand. "I can tell you that I will try, but you must realize that what you ask of me is virtually impossible. Though Rafael will believe me, Duke Henry might think I am making up a story to save the rabbi."

Color rushed to Leah Sara's pale cheeks. "Assure me that you will try."

I bowed my head. "As a woman of my word, I swear I will try with all my might. If I fail, you must believe that it will not be for lack of effort. Natan knows about his wife, so, despite his standing apart, I can confer with him?"

"Yes, him and Baruch. None of the other family members knows the full story."

"I must go." If I did not get Rafael's counsel soon, I feared my head would burst. "As soon as I know what is happening, I will let you know."

She sighed. "God go with you."

My thoughts clashing with the truth and with the questions that truth brought up, I rushed from Leah Sara's home out into the storm to meet Rafael. Together, we would need to gain an interview with the duke—and find a way to make sure the rabbi was not with the other prisoners on the next transport to Palermo. Together, we would decide on a path to the best justice we could obtain.

Or so I hoped.

Thirteen

R afael awaited me within the guard's station outside the dungeon. "I know who murdered the crusader," I whispered to him as soon as I was close enough.

He did not waste time by doubting me. He took hold of my arm and steered me to a quiet corner of the hall. "Who did it? Why are you waiting another moment to reveal the truth? Do not keep me in suspense."

"Prepare yourself for a great shock—several."

He snorted. "Who?"

"A woman. I can tell you who, but I have promised to keep her identity confidential."

Rafael reeled backward, away from me. "So, a woman *really did* do it!"

"Yes, one driven to murder by grief and insanity of the violation and then suicide of her daughter. Malka Freya Mendoza."

His eyes flew open and he muttered an oath I had never before heard him express. "*My God*. Natan Mendoza's wife did this? And their daughter was raped and committed suicide! I can scarce take it all in!"

Neither can I, and I witnessed Malka Freya's current state. "Let us go to the castle right now. Maybe when we tell the duke that we

have identified the actual culprit, without, of course, naming her—"
I began.

"Have you taken leave of your senses? You propose that we go to
the duke with this preposterous tale, saying we know who is guilty
but that we must keep the identity secret. You think this is a viable
plan? If so, the killer is not the only madwoman around."

*He is responding as any other intelligent person would. Still, his
comments unnerve me.* "Is there any way we can use the truth to save
the rabbi?"

Rafael shook his head. "Rebecca, listen to yourself. I want to hear
everything, including how you learned such incredible information,
but that is for later. As to making your plan work, I do not see any
possibility. Please use the good sense I have come to expect from you
and admit you will have to tell the duke the whole truth."

"This is the truth, at least of who committed the act and what
motivated it." I sounded unconvincing, even to myself. How to rec-
oncile what we now knew and what had to be done?

He exhaled hard. "What you propose is impossible. For one, it will
be difficult to convince anyone a woman could do the act. And the
duke is not going to see any solution in simply identifying a woman
as the murderer. Such a pronouncement would probably enrage the
crusaders even more and spur the pogrom we have so far managed
to avert."

"There must still be a way—"

He shook his head. "There is no point in seeing the duke if we are
not going to identify the killer. Even doing all that may not convince
him of anything. Do you agree that we will need to reveal the full
truth to have a slight chance of saving the rabbi?"

"I did tell the person who revealed all this to me that we probably
would not be able to keep the killer's identity secret from the duke."

He nodded. "I will go with you to the duke, though we need to be prepared for disappointment, even after we have told him everything. I fear that hearing what we have to say will not change his mind about the rabbi."

I prayed for the best possible outcome—whatever that might be.

We were fortunate that the bribes—with promises of more to come—"convinced" the guard to secure us an audience with the duke sooner than was his habit.

Though I was no stranger to the surroundings favored by the rich, the extreme sumptuousness of his quarters impressed me. Our duke clearly loved luxury and comfort.

"I understand you want me to refrain from putting the Egyptian rabbi on the ship to Palermo that is now scheduled for Friday. The regent's men are expecting him to be on that transport. Why should I consider not sending him?" The duke, regarding me with some cynicism, lounged back in his chair.

"Your Grace, with all due respect, we now know who murdered the crusader. Please free the rabbi before any more injustice is committed." I tried to keep my voice calm yet strong.

"Why did you not say this first?" The duke's eyes widened with surprise as he sat forward. "Tell me at once the name of the guilty man. We will arrest him and free the rabbi."

"This is where the story becomes complicated." I glanced over at Rafael for support. He nodded. "The guilty person is a woman."

That news, evidently as much a surprise to the duke as it had been to me, was at first greeted with silence. Then he said, "A woman? No. Not possible. Why would you say such a thing?" He shook his head, made a sour face, and sat back in his chair. "A woman could not commit such an act. Why are you wasting my time?"

Breathe deeply. "A woman. A crusader robbed this mother's

daughter of her innocence, which ended in her suicide. The mother, in her grief, sought to avenge the assault and suicide of her beloved child."

From the expression on the duke's face, it was clear he did not believe me. "I am listening, Magistra, though I am losing patience. Tell me who this so-called murderous mother is." The duke's tone was cool. "Even then, I will probably not believe you."

What to do now? Can I protect Malka Freya's life once I say her name? Is there any other way to save the rabbi? "Her name is not as important as her story. This woman has lost her reason. She is incapable of understanding her actions and their consequences. Perhaps in time, with medical attention to bring her humors back into balance—"

With an imperious hand, the duke waved away my words. "First of all, I do not expect we can charge a woman with such a crime, let alone execute her." He peered at me through narrowed eyes. "I might almost suspect that you have come up with this story to cloud the situation and try to see that no one is blamed for the crime. Whatever your motive, we must face the basic truth. Everyone knows a woman is no match for a warrior in any sort of assault."

Everyone knows. How often is this the prelude to information that is, in fact, not true? "Nonetheless, the truth is that a woman, driven insane, committed the murder."

He growled his disbelief and rolled his eyes. "Maybe there is the slightest possibility that such a thing might have happened, but I will not listen to another word until I know who this woman is. So if you continue to refuse to name her, the current situation will remain as is."

I was bargaining from a weak position for life-or-death stakes. "May I have your pledge, sir, that this woman will not be tried and executed for the crime?"

Duke Henry cleared his throat. "I do not have to pledge any such thing. Nor will I. In fact, I can command you to tell me this information now." He paused, then continued, "I shall not. I shall give you until darkness falls to reconsider your stand. If you continue to insist on secrecy, the rabbi will go to his fate, and we will have an end to this troublesome matter, which has already taken too much time and consideration."

He went on, "This I will do for you. If you tell me what I ask, I will consider delaying his passage to Palermo." He rose. I had known, even when I gave my word, that the vow to safeguard Malka Freya might be impossible to keep. But at least we had gained some time.

Once Rafael and I were outside the castle, we looked at each other in consternation, and yet something more. He regarded me with such tenderness, my heart nearly melted. And then, without thinking, I went to him and he took me in his arms. We stood together for several moments. I so savored his warmth and his strength that I longed to linger there.

Life, after all, is so fragile. For Gabriela, for Malka Freya, for Shoshana, for the rabbi, even for the dead crusader, everything had turned in a matter of moments. Not one of us is immune from such catastrophe. Here I have this loving and caring man who wants me to be his wife. And what stops me is the broken heart I suffered as a girl not much older than the one I recently treated. I have been such a coward, have I not? Not a word I like to hear describe me. A cowardly child who has held back from being a full adult, growing in love with a beautifully adult male.

We regarded each other with a new understanding and longing between us. But other matters called before we might act on these feelings. "Please come with me to Leah Sara's house."

"Of course."

She was waiting when we arrived. Though she showed some surprise that I had brought Rafael, she ushered us both into her sitting room.

Clutching her hands, I said, "There is no time. I told Rafael all. We saw the duke. He has given me until the fall of darkness to tell him the killer's name or the rabbi is finished. Further, he can command me to tell him what I know."

She let out a cry. "There is no choice, is there? But what will he do to my poor sister?"

Rafael cleared his throat. "It seems he would not consider having her prosecuted and executed for this crime. But someone has to be. And the duke demands to know the whole truth as he makes up his mind."

Leah Sara sat thoughtfully for a long moment and then spoke. "You must tell him. And then I leave it to God for there to be justice, especially for my poor sister."

What anguish this woman faced, and what courage she showed. I hugged her and promised to keep her informed. Then Rafael and I rushed back to the duke.

"Your Grace," I began, choosing my words carefully. "I have permission to tell you the identity of the woman who was driven to commit the crime. I speak of Malka Freya Mendoza."

The duke's eyes widened. "Mendoza?" He looked to Rafael, who nodded in agreement.

The duke's mouth twisted in disgust. "Is she the wife of Natan or Baruch or one of the others?"

"The wife of Natan."

The duke looked heavenward before returning his steely gaze to me. "Leaders of your Jewish community, the Mendoza family. Jews. How can they ever be trusted!" He shook his head and glared at me. "You would expect me to charge the wife of Natan Mendoza, a woman conveniently gone insane, with the murder of a crusader? Can you think how the pope and the regent would greet such news? The crusaders themselves?"

"No, Your Grace. There are circumstances that argue you must not arrest her. A crusader raped her daughter, and the child committed suicide." I paused to allow space for him to take in the gravity of what happened. "The mother of this poor child has lost all reason and cannot answer for anything she has done under the force of her madness."

"Well, I can take solace in that thought." He looked heavenward with an expression of disdain. "Do you seriously expect me to believe this tale of yours? Perhaps you think I am the one who has gone insane?" His voice dripped with irony.

"The magistra is a woman known for her honesty and integrity," Rafael said.

Thank you, Rafael.

"Such qualities exist in the Jewish community?" Duke Henry asked. "Certainly not with the same meaning we Christians attribute to these values."

I dug my fingernails into my palms to keep from saying something that might further inflame the situation. Rafael's gaze met mine in mingled misery. We had to set aside our feelings to continue with our quest.

"Your Grace, difficult as it is to accept, this is the truth of the situation." Rafael spoke softly and civilly despite the growing ugliness of the exchanges. "Along with truth, we seek justice. We cannot believe you would try and execute an innocent man for this crime when you know someone else committed it."

I swallowed hard and waited. Never before had it been so difficult to remain silent.

At last the duke narrowed his gaze at me and his smile sent a shiver down my spine.

"I see you make of this complex matter a simple story. A crusader has been murdered in Salerno, but no one should be punished because the murderer is a woman driven crazy by her daughter's misadventure, according to your preposterous tale."

Misadventure. As if her dress had torn while she was frolicking with friends. "We must return to the overriding concern here. Justice." My voice faded as again his harsh laughter assaulted my ears.

"What gives you that idea?"

"'Justice, justice shalt thou pursue,'" I murmured.

Duke Henry shook his head. "Even the devil can quote scripture to his own ends. Never have I seen this better demonstrated. Ah, now I understand your goal. Governance according to the dictates of Deuteronomy. As if we were back in the old days, in a desert country far from the civilized world."

"Justice is fundamental to us all, in all the different faiths." Even as I said the words, the tightening of my stomach and a lump in my throat warned me to prepare for the duke's ultimate rejection of that notion. Indeed, Rafael signaled that I should back down.

"Tell me, Magistra, if I free the rabbi and neglect to hold the murderer of a crusader responsible, how do you see that as a pursuit of justice? A man on a holy Christian mission was murdered when he was merely sitting at a table outside a tavern, a place open to all. Do you think the citizens of Salerno and the crusaders will have their need for justice satisfied by my telling them to forget about punishing the murderer? If by chance they are willing to consider the case resolved, what about the pope, who champions the crusaders? What about our young king's regent, who also holds the crusaders in his favor and expects me to keep order here in Salerno?"

I took a deep breath. Despite Rafael's signal for me to pause, I responded. "You are asking difficult questions, but I have some too. This murder was committed by a mother whose daughter was brutally assaulted. A young woman's life ended in disgrace and suicide because of the crusaders' crimes. How is a loving mother to bear such agony? And where is the justice for the other young women of Salerno who have been raped by the crusaders?"

The duke shrugged away my protest. "Do not try to divert me from the main point of our discussion. Unfortunately, Signora Mendoza will not serve as a satisfactory sacrifice to the greater good, which is what I must think of above the fate of individuals. The Egyptian rabbi still appears to be the best candidate to play that role."

Rafael shook his head. "That is an impossible exchange. It would pile one gross injustice on top of other gross injustices."

"Justice and injustice are abstract qualities," the duke said. "We are not short of those. What we are short of are suitable candidates, other than the rabbi, to be held accountable for the murder of a crusader. Someone must be punished. How can we call ourselves civilized if we let murders go unpunished? What if the pope or the regent or the crusaders decide to pursue their version of justice and punish all of Salerno for this one crime?"

Much as I disliked the duke at this moment, I understood the force of his logic. "So guilt must be assigned and lead to an execution."

"Exactly. I do not consider the Mendoza woman or any other female suitable for this role. The Egyptian rabbi much better fills the need. And he is expendable."

"No one is expendable," Rafael replied, his distaste evident in his tone.

The duke's sigh made clear that his patience was growing thin. "You both see individuals," he countered. "I see the greater tapestry of concern for all of Salerno. What I can do for you, and I am being extraordinarily generous, is to delay transporting the rabbi to Palermo. The initial transport was delayed by the storm, as you well know. If you do not come up with an acceptable solution to this dilemma by Friday, you must say your farewells to him and the matter will be closed."

"Can you give us more time? There are several people we need to consult."

He shook his head. "I have been more tolerant than might be wise, but there is an end to my forbearance. And an end to what the citizens of Salerno should or will accept. Now, you must be on your way. I will grant you another audience tomorrow evening to hear your solution."

With that, he swept from the room. Servants ushered us out. We were not permitted to see the rabbi again or even to send him word of what had happened. Although, perhaps it was all for the best—that his hopes not be raised.

We went quickly to my house and slumped down in chairs in the parlor.

"I do not think I can face going to Natan Mendoza's home, not yet, though that must certainly be our next destination," I said to Rafael.

"What else can we do to save the rabbi?" Rafael asked.

"That is the question. The duke appears determined to execute him to mollify the crusaders and their supporters." My voice cracked. "Well, despite what I said earlier, perhaps it is time we went to the Mendoza family. I am thinking as I speak. We must first talk to the husband and see how he and his closest kin plan to proceed. They must take responsibility for what has occurred, but I am unsure where this will lead. Do you think the family will allow a truth so damaging to their honor to come out?"

"I think they would not merely for the sake of the rabbi," Rafael stated.

I nodded. "Nonetheless, I see no alternative except to try to convince them to get involved."

Rafael wrote a quick note, which Manuel took to Natan Mendoza, the father of the dead girl and the husband of the killer who had lost her mind. Manuel returned with the message that both Mendoza brothers would see us, but we would have to wait until the following afternoon. Since we would see the duke tomorrow evening, our schedule to make this work would be tight.

⁂

Meanwhile, I had an appointment to meet with my student Laura at the Scuola. As I was walking there, I saw a street fight erupt between a crusader and one of the apprentices who worked for a silver merchant. This drew first a crowd and then members of the duke's guard. From the calls of the onlookers, it was clear the crusader had earned the crowd's contempt. I had too much on my mind to pay attention, other than to mutter at the inconvenience of having to wend my way through the mob-filled street, causing me to be late for my meeting with Laura.

When she got a look at me as I entered the small meeting room in the Scuola, Laura's smile faltered. "What is wrong, Magistra?"

I had never grown adept at hiding my feelings from people who knew me well. "I have a serious matter in my life right now, but we are here to talk about your reading and your questions."

She sighed. "Of course I have many questions about the work of our La Trotula. However, they can wait. Tell me about this serious matter."

"No, Laura. This is the time for your work, not my worries."

"Please tell me. Perhaps I can help."

I squeezed her hand in grateful appreciation. "This is most kind and generous of you, dear Laura. I will tell you, but let us use up only a few minutes on this matter." I went on, "You remember when I spoke of the arrest of a rabbi from Egypt?"

"I have. He is to be transported to Palermo for trial and execution."

"Yes, even though I know for a fact he is innocent." I very briefly confided the story to her without revealing Malka Freya's identity.

She listened attentively and looked shocked. "I do not expect the Holy Father in Rome would be pleased to learn that the justice for the crusader comes at the cost of an innocent life, even of a non-Christian."

How young and naïve my student was. How sad that such innocence would not be sustainable for many more years. It was not my role in her life, however, to cause her to question her beliefs, especially as a Jewish teacher working with a Christian student.

Keeping my tone neutral, I said, "In my conversation with the duke, I discovered that he does not share this view."

She frowned. "That is unfortunate. Nor would the Holy Father agree to the death of one who cannot be held responsible for the crime she has committed due to the state of her sanity. If she murdered the actual crusader who assaulted her daughter, she might have made a case for avenging the honor of her child."

I agreed with her at the unlikeliness of this scenario.

"This is a dilemma," Laura said. "Perhaps there is a law that would apply."

As she spoke, I thought of my patient, the avvocato Mario de Rienzo. He often expressed interest in being able to provide me with his professional expertise. He might be of help in this situation.

"That is a good idea for me to ponder. But now it is time to return to the writings of La Trotula, our topic for the day."

"I was hoping to persuade you to forget that."

"And there your powers of persuasion reach their limit. Time to get to work." And so we did. But it soon became apparent that her mind also was elsewhere. "Now it is my turn to ask if you have some concern distracting you."

She frowned. "There is a problem in my family," she said softly. "I hesitate to take our time with this."

I patted her hand. "You are such a good student, I know you would not waste our time. Please, tell me. Perhaps I can help."

She sighed. "It is my cousin Benedetta. We are so close. Both of us have only brothers. Too many of them. We are each the sister the other never had." Her nervous laugh at this gave me gooseflesh. "To make our connection even closer, both of us are engaged to marry two brothers."

I nodded to show I was listening closely. When the silence grew oppressive, I prompted Laura to continue.

"Benedetta, usually the happiest of girls, has grown morose and refuses to see her friends, or her betrothed, or even me. We used to see each other several times a week, but it is more than two months since we last visited. Now, when I try to see her, her mama tells me she is sick and wants to be alone. I, the one who is supposed to be learning the healing arts, have no idea what to do for her because I have no opportunity to know what is wrong."

Hearing this story, I shivered. "Do you know if something happened to her?"

Laura shook her head. "There has been no communication since weeks before the Easter holidays."

I must not leap to conclusions. Any number of conditions could affect a young woman like this. "Have you spoken with her betrothed?"

"He is as baffled as everyone."

"I hope that you can find a way to communicate with your cousin soon, for everyone's sake." I winced at the weakness of my advice.

"I hope and pray so too." She sighed. "Thank you for listening."

"The least I can do. Now if you can face it, let us get back to La Trotula for today. But, Laura, please let me know what happens with your cousin. Maybe I will be able to provide actual advice once you know more of her situation. Maybe when you are together, you will be able to convince her to be examined. Then I might really be able to help."

"Thank you. I hope that can happen soon."

Fourteen

After another sleepless night, I faced the next day with hope that Rafael and I could succeed at saving the rabbi. I thought about the conversation with Laura as I hurried to Rafael's house. "I know a very successful avvocato, a Christian. Perhaps he can help us find a way to use the law to help us." I saw no reason to identify Signor di Rienzo as a patient.

Rafael looked surprised and pleased. "This is a good idea. I was going to ask how you know him, but it is better not to, is that correct?"

I smiled. "Let us go together to his office and see if we can see him soon."

We quickly went to the office, which was in the avvocato's house. When his clerk opened the door, he recognized me right away. "Did the avvocato summon you?"

"No. I am here with my colleague to see him on a professional matter."

He nodded. "Come in, Magistra, Signor. I shall see if the master can meet with you now. His schedule today was not very full." We did not have to wait long as the servant returned to usher us to the office. Avvocato di Rienzo stood and greeted me most warmly. "Seeing you is a pleasant surprise. And your companion. But tell me, why this visit?"

I introduced Rafael and told the avvocato that we sought his professional expertise.

"I am happy to give you something back for all the good you have done for me." His generosity warmed me. "Now, how may I help you today?"

Rafael and I provided a brief overview of the situation without naming the Mendozas.

When we were done, the avvocato's visage no longer looked quite so merry. "Well, I can see you must hold my skills in great esteem, to come to me with such a complex story." He sat back in his chair and was uncharacteristically quiet for a brief interval. My eyes locked with Rafael's as we waited.

The avvocato nodded, as if he had been in conversation with himself. Then he said, "What you ask of me is so strange, I may have to look beyond our usual code to come up with a solution. 'Justice, justice shalt thou pursue.'" The avvocato quoted the same verse that I had recited earlier to the duke. "Once, in my younger days, this verse was what inspired me to choose my career." His eyes took on a faraway expression.

"And this is the idea that impels us to try to find the path to justice in this situation," Rafael said.

I nodded in agreement. "How do we begin?"

The avvocato shrugged. "The first thing is to make an evaluation—which can seem like too big a challenge when the challenge is desperate, as you say this one is. Desperate problems call for desperate solutions. You must first deal with the family of the person who committed the act and convince them that they are, indeed, involved and responsible. Then you must persuade the duke to take his portion of responsibility. After all, he has let the politics of the situation lead to lawlessness—both of the crusaders and now of a Salernitan." He smiled. "If you would like, once you have gotten the family involved, I am willing to go with you to the duke."

"Thank you. That would be great and so helpful. The truth is, your being a Christian and an avvocato might mean that we have a greater chance of getting the duke's agreement than Rafael and I alone do."

The avvocato nodded. "I am not happy to say, as things are now, what you say is probably true."

We both thanked him. We were walking away from his office with the start of a plan. If only it would work and be in time.

⤐

As Rafael and I entered Baruch Mendoza's house that afternoon, it seemed very quiet. Natan and an ill-looking Baruch sat shoulder to shoulder on one side of a table. A servant motioned for Rafael and me to sit across from them.

Natan started, "Our loss has created a hole in our family. While it is usual practice to look to our community for support during such times of grieving, what happened was so difficult and painful that we have chosen to remember Gabriela in private."

And to forget about the unwanted attention her death might bring to your family? However, I felt he spoke from his heart, as much as this man could.

Natan went on, "Perhaps if we had done things another way after the attack on Gabriela, the consequences would have been different for my beloved wife. Perhaps other victims would have been spared. How can we possibly know?"

Despite the seeming sincerity of his words, I did not feel I could trust him completely. On the other hand, he was allowing us into the most intimate of family matters.

"My poor wife broke down after Gabriela's death. Her sister is the only one she will allow to care for her," he added.

"You mean she broke down *after she murdered the crusader.*" I said the inflammatory words in the most level voice I could summon.

"What?" Natan slammed his fist down on the table, and Baruch, weakly, did the same. "Magistra, do you know what you just said? You have accused my fragile wife of murder. How can you entertain and express such a bizarre untruth?"

This conversation would be more difficult than expected if they were committed to maintaining this lie, even now, when the truth was known.

Rafael started to say something, until I motioned for him to hold back.

"Please listen." My voice trembled. "I have spoken with Leah Sara Garcia, who told me the truth. That Malka Freya killed the crusader. Let us put aside any uncertainty as to the identity of the killer."

Baruch promptly went into a seizure of coughing and seemed to have trouble catching his breath. I ached to provide him care, but when I started to get up, he signaled I should back away.

"Shall we interrupt this talk for your brother's sake? Surely he has medications to help him," I said to Natan. When the coughing fit continued, Natan called for a servant to usher Baruch away. I hoped this meant he would receive treatment and relief.

I also hoped that Baruch's absence would not signal the end of our having a useful conversation. "We must address the most urgent of challenges—the matter of the injustice to the rabbi. Rafael and I revealed the truth to Duke Henry that Malka Freya killed the crusader. The duke has stated his unwillingness to prosecute and execute a woman for this murder."

"You spoke to the duke about my wife?" Natan screamed out

from a face suddenly bright red. He lunged toward me, which caused Rafael to rise and interpose himself between us.

"How dare you say such a thing!" Natan demanded as he backed away.

"In order to save an innocent man from being executed for a crime he did not commit."

He shook his head. "You had no right to talk to the duke about my wife. This is a private matter, to be handled by our family."

"Do not talk of rights," Rafael countered. "You who have known the truth all along and have had several conversations with the duke. How can you have maintained such a lie, one that will cost the rabbi his life?"

Natan glared at him with an expression of pure malevolence. "I should throw you both out of my house now."

"It would give me relief to leave," Rafael muttered.

The atmosphere in the room had grown so thick with menace, I needed a way to calm us all or risk an impossible breach. Later, I would think about the insanity of this interview. Right now, however, my concentration was solely on saving the rabbi and for that to happen, how to keep Natan in the conversation. So, speaking in even tones, I went on, "Gentlemen, please let us keep to an orderly discussion."

"It is not clear why you are involving us." Natan's color slowly returned to a more normal hue. "Given that the duke will not prosecute my wife, she will remain where she is, with her sister. Perhaps in the fullness of time, she will once again resume—"

I shook my head. "We are here because Duke Henry insists the murder cannot go unpunished. He is willing to see an innocent man executed because of the demands posed by Palermo and Rome, which unconditionally support crusaders."

Natan waved his hands as if brushing off a fly. "Look. The Egyptian rabbi is not the first man who will be unjustly punished to meet Christian demands, nor will he be the last. Because his sacrifice, although unjust, would be for the good of the greater Jewish community, we will venerate him as yet one more martyr to the injustice of the Gentiles. Our family can join in this veneration, perhaps contributing *tzedakah* to a worthy cause in his memory."

These bland words—calculated and cold—caused me extreme emotional distress. "Even if Rabbi Isaac ben Shmuel agreed to being martyred," I said, unable to keep the sharp bite from my words, "we cannot support this. No moral human would."

Natan shrugged away my words. "The rabbi has no place in our community, so we will not feel his loss greatly. And now, we must finish this conversation because I have another matter that needs immediate attention. You will please take your leave."

I scowled at him with the most overwhelming frustration. "We have not yet come up with any satisfactory solution for dealing with the crime."

"That is not the concern of our family. We have enough of our own problems without taking on this matter." He stood. "We talked and came to realize there could be no satisfactory solution to the dilemma that brought you here. We will join you and the community in mourning for Rabbi Isaac ben Shmuel. More than that we cannot do."

"This is not acceptable," Rafael began.

Before he could finish, a servant announced the arrival of several more Mendoza men.

"Show them in," Natan said. "I told you I have other business. Please have the decency to leave."

But two other men came into the room before Rafael and I had left. *Good. Now we can present the case to more of the family.* There was the third brother, the reclusive Shimon, and Yossel, a cousin. Once he realized we were not leaving, a sour-faced Natan indicated that we should all sit at the table.

"Where is Baruch?" Shimon asked.

Natan frowned. "He is resting. I would prefer not to disturb him. I have asked these two to leave, as our discussion is at an end. But they transgress courtesy and remain."

Rafael shook his head. "The magistra and I would not insist on being heard, were this not for the gravest of matters. Your brother Baruch has been resting for a while. Can we see if he is better? It is important that he join us for what we will talk of."

Natan glared at me. "Good God, Magistra, you are *supposed* to be a physician. I would expect you to know better." The two other men joined him in frowning at me.

"I am indeed aware of the demands illness puts on a person, and I respect Signor Mendoza's need for rest and peace. To that end, we hope to make our discussion short. However, as Signor Lopes Dias said, this matter is extremely important. It is fortuitous that there are already three of you here." I glanced at each man in turn, then spoke to Natan. "If your brother cannot join us in this room, perhaps we can all adjourn to his bedchamber and meet with him there."

Natan's face puckered in an incredulous expression, as if I had suggested serving a roasted pig for a Shabbat dinner. "We will certainly not invade his bedchamber to satisfy your unreasonable demand."

"What we ask is not unreasonable," Rafael said. "We are hoping his presence here now will forestall the need for even more distasteful action."

"Very well. However, I firmly insist you not overly fatigue him."

"Thank you. We will make every effort not to exhaust Signor Mendoza."

As Shimon left the room to bring back his elder brother, Natan, Yossel, Rafael, and I waited in uncomfortable silence until we at last heard shuffling footsteps. Baruch, though properly dressed, looked so greatly reduced in size and vigor that I had to stifle a gasp. He was leaning heavily against Shimon as he made his way to a chair at the table. The brief exertion had left the oldest Mendoza breathless and shaky. My heart went out to him.

"Thank you so much for joining us." Rafael broke the strained silence that had settled around the table like an additional participant.

"When it comes to the honor of the Mendoza family, I have no choice but to attend," he gasped between wheezes.

I hoped we could spare him the need to say many more words. Would he permit Natan or one of the others to take on more of a leadership role?

All eyes riveted on Rafael.

"The time is growing short for your family to act," he said. "Once the Egyptian rabbi is on the ship to Palermo, he is a dead man. Unjustly to be executed for a crime committed by a member of the Mendoza family. Malka Freya."

Natan regarded us with disgust. "We have already spoken of this and rejected these claims." He rose.

"Please be seated," Rafael said. He spoke softly, but with such natural authority that Natan did as ordered.

In a moment, though, he appeared to realize what he had done and scowled. "How dare you come into my brother's home and issue orders."

"I dare because an innocent man's life is at stake. We have not completed the necessary discussion of this matter nor of the threat to the honor of the Mendozas. A threat that also endangers the whole Jewish community."

Natan looked around him at the three other members of his family. "We all agreed that, even if my wife were responsible for the heinous act of which these two have accused her—and we have not admitted to this—we cannot be held responsible for what her unfortunate madness might have led her to."

"Be that as it may," Rafael said, "a number of us know your wife's culpability as a fact. We do not agree the Mendoza family is free to let an innocent man proceed to pay for her crime. And we could not, in good conscience, allow such a breach of justice to remain hidden. The Mendoza family must participate in saving the Egyptian rabbi. The magistra and I will provide every possible aid."

Natan struck the table with his fist. "Preposterous."

"You cannot completely silence the truth. We know about Moshe ben Shlomo, who saw what happened and has been paid off to stay far away until the execution is completed."

"I know of no such person," Natan spluttered.

Baruch, wheezing, asked, "What is it you want from us? Speak up, man. I must rest soon." It was not difficult to see how much the situation taxed him.

Rafael held out his hands. "We are determined to save an innocent man and see justice done. The Mendoza family is renowned for a deep knowledge and love of Torah and our other sacred texts. Let us put our heads together and come up with the best possible solution to this difficult situation. For the sake of both justice and honor. The Torah tells us we must do all we can to preserve life."

I nodded in agreement.

Natan spat back with contempt. "You deign to talk to us of what the Torah teaches."

A new voice now entered the conversation. "I agree with the two overriding concerns—justice for the rabbi and maintaining the Mendoza family honor, but truly, not just in public reputation." We all turned to look at Shimon, who continued, "The conundrum is that the duke, because of his concerns for Salerno's stability and his need to satisfy the pope and regent, requires a man's execution for the crusader's murder."

Natan exclaimed in frustration, "What can we possibly do in this impossible situation other than to accept the injustice of the rabbi's execution?"

After a long moment of heavy silence, Baruch, with a wave of his hand, signaled his intention to speak, but instead began to cough and choke. We all sat quietly while a servant brought him a cup of water, which Baruch sipped without great energy. When he regained his composure, he was able to speak—quietly but now with a solemn firmness. "There is one way to spare the rabbi that also is truly honorable for this family I love and lead." Here he took a relatively deep breath and continued, "I will, as head of the family, take responsibility for the act my sister-in-law committed."

Natan jumped up, but before he could speak, Shimon put a restraining hand on his arm and asked, "Dear brother, what are you suggesting?"

I regarded this quiet and intelligent Mendoza brother with gratitude.

Natan got red in the face. "So we should sink to their level? I would expect better for us."

Shimon waved his hands. "Natan, face reality. Malka Freya has lost her wits and somehow managed to murder a man. Of course the reasons for all this are horribly tragic. We do not want her to pay for this crime, granted. And, because she is not fit to do so, the duke and others would not even consider that. And, the Mendoza family cannot allow the innocent rabbi to die for something a member of our family has done."

"My brother the philosopher," Natan said in the same tone he might have used to label him a robber of widows and orphans.

Shimon made a short ironic nod. "These people have brought us a puzzle. Now Baruch says he takes responsibility on behalf of our family. What do you mean, Baruch?"

Somehow Baruch summoned the energy to rise out of his chair and stood, erect, to his full height. "I will take the place of the rabbi and be executed." After this startling pronouncement, he collapsed back into his seat.

Total silence greeted these words. Then Natan began to laugh, a harsh sound that bordered on hysteria. "I am sure that my beloved brother did not just say the words I thought I heard him say."

"I heard them," Shimon said. Yossel nodded.

Natan shook his head. "Now it is my beloved brother who has lost his wits. Brother, you will not do any such thing."

Baruch turned to Rafael and me. "You have heard my offer. Go, quickly. Tell the duke I shall take the rabbi's place on the gallows."

Rafael and I regarded each other in shock. We started to rise, when Natan bellowed, "You are not to go anywhere now. Certainly not to the duke with this preposterous idea."

"Natan," Baruch pleaded. "I am sick and old. I shall die soon anyway. Let my death serve a purpose."

Natan angrily scrubbed a hand across his face. Could those have been tears in his eyes? "You are not so old, not so sick. Your physician will bring you back to health. You are not to sacrifice your life."

"I am dying, and shortening the little of my life left to me is a sacrifice I am willing to make, for what is just and for the honor of this family." Baruch's voice faded on the last words.

Natan snorted. "A sacrifice. If we must spare the rabbi, we can find people who need money. Someone who would be willing to die for whatever we would pay him—or, rather, pay his family."

"You would try to *hire* someone to give up his life?" The idea struck me as being as monstrous as the murder itself.

Natan shrugged. "Do not be so naïve, Magistra. There are people whose misery would lead them to make such a sacrifice gladly—for their loved ones or for some other reason. I am not about to volunteer to replace the Egyptian rabbi and face the royal court for justice, nor would I want anyone from my family to step forward and take this on. Some poor wretch, though, could sacrifice himself so his family would be provided for—

"It would have to be someone the duke believed the king's regent would deem acceptable," he continued. "Also the pope. And the crusaders would have to be mollified."

"Think what would happen if the news came out that criminals could successfully avoid punishment by supplying people *willing* to sacrifice themselves. The criminals might add abduction to their other crimes—so as to have a designated sacrifice available to help them avoid punishment," Shimon said.

"What is that to us?" Natan asked. "We do not make it a practice to commit crimes. This one is only because of a freak set of circumstances that will never happen again." He took a long look at me. "Will you be satisfied and leave us alone if we deliver an acceptable sacrifice to the duke?"

Rafael and I shared a look of horror. I was about to refuse when Baruch cleared his throat and, in a voice barely above a whisper, said,

"I meant what I said. No one else will be involved. I am ready to save the rabbi and be executed."

Total silence again greeted his pronouncement. Then Natan once again sprang to his feet. "You will not."

Baruch went into another spasm of coughing. With shaking hands, he raised his cup to his lips and sipped. "I will go. You see," he said to everyone, "I am dying. What does it matter if I do it a bit sooner?" He subsided into his chair.

"You are not dying," Natan insisted, going to his brother's side. I could see the tortured love on the healthy man's face. "Magistra, tell him. He is not dying."

"Signor Baruch, has your physician so diagnosed you?" I asked.

Baruch appeared to gather a bit of strength. "He confirms what my body tells me every morning and night. My days on this earth are numbered."

"Nonsense," Natan blustered. "Magistra, you will recommend another physician. Ten more. A hundred more. We are in Salerno, after all, the center of the world for physicians."

Even at this extreme moment, I served only to recommend *another* physician, a man. Shimon caught my eye, and I could see compassion in his gaze.

"It matters not how many doctors see me," Baruch panted. "I am a dead man. I will say farewell to my loving family and board the ship to Palermo. Let the king's hangman execute me, the eldest of the Mendoza men. With my sacrifice, let me save the life of the rabbi and safeguard our family's honor."

"I will not permit this," Natan repeated, but this time with a deflated air of resignation.

Baruch shakily drew himself to his feet. "Both as the leader of the Mendozas and as myself the individual, I make this decision.

However, I pray that you, my family whom I love, can understand." With that he looked at his family members, waiting as the expression of each of them in turn showed a sad resignation and acceptance.

Then Baruch Mendoza turned to Rafael and me. "Thank you for bringing us this matter so clearly. Now, please, go tell the duke and get his approval of the plan." Then he turned to his servant. "Prepare me for my final voyage."

My heart now went out to Baruch and to the Mendozas. As the curtain was about to come down on the rabbi's chances, this glimmer of hope shone through. "The magistra and I will go to the duke," Rafael said.

He and I started to rush through the busy streets of the city intent on seeing the duke immediately, when I remembered the avvocato's offer. "Let us bring him too."

Rafael frowned. "We have a strong argument and there is not much time. But, yes, he might be helpful in convincing the duke, so let us take him along. We must do everything possible."

Thank goodness it was not much of a detour to alert the avvocato, who, after we explained what was happening, agreed to join us and was able to get ready quickly. For expediency, we now went in his carriage to the castle. En route, we gave him more details of the situation and of Baruch Mendoza.

He raised a brow. "Extraordinary. We may just be able to pull this off."

The three of us brushed past the guards posted at the entrance. Because of the presence of the avvocato, the inside guard let us in without the usual delaying tactics.

As we entered the duke's chamber, I noticed he was not alone. He and his companion, in a formal uniform I did not recognize, regarded us with the curiosity they might have accorded a creature risen from the depths of the sea who deigned to soak their rugs with foul waters.

"Excuse me, Your Grace," Rafael said. "The guard did not tell us you had company."

The duke murmured a few words to his guest, who glanced over at us, nodded, moved to the back of the room, and poured himself a goblet of wine.

"Lopes Dias, have you come with a new suggestion for the situation of the rabbi?" he asked. "And, my friend Avvocato di Rienzi. You are now allied with these two?"

He took a deep bow. "They have a most intriguing legal situation about which I have advised them. I am happy to provide my best legal opinions to you too."

The duke snorted, but he indicated we should continue. "Given that you are here, Avvocato, I will listen. But please get on with it. I have a very full schedule."

Rafael started, "As you asked us, we have come up with a solution to save the life of the innocent rabbi while still bringing the appearance of justice for the murdered crusader. I would like the magistra to describe it."

Please, dear Lord, be with me. Guide me in my words as I attempt to convince the duke to allow what we ask. "As we told you yesterday, a distraught female member of the Mendoza family killed the crusader. We have just come from Baruch Mendoza's home." I took a deep breath. "A male Mendoza is willing to take the punishment in place of the guilty female, to preserve the family's honor and to save the innocent life of the accused rabbi."

The duke, who looked somewhat taken aback, set down his goblet of wine. "Magistra, did you say one of the Mendozas is going to allow himself to be executed?"

Clearly and carefully, I repeated what I had said before, adding that the man willing to lay down his life was in fact Baruch Mendoza.

"Baruch Mendoza?" the duke repeated, his voice signaling surprise. "He is the leader of the family and the Jewish community, and he is an honorable man." The duke looked incredulously to Rafael.

"Yes, he is all that." Rafael paused. "And he is dying."

Duke Henry's face reflected surprise. "I did not know this, but his imminent death sheds light on his decision. On the one hand, it is more understandable that a man facing death should step forward in this fashion. On the other hand, it makes his sacrifice less significant. So you propose that we deliver a dying man to the hangman?"

Would the duke not accept him because of this? "Signor Mendoza is sick, true, perhaps fatally. But surely his role as a leader of the Jewish community should compensate for his lack of good health in making him an acceptable substitute." I considered further. "And as far as the crusaders are concerned, they would probably sooner accept that one of their number was felled by a sick but powerful man than by a sick woman or a frail rabbi."

After a pause, the duke replied, "Yes, I would say the crusaders and the pope might be satisfied with being able to show that a Jewish leader was executed for the murder of the crusader."

I started to feel that this strange bargain might work, even though the idea of such a sacrifice continued to trouble me.

Duke Henry paused again, this time picking up his wine and taking a long draught, clearly considering the situation. "No," he said at last, making my heart seem to stop. "What you propose is not sufficient. Before I accept this change, I would demand more."

We are not bartering over vegetables in the marketplace. We are dealing with a man's life. "More? What more can you want?"

The avvocato caught my eye and shook his head. Rafael stepped in. "We are glad, Your Grace, to be so close to a resolution. What would suffice to make this switch possible?"

The duke favored us with a half-smile. "The Mendoza family has control over a fleet of ships. They could provide the crusaders free passage to return to France. That way we could generously enable them to return home." He nodded to himself. "Yes. Providing passage to the crusaders and a small gift of gold to me would allow me to agree to this offer."

I could not believe that Duke Henry was adding personal profit to this. I nearly spoke up, but Rafael signaled me to remain silent.

"Your Grace, this is a large forfeit to charge the Mendoza family," the avvocato pointed out.

"What price honor, even for Jews?" the duke asked.

The ugliness of his remark stung.

"All Salerno would be thankful to see the end of the crusaders in our midst," the duke went on. "Just think—the Mendozas would be celebrated as heroes despite their role in the crusader's murder!"

"We would have to see if they agree to this plan," Rafael said tightly.

"Yes, you do that. However, I must tell you, there is one more problem."

No. "What else?" I asked before Rafael could even attempt to be diplomatic.

"The rabbi is already on a ship to Palermo."

No! Solid ground seemed to be crumbling beneath my feet.

"What? How can this be?" Rafael's voice rose the smallest bit, an unusual show of emotion for him. "You said you were not going to send him off until tomorrow morning."

The duke's brow shot up. "You are questioning me, Lopes Dias?"

I jumped in to answer before Rafael could. "We thought we had more time, Your Grace. You *told* us we had more time." I looked from the duke to Rafael.

The duke shrugged. "If you remember, the prisoner was supposed to be on a ship Wednesday morning. Bad weather held up that departure. The sailors determined that the weather was sufficiently better to sail today instead of waiting yet another day. They feared another storm might be brewing and would come upon us by tomorrow. I saw no reason to delay transporting the accused." Now he shook his head and looked at the avvocato. "I am the one you should feel sorry for. Without the rabbi to bargain with, I may not get what I want from the Mendozas. Unless I can think up another scheme."

"This cannot be. You are talking about executing an innocent man as if you were merely discarding a bit of rubbish. Can you not do something to save him? Send word to the court to delay the execution?"

Rafael shook his head at my headstrong words and put a restraining hand on my arm. The avvocato said, "Will you go along if my companions can discover a way for you to have all you want if you agree to the substitution?"

"I would, of course. But what you ask is likely infeasible." The duke waved his hands in dismissal. "By the time any message would arrive, the execution will already have taken place. Is that not right? Duke Otto, my *invited* guest, has just come from the court in Palermo. He knows more about its doings than anyone here." He looked to the other man who stepped forward out of the shadows.

Duke Otto nodded. "Yes. Justice in Palermo is very swift, especially in such important cases."

His Grace shrugged. "There you have it. You have fought a good fight, but it is over."

Oh no, it is not. "What if we can get Baruch to Palermo on a fast boat? What if we can have him arrive in time, before the execution?" Rafael asked.

"Your Grace, think about this possibility. What if somehow there was success in transporting Baruch Mendoza to Palermo in time? May my companions have a document showing your approval for the scheme—even if it is impossible to put to the use they desire?" the avvocato asked. I regarded him with gratitude.

The duke shrugged. "It is probably a wasted effort, but yes. I will provide such a document with the understanding that I get what I ask for, *even* if the substitution fails."

The avvocato gave Rafael and me a solemn nod. Though agreeing went against notions of fairness and justice, we acquiesced.

After summoning a servant to bring vellum, the duke scrawled a few words and affixed his seal. After Rafael and the avvocato reviewed it and nodded their acceptance, the duke dismissed us.

Once outside, we thanked the avvocato, who favored us with a lopsided smile. "I find this matter most interesting. Please apprise me of what happens and include me if I can be of any further aid." On that note, we parted ways and moved with the greatest of speed.

How can it all fall apart precisely when we see a solution? I fought not to surrender to complete despair. *If only the timing had worked out more fortuitously.*

Fifteen

"Rebecca, look how far we have come." Rafael, sensing my internal turmoil, tried to calm and reassure me.

"Is it really possible to move with the speed we require?" I hissed at him. "When is it appropriate to give up?"

"We are about to see."

We rushed to the home of Baruch. Once the servant brought us to the sitting room, Natan was the first person we encountered.

"Have you not done my family enough harm?" he growled.

I understood that he wanted to blame someone for his troubles. Right then, Shimon joined us. Moments later, Baruch, dressed for travel, came. A servant brought a small chair, for even taking a few steps exhausted Baruch.

"Now that you are all here, we shall explain what has happened," Rafael said.

"He is gone." My voice carried my discouragement. "The rabbi is already en route to Palermo as we speak. Duke Henry says it is too late to send a messenger. Too late for the rabbi." I swallowed hard.

Natan shrugged. "We tried to help. Lopes Dias, Magistra. You cannot fault us for the duke's action. You cannot carry out your threat to dishonor our family by disclosing what Malka Freya did just because the duke did not stay true to his word as to when the rabbi would be sent. Now, the arrangement is cancelled and the entire situation is settled."

"We disagree," Rafael said calmly. "You see, there is more to Duke Henry's conditions." He then articulated each of those demands.

Natan sprang up and began to pace. "Outrageous. Not only would he kill our Baruch, he would bankrupt the family as well. Free passage to the crusaders." He grunted, his face puce with emotion. "Those animals would wreak havoc on our ships. And how much gold does he plan to extort? No, I say, no to it all."

Just then another voice chimed in. "We can take our newest ship, the *Ester HaMalka*, the Queen Esther, which is now here in Salerno and is faster than any in the duke's mediocre fleet." Baruch Mendoza regarded us. "Yes—I will go to Palermo on that one. If we leave immediately, I believe we might reach Palermo first." He spoke with a clear voice, though as soon as he said the last word, he collapsed into a fit of coughing and choking.

Natan looked stricken. He put a hand on the older man's arm. "Brother, you do not have to make this sacrifice, to do further injury to your health by going to sea. Stay here. Recover your health."

Baruch shook his head. When he could speak again, he said, "You must accept the truth, Natan. My life is over, whether it goes to save the Egyptian rabbi or I succumb here in my bed. For the sake of the family honor, I must try."

What bravery in the midst of suffering! What nobility! My eyes filled with tears of admiration. I nodded to him and said, "Thank you, kind and generous sir."

Natan held up a hand. "There is more you have not heard." He sputtered, repeating the duke's demands.

"I did hear it. I agree to it all," Baruch said. "My parting gift to Salerno, which has been such a good home to us. I pray it will become a safe haven once again. Perhaps if we had acted in such a way to rid our city of the crusaders earlier, we would not be in such a situation. Perhaps your Gabriela and the others would not have suffered as they did."

Then he turned to Shimon with surprising dignity, considering his condition. "You have heard what to do. Give the orders to prepare the ship for departure at once. Everything that I am taking with me is packed. I have put my affairs in order. Let us go to the pier and sail while we still have a chance of not being too late." Then Baruch glanced at me. "After all, if all you can deliver to the regent is my corpse, I doubt we shall accomplish our mission."

Shimon embraced his oldest brother, nodded to Rafael and to me, and rushed off to do Baruch's bidding. Weak as he was, Baruch retained the full authority of a man accustomed to having his orders as the head of his family obeyed.

"With my whole heart and soul, I thank you, sir. Of course, Rafael and I will accompany you. As a physician, I can help to make the trip as easy as possible in light of your condition. And Rafael will help with necessary negotiations once we reach Palermo."

Both Natan and Baruch balked. "A woman on our ship? Impossible. This cannot be allowed."

However, I would not be dissuaded, and Rafael stood his ground. I could see Baruch weighing its merits. Finally, he came around to concur with us.

"I wish her to accompany me," he said in a voice barely above a whisper.

"Baruch, my beloved brother, this is such a wrong idea. Stay here. Regain your strength. Do not give up on your life." Natan's voice took on a pleading note.

Baruch, with what seemed to be the end of his strength, refused. "My dear little brother Natan, let me do this. Let our final memory of each other be one of peace and harmony, not discord." He lifted his arm with great effort and patted the other man's cheek.

Natan closed his eyes for a moment. "If this is indeed what you want of me, then, yes. Go with God."

"And what of me," a woman's voice quavered. "Were you going to leave without bidding me farewell?" Raquela Susanna stood before us, tear-stained yet dignified. "And the children?"

"My darling wife," Baruch sighed. He touched her face. "I had hoped to slip away without this hardest farewell. Let the children remember me as I was, not as I am now. Broken, dying. And you too, my love. Until we meet again in paradise."

The two shared a tender kiss. Who could see this scene without being moved?

Finally, the two brothers embraced. I took my bag with my medical supplies, and we all set off in a horse-drawn wagon to speed us to the pier.

❧

The emotional leave-taking must have sapped Baruch's strength almost unbearably. Fortunately, with a speed and efficiency I marveled at, we were on the Mendozas' ship the Ester HaMalka en route to Palermo, on which his servants and I made him as comfortable as possible. My prayers to God now concerned our arriving at the royal palace in Palermo in time.

When Baruch was not coughing, the poor invalid fell into a fitful doze. I kept vigil by his side and prayed our efforts should not be in vain. Alas, my old difficulties of travel by sea returned, and the movement of our ship in even relatively calm water had the usual ill effect on me. Having Rafael on board somehow helped, but it was not a miracle cure.

I concentrated on my tasks and my patient's needs to try to distract myself from my misery. A lozenge of ginger and mint provided some relief. The wind and seas were favorable and the crew was most adept, so our ship moved along at a steady clip with a minimum of turbulence.

Although one sailor kept watch for the duke's vessel, we did not see it. This itself was not deeply worrying because, as we were told by the captain, all ships on this route had to make frequent tacks back and forth to respond to the winds and seas, so it would be unlikely to see the other vessel even if we were able to arrive in Palermo sooner than it. Even with that knowledge, I could not keep myself from peering out at the horizon to try to catch sight of the other vessel. But the sea and the sky soon lulled me into lethargy.

As we had done the night we spent caring for the rabbi after he was attacked, Rafael and I alternated watching Baruch and taking short naps. Fortunately, Baruch had a calm night.

At this point the success of our mission truly was in the hands of the Creator of the Universe. He had reasons that were beyond the capacity of mere mortals to comprehend, but that did not stop me from praying to convince Him of the justness of our cause.

Early the next morning, we reached our destination and disembarked. As smooth as the journey had been, still it exacerbated Baruch Mendoza's condition with frightening effects. As a physician, I noted the deterioration of his mien and his stamina. Surely if we delivered Baruch as a corpse to the palace, the regent would be loath to accept him in exchange for the executioner's intended victim. Perhaps once we showed the regent the document with the duke's full plan, to link the use of the substitute with transporting the crusaders from Salerno . . . but first things first.

No matter the urgency of our mission, we needed to follow the rules of landing in the port. While the captain went through that protocol with the harbormaster, Rafael had the clarity of thought to make inquiries if the duke's ship had already landed. And so we learned, alas, that the ship transporting the rabbi had arrived just a short time before and the prisoner was en route to his fate in the city.

As soon as we were cleared to disembark, we did so. "We need to get to the castle immediately and demand an audience with the regent!" Rafael barked his words to the servants supporting Baruch Mendoza.

Despite the bustle of the docks, we were able to hire a horse-drawn carriage whose driver claimed his conveyance to be the swiftest in all of Sicily. "We hope you can also provide a smooth ride. As you can see, one member of our party is quite ill and cannot be made to suffer passage over a rough route."

Gesturing expansively, with a smile that would probably guarantee anything under the sun for the right price, the driver assured us he was, indeed, our man. With great care, we bundled Baruch into the carriage. His two men climbed in to help support him. Rafael and I took the remaining spots in the wagon.

Even for our experienced driver, navigating the streets of Palermo was not a trivial task. Used as I was to urban settings, I nonetheless marveled at the crowds filling the streets and impeding our progress. "Please, God, do not let Rabbi Isaac ben Shmuel meet his end in this unjust manner. Be with us as we rush to his rescue, in the name of all that is holy and pure. Amen." Unbeliever that he was, Rafael merely observed me, with no comment.

As we hurtled through Palermo's narrow streets, I also had to attend to my patient. The poor man moaned when he was not coughing and wheezing. I gave him herbs for the pain, which helped some.

I also directed his men to try shifting his position to see if that would help. However, little any of us could do brought him real relief.

We finally reached the royal castle. While one of the servants paid the driver, Rafael, the other servant, and I helped Baruch down from the carriage. Every move elicited groans of agony from the poor man.

As we approached the entryway to the castle at a drawbridge over the moat, a guard challenged us. Rafael showed him the written document from the duke explaining our mission. He looked at the vellum and shook his head. "I cannot read this."

Rafael lost patience, a most rare happenstance for him. "For heaven's sake, man, we have an emergency situation, and you can see that one of our party is gravely ill. Stop wasting time and find someone who can read this."

The guard peered at us with disdain. Fortunately, God had not abandoned us. One of the other guards, clad in a grander uniform, approached. "What is the trouble here, Geismar?"

Geismar made a sneering expression and thrust the document at the new guard. "They just arrived from Salerno, claiming the duke there himself sent them."

The new guard frowned as he read the words, then looked at us. "The duke says you must have an audience with William of Capparone, the young king's regent, immediately." He shook his head. "The duke should know better than to make such demands. Our regent is a very busy man. He cannot adjust his schedule to accommodate everyone who comes along."

"This, sir, is a matter of life and death," Rafael said. "With all due respect, that is why Duke Henry is requesting this audience for us. His Majesty's regent will want to hear our proposal because it will allow him to avoid the injustice of executing an innocent man." Rafael's measured speech showed that he had, thank goodness, regained control of his temper.

The guard looked at the two servants and the nearly collapsing Baruch Mendoza. "I see four men. Three are able-bodied. Who is the woman?"

I bit my lip and decided I had better keep quiet, no matter how much I hated this.

Rafael sent me a reassuring look. "She is one of Salerno's finest physicians, who is ministering to the patient. Now we must move quickly or all will be lost."

The guard assessed me and smirked. I clenched my fists even harder and forced myself to keep quiet.

"Tell me what makes this woman special," the guard leered. "Sometimes these older ones have a few tricks that can make you forget they are not young. Is that what you mean?"

Rafael glared at him. I saw his fists were clenched even tighter than mine. "None of your disrespect, or at the gate I shall inform the regent of what an insolent dolt you are. Surely young King Frederick, his regent, and all the court know of Salerno's medical school and our doctors—the best in the world. Now, do your job."

Taking a step back, the guard turned and said something to one in their group, who took the letter and left us. Then he said in a more formal voice, "Alexios will go to the regent's counsel, and we will await his answer. William of Capparone is probably not seeing anyone else today as his schedule is full, so I expect your request will be denied."

My self-restraint cracked. "He must see us. We have come all this way on a matter of the highest urgency. An unjust death will ensue if we cannot see him now."

The guard shrugged. "Do you know how many matters of life and death arise in a single day, let alone a week? If William of Capparone stopped what he was doing every time someone comes from the provinces and demands an audience, he would get nothing else done."

He pointed to several hard benches a little way into the anteroom. "Wait over there until Alexios returns. That is all I can do for you until we hear from the court."

Baruch Mendoza could barely stay upright even leaning on his strong young servant. I went to them and put my arm out to help. Despite my care for him on the voyage, he withdrew and, with a slight shake of his head, rejected my assistance. *Very well. Let him lean on his servant.*

The anteroom was filled with people who, based on their physical forms and colors, dress, and speech, were from many places. I listened to the mix of tongues. There were crusaders, probably Franks from the look of them, whom I tried to ignore. Several Byzantines, some Africans, some Sicilians from other parts of the kingdom. I was one of the few women.

As the time dragged on, marked only by the coming and going of more supplicants, I resorted again to prayer.

Finally, Alexios returned to where we sat huddled together. "William of Capparone will see you tomorrow afternoon. At first, he said no. When I showed him the note from the duke, he relented and made room in his appointments."

I jumped to my feet. "Tomorrow afternoon! No! That is far too late. By then the rabbi—" My voice cracked, and I took a breath to regain control. "By tomorrow, an innocent man may have already paid with his life for this unfortunate delay."

A mask of cynicism slid across Alexios's face. "It took some effort to secure this appointment." He nodded to the people in the room.

"Most of the others here would reward me with gold for coming back with such an offer."

Understanding the guard's clear message, Rafael nodded to Baruch and responded, "My companion here is near death and must see the regent while he is still in this world. He is one of the wealthiest men in Salerno. His heirs will give you gold if I tell them what you did to ease his last hours."

Alexios's brows shot up and he smiled wryly. "You must think me very naïve to believe in such a promise."

"I will provide this 'gift' now," Rafael said, placing a coin in the man's palm, "but only if you act swiftly."

Alexios frowned. "I deserve more than this for what I have managed already."

"So you do. You will get much more if you do as we ask," Rafael spoke firmly.

"I hope I shall not regret my generosity in trusting you," Alexios muttered. Much to my relief, he turned and made his way once again through the noisy, crowded room.

Baruch Mendoza was, I thanked God, asleep at this moment. He did not seem to be coughing as much now, for which we all were grateful. I prayed he would not slip from consciousness, as I believed it was vital for him to be able to talk with the regent.

Time seemed to drag on, and I felt as if I was in the anteroom to Gehenna, the pit of hell. If only I could hurry outdoors for a breath of fresh air, relief from the malodorous presence of so many people in close quarters. But I did not want to go too far from Signor Mendoza. I could not continue to sit, so I rose and paced as much as I could in the crowded room.

I wondered where the rabbi was. Perhaps he was now in the legal pretense of a trial that would condemn him to execution. For all I knew, he might be dying at this very moment, or he might already be dead.

No. With my whole heart and soul, I believed that, after all our efforts to save the rabbi, I would know if hope was gone. All my instincts told me he still lived. Only this thought made it possible for me to wait. The hope for justice still flickered, like a candle using up its last bit of wick near the bottom of its wax.

"How are you holding up?" I asked Rafael.

He shook his head and laughed. "We had to rush to get here to Palermo, and now we are condemned to wait. How are you?"

"Anxious. Wishing this ordeal were over, and we were going back to Salerno with the rabbi."

"A good thought. How is our patient doing?"

"He is dozing but seems to be staying steady."

"Good."

While we had been waiting, the anteroom had slowly begun to empty. How late was it? I had lost all sense of time. Finally, when I was sure to go mad if another moment passed without some movement, Alexios returned.

"Are we going to see the regent now?" Rafael asked.

"Sit down, sir, and I will tell you what I have on offer, which is the best for your situation. Deserving of much gold."

"Tell us something of value first," Rafael said.

"For the matter in your document," he intoned, "the best man to see is the Minister of Justice, Roberto von Gruenwald. He is the one the regent would refer such a matter to. So, as the regent is so busy now, I was able to secure a short meeting with the minister. I will take you to him."

"How far must we go?" I asked with an eye on Baruch, who would not be able to travel any great distance.

"The other side of the castle, up several flights. It is a bit of a walk."

"Then we must have a litter to transport Signor Mendoza, who is not capable of walking much."

Alexios frowned. "Getting a litter here will slow us down."

"We have no choice," Rafael said.

"Very well. I shall make the necessary arrangements. As soon as you give me more gold."

Rafael gave him another coin.

Fortunately, two servants soon brought what looked like a royal litter. I stifled a smile at the prospect of Baruch Mendoza in a royal litter. His servants took charge of bundling him into it. As gentle as they were, he moaned most piteously. Alexios then led the way to the chamber of the Minister of Justice.

The man I took to be Roberto von Gruenwald sat at the center of a long wooden table in an ornately carved chair, in attire so opulent as to be almost regal. Several other men, dressed somewhat less richly, sat on either side of him.

A clerk announced us. The Minister of Justice gazed at us from deeply set eyes over cheeks swollen with privilege. "You are sent by Duke Henry, ruler of Salerno?'

"Yes, sir," Rafael said.

The minister cocked a brow. "I will have to speak to him about his selection of worthy representatives."

A reference to our being Jews? Ignoring the comment, Rafael, in an unemotional voice, related the story completely but succinctly. The Minister of Justice and his attendants did listen attentively throughout.

During Rafael's monologue, I had remained silent, eyes respectfully cast downward. The minister now turned his attention to me, as he stroked his bearded chin, then poured himself a goblet of deep red wine.

"So, Magistra, you and your companions seek to prevent the execution of Rabbi Isaac ben Shmuel by substituting Baruch Mendoza. Did the mad woman at least get the right crusader?"

I frowned and answered, "Almost certainly not. That would indeed have been a rough justice bordering on divine intervention. Apparently, some unlucky wretch who happened to be in the wrong place at the wrong time, when the poor woman went berserk."

The minister's face creased with distaste. "Nonetheless, I agree that the crusaders would not be pleased to know that one of their number met a grisly death at the hands of a mere woman. I suppose even Jews would find it more acceptable to believe one of their men was felled by another man than by a woman." He spat out the last words.

He now turned back to Rafael. "I find your plan interesting. Ingenious. Almost biblical. And I applaud you for coming up with it."

"Then you will agree to release the rabbi and allow Baruch Mendoza to take his place?"

The minister brought forth a smile that I imagined being similar to that of the snake that seduced Mother Eve in the Garden of Eden. "Your plan might have had more appeal had you chosen a worthier candidate who truly offered to sacrifice himself. This man," he gestured toward Baruch, whose eyes remained closed and his head bowed, in a state somewhere between life and death, "is going to be dead in a matter of days if not hours. Not much of a sacrifice to go to the hangman instead of dying in his bed."

"This man is the patriarch of the leading Jewish family in Salerno, one of the reasons the exchange is acceptable to the duke, in whose land the murder occurred," Rafael pointed out.

The minister held up a conciliatory hand. "I am only speculating aloud. The sad fact of the matter is, you are most likely too late—the execution is likely to have already occurred." He smiled in a parody of sympathy.

"Too late?" I blurted out, keenly aware of the time we had spent waiting to speak to this minister who sat like a sloth drinking wine. "It cannot be! The rabbi cannot be dead."

"This man was your husband? Father? Uncle?—Lover?"

I somehow managed to contain my outrage and reply with just "No, sir."

"Then who is this man to you that you should go to such effort to save him?" He lounged back in his chair.

"He is an innocent man being executed, and I care about justice in our world."

I went on, "Where is the rabbi? I want to see him."

"Even if he has already been executed?"

"Yes. I must have the chance to bid him farewell." I sobbed on the last word then pulled myself together. "Even if it is too late to ask his forgiveness for our failure to save him. And we want to see that his body is buried with proper honor."

Roberto von Gruenwald looked heavenward and shook his head. "He cannot be buried with honor. I am, however, willing to see that you are taken to him before his body is disposed of. And now you will all go—you have already taken too much of my time."

Disposed of? What does he mean?

"One more thing," Rafael interjected. "If somehow the rabbi is still alive, will you allow us to make the proposed switch?"

The minister snorted. "Though it is probably a moot point, I will allow that." He scrawled something on a scrap of vellum, which he handed to Alexios along with hurried instructions.

Alexios then led our entire party, including Baruch Mendoza on his litter, back through the labyrinthian castle, to the execution site gallows, not far from where we had waited earlier.

In the gruesome courtyard, my heart froze at the sight of five wooden gallows topping sturdy posts. Nauseated, I saw four bodies sickeningly swinging in the small breeze to the apparent delight of some men in the crowd. As a physician, I had grown accustomed to sights that caused less trained people to avert their eyes. No matter what crimes these men committed, they deserved better than to be reduced to entertainment for a mob. And as hideous as these corpses were, even uglier was the jeering crowd that filled the space around and between the gallows.

After a quick, agonizing look at each of the executed bodies, we saw that the rabbi, thank our merciful God, was not one of them. Alexios, who was also taking in the scene, turned to us. "Not too late, but almost. Look there—the hangman saved your Jew for last—the one most of the crowd has especially been waiting to see swing. He is just mounting the steps to be hanged." With the minister's permission in hand, we could still save the rabbi!

"Kill the dirty Jew! Kill the dirty Jew rabbi!" The screaming grew louder. Some from the crowd threw fruits and vegetables that smashed on impact with the infernal posts.

A man led the rabbi up the wooden steps to the platform.

My rigid self-control wavered and evaporated. "No!" I screamed the word and agitated my arms like a mad woman. At the sound of my voice, I thought Rabbi Isaac ben Shmuel turned in my direction—but that might have been wishful thinking on my part. After the briefest of hesitations, the guard with the rabbi urged him on, as did the jeering mob.

Rafael and I attempted to run toward the scaffold. However,

Alexios detained us. "To do what you want, you need gold for the executioner."

"Of course," I flung back at him as Rafael gave him a bag of coins. "Only tell him to stop."

Sixteen

As the rabbi reached the gallows platform, the crowd attained a level of hysteria. Evil screams and taunts raised gooseflesh along my arms and terror in my heart. Alexios ran toward the gallows at, *thank God,* a great speed and, holding out the purse of gold, remonstrated with the executioner. However, horror of horrors, the latter shook his head. Without any further pause, he then pulled the cord, releasing the trap door beneath the rabbi, completing his hellish job—to the crowd's now even louder roaring approval and laughter.

Our party of Salernitans stood in stunned shock, unable to comprehend what we had just witnessed. Time seemed to stop. . .

Alexios returned to us, the rejected purse of gold in hand. "What happened?" Rafael thundered as he took it.

Alexios shrugged. "The executioner said it was his life or the Jew's. If he let the Jew go, the crowd would have strung him up in his stead."

"But there was another Jew to take his place," I cried out, sick at what I was saying. Sick that a crowd would have such hunger.

"The word was out that the man to be hanged was a rabbi, a man holy to the Jews. A rabbi who killed a good Christian crusader. And, of course, as a Jew, he's also a Christ-killer."

"But he did not kill the crusader," I protested.

Alexios shrugged again. "Maybe he did, maybe he did not. As far as the people are concerned, this does not matter."

The rabbi's lifeless body now swung in the slow rhythm of the other corpses, as if they were dancing together. After more cheers and insults to Jews, the crowd began to disperse.

I swallowed hard. *I cannot believe it.* All that we had been through—to what good?

Alexios now addressed Rafael in a surprisingly soft voice. "You must go to the Minister of Justice with this man," he nodded to the teetering Baruch, "and the rest of the party. You must tell him what has happened."

Rafael, grown quite pale, nodded and moved to Baruch Mendoza, who looked scarcely more alive than the rabbi. Of course, there was now no reason for him to expire in this terrible place.

Still looking at the rabbi's corpse, I came back to the reality of the situation. The rabbi must be given the ritual bathing to be prepared for burial—at least we could do *that* for him.

"When might we have the rabbi's body to arrange for a decent funeral?" Rafael asked, as if reading my thoughts.

Alexios shook his head. "Not possible. The punishment for those executed includes being on display in public for one week and then burial unmarked in unsanctified ground."

I now understood the full meaning of Roberto von Gruenwald's words, that the rabbi's body would be "*disposed of.*" Like a piece of rubbish. *No. Not this indignity too.* My eyes filled with tears.

Alexios warned that we should not waste our effort. "The Minister of Justice will not make an exception for the Jew—not even for a large gift."

I bit my lip to try to stifle my tears when I heard this final degradation.

Alexios said, "You can do nothing more here. Indeed, you must return immediately to the Minister of Justice."

"Why?" Rafael looked as drained as I felt. "It is too late for everything we came for."

"This is a mandatory formality. For the minister's records. Here in Palermo, we must keep careful records. Also, he will tell you when you can return to Salerno, including this man." Alexios nodded toward Baruch.

With Baruch Mendoza on the litter carried again by his servants, our party returned to the chamber of the Minister of Justice. "The rabbi has been executed," Rafael said. "We request access to the rabbi's body for a proper burial according to our laws."

"No. He will be dealt with as all of his ilk. That is one rule that is never broken, no matter how many others are," the minister said. "Anything else?"

Rafael and I looked at each other blankly, feeling stunned and enervated by all that had occurred.

"Then you are free to return to Salerno tomorrow and report to the duke that you found all satisfactory in your dealings with this court."

Satisfactory? The word left a bad taste in my mouth. I expected Rafael and I would have many conversations about this episode in the future. *Will I ever find peace in my soul over this?*

The minister went on, "The regent has instructed that you will come to him tomorrow morning before you leave."

Rafael asked, "Why does the regent wish to speak about a matter that has been concluded?"

"I will leave that for him to explain," he said.

"If we must stay tonight, we shall have to find appropriate lodging for our whole party," Rafael pointed out.

Especially because tonight will be Shabbat.

The Minister of Justice held up plump, bejeweled hands. "Not to worry. After all, there are also rich Jews here in Palermo. One family has offered to host you and can meet all your needs until you leave on the morrow."

With that, the minister signaled our dismissal.

๖๙

And so, escorted by royal guards, we went a short distance from the castle to the home of Meir ben Levi. As soon as we arrived, I had Baruch Mendoza taken to his room and saw to it that he was comfortable. I instructed his servants, who would stay with him, to fetch me if his condition grew any worse.

Rafael and I were then taken to separate rooms where we washed ourselves and were given fresh clothing. Following this, we joined for dinner the entire family, who had assembled at the patriarch's home for Shabbat. Baruch was also invited, though he declined. Though Rafael and I were exhausted and drained, and we would have preferred a simple quiet meal alone together, it would have been rude for us not to accept the generous hospitality of these strangers. So we went to the parlor.

We were introduced to the ben Levis. The family included mother, father, five grown children and their spouses, the eight eldest of the grandchildren, and the aged mother of Signor ben Levi. Here we gave a very brief description of what had brought us to Palermo and what had happened here, avoiding as much as we could of the horrible details. We all then went to the dining room.

When everyone was seated around the large dining table, and after the blessings over the candles, the chanting of the Shabbat *kiddush*, and blessings over the wine and challah, Signor ben Levi again called for everyone's attention. "We have heard the sad and horrible tale of the past several weeks of our guests, and we give them our thanks and blessing for the noble attempt they made. However, I also want to call attention to who these visitors from Salerno are, and who honor us with their presence. They are two physicians from the faculty of medicine of the famed Scuola Medica—Rafael Lopes Dias and Magistra Rebecca."

Rafael nodded in acknowledgment of the gracious introduction. "My companion is, indeed, a superb practicing physician—I would venture to say the finest in all of Sicily. However, although I did complete the course of studies at the faculty of medicine many years ago, I have never practiced medicine. Rather I use my knowledge in the more humble occupation of translating scientific and medical works from Arabic, Greek, and Latin into Hebrew, in the hopes of helping Jewish physicians and others in their practices and advancing the formation of Hebrew vocabulary. I am very pleased to add that the magistra partners with me on some of these projects, bringing her greater and more recent knowledge to this work. One of my many reasons for which I am grateful to and admire her."

By the time Rafael finished with his talk, people were regarding me as if I were the incarnation of Queen Esther of Persia, who saved the Jews. Ironic, because I had failed in my mission to save the rabbi.

And then they treated us to fine hospitality, encouraging us to partake despite our grief. All ate and drank of excellent fare, which Rafael and I were able, in spite of the day's events, to appreciate if not deeply enjoy. We also shared news of our city and theirs, and other such topics, avoiding unpleasant ones.

Along with the food and the drink, we talked. It soon became clear that the women—probably the men also—did not understand my relationship with Rafael. After dinner, my hostess enfolded me in a warm embrace and took me to a quiet corner of the room where we could talk alone. "Though we have just met, I feel as if I know you. May I call you Rebecca and speak frankly with you?"

"Of course." Any other response would have been ungracious. And, in truth, I welcomed hearing words of wisdom from a woman of her generation—even though I suspected what she would choose to talk about.

"Tell me, darling girl, is it true that you and the gentleman are not married?" Eyes twinkling, she studied my face as I prepared to answer the question yet again. At least I had practice in responding to this question.

"We are not. We work as colleagues and we are friends."

She looked almost as if I had confessed we each had three heads. "What is this, work colleagues and friends? I have never heard of men and women speaking thus of one another."

I sighed. "In Salerno, where there are other women physicians at the university, it is not so uncommon for men and women to work together. Sometimes we also become friends."

She looked at me questioningly. "Does he refuse to marry you? If so, I will have my husband talk to him."

I bit my lip to keep from smiling. Though I might have enjoyed the prospect of Rafael being harangued by a Palermo papa regarding obligations to women, I could not be that unfair. "Please, Signora, I ask you not to do so. The truth of the matter is that Signor Lopes Dias has offered to marry me. Many times. It is I who chooses not to marry."

Her eyes flew open even wider, and she made a sound somewhere between a gasp and a groan. "My dear, why would you turn down such an offer? Is he not a good and honest man? You may speak frankly."

I expected I could speak very frankly with her, but what good would it do to shock the old dear with the extent of my perversity when it came to my duties as a Jewish woman? "He is a very good and honest man. I am sure he was a good husband to his late wife, she should rest in peace. He is an honorable member of Salerno's Jewish community. Also a very talented and able translator."

She smiled as I enumerated all of Rafael's sterling qualities. "All good and well, Magistra. And he is comely to look at. Do you not agree?"

My face heated with a blush. "Yes, I do agree."

Her brow wrinkled. "From what you say, I see no reason for you to refuse to marry him. But perhaps it is that you have no feelings for him?"

A wave of heat nearly forced me to fan myself. "I care greatly for him. I am deeply satisfied in his company and I miss him when he must travel to distant places."

Her arms opened in a gesture of "So? What is holding you back?" She then said the words I expected. "With all his good qualities, your deep fondness for him, and his desire to marry you, I do not understand why you and he are not wed. Such a man is a treasure it would be a sin to lose."

"If I may confide in you, Signora."

She placed a reassuring hand on my arm. "You may tell me anything. Please unburden yourself."

"I cannot marry Rafael because my heart belongs to another man, from my past." *As I listen to these words, I am suddenly aware that they now ring strangely hollow.* And then a new thought appears—*My heart also belongs to Rafael!*

She sighed and shook her head. "Why did you not marry this other man? Was he already married?"

"No, not yet then. But I neither could nor would marry him."

After a long pause while she studied my face, a sudden expression of revelation lit her eyes. With a lower voice she said, "He was a Gentile."

With a mixture of relief and resignation at finally making my full admission, I replied, "Yes, Signora."

She waved a hand in dismissal and gave a quiet, amused laugh. "You are not the first nor will you be the last to give your heart where you should not." She sighed again. "So you chose duty to your faith and our heritage over love."

"Yes," I whispered. "We both did."

"Yet, my dear, rather than looking at what might have been, you should look at what is and might be. So, Rebecca, regard this man in front of you." She paused and waited until I looked over at Rafael on the other side of the room, talking animatedly with Signor ben Levi and one of his sons. Handsome, smart, dependable—who also has my heart. As I looked at him, he seemed to sense it and turned his head, caught my eye, and smiled, raising his wine glass in silent toast. To us. To our strange relationship.

Signora ben Levi then said, "You still have a chance to enjoy the fruits of both love and the fulfillment of duty, and yet you refuse to do so. That is not God's way. And you have not many more years when you will be able to bear babies."

Of course that remark deepened my blush. I had feared she would find my conversation surprising. Instead, she turned the tables on me. I put my hands over my heart. "I have resigned myself not to bear any children but to care for those of others. As to the rest, how can I marry one man when haunted by the memory of my love for another?"

"Are you sure it is love and not nostalgia? You have a very strong memory of this Gentile man whom you loved in your youth?"

"We were present for each other at crucial times."

"Can you not say the same for yourself and Signor Lopes Dias?" she probed. "Has he failed you in some way?"

I thought of the past several weeks, and then of the earlier years of our intense relationship. "No, not that. Rafael has never failed me—quite the contrary. Yet my heart . . ." I faltered, as I felt warmth at the mere thought of him. ". . . it is closed to him as a lover. As a husband."

She smiled. "Here, I must beg to disagree. Your words say one thing, but your eyes say something else. I believe that, alongside your love from the past, your heart has opened to another love in the present. You are a woman with a great heart. Do not be afraid to follow its messages. Do not be afraid."

Why did so many people feel free to interfere in my life? "Signora, much as I respect you and value your hospitality, I cannot accept your understanding of who I am."

"Yes, I know. Although you are doing so quite politely, you are not the first to tell me that I am a meddling old lady."

And yet, how can I not cherish this woman? Perhaps my mother was like her, would have been like her for me now. "Such harsh words to describe a warm and loving woman. I am sure no one would think or say such things about you."

She laughed. "Thank you for your kindness. My dear, I am very glad we are able to host you and Signor Lopes Dias tonight, after your ordeal."

I shivered at the reminder of how we came to be enjoying this respite. "If I can ask your indulgence even further, may I ask you about a different subject?"

"Certainly, my dear."

"Today, I was shocked to hear so many crying out for the death of a Jew. I did not expect this here in Palermo, which I considered almost as much of a haven as Salerno."

The signora's smile dimmed, and she shook her head. "An ill wind has blown into our beautiful homeland with the coming of the Hohenstaufens, who forced out our much more tolerant Norman rulers. Will their like ever be seen again?"

"Things have gotten bad here," I murmured.

She thought for a moment. "From what I understand, not as bad as England and France, at least not yet. But certainly not as good as it had been for many years. I have a slim hope that perhaps young Frederick will grow to be a wise king, but the regent and other nobles around him have caused us to be troubled."

"I am sorry to hear this. Are you concerned for the future?"

"Always, of course." She moved toward me and her voice grew softer, more confidential. "In this situation, I am relieved to be old, so that I will not have to witness what I expect to be ever more such troubling changes. However, as a mother, I am very concerned for my children and theirs . . . my hope is that they will be smart and capable enough to make good and happy futures, no matter what the challenges. And if the time comes when they need to find a new home, I hope they will recognize that and not tarry overlong in doing so."

I admired this woman's heart and mind more than I could say.

She patted my hand. "Let us not use our time while you are under our roof for either sadness of what has happened today or for concern for the future. Let us deal with the here and now. There are practical matters to be seen to. First of all, did the minister refuse to allow the rabbi a decent burial?"

I gasped. "Yes. We were shocked and dismayed that we could not provide this final service for the rabbi."

"Have no further concern over this. My husband and his brothers will make sure the rabbi is provided with acceptable last rituals."

"How can this happen?" I stammered in amazement.

She squeezed my hand. "Trust me—they have the influence and means of doing it."

Tears of gratitude came to my eyes. "Thank you." Rafael would also be relieved.

"You listen to me, Magistra Rebecca of Salerno. Never give up what is close to your heart." She pursed her lips, and I understood that she spoke once more of Rafael.

I glanced over at him once again and could not doubt that the sensation filling my chest, even my whole being from head to toes, was love.

She squeezed my hand, this time with surprising strength. "I hope the brightest stars light up your future. Most of all, I hope you will choose not to forget what I have said, but rather think seriously about my words. This man who is in your life, he is your *bashert*, your fated one. I know this from the depths of my soul. And I hope one day soon to hear that you have come to see the same and have accepted him."

What she spoke of did not seem so entirely impossible to me as it once had. After the strange and improbable happenings of the last weeks, anything could happen. Even a change of heart. I wiped the tears from my eyes and embraced this woman. "I appreciate your caring and your generosity more than I can express."

She nodded. "In the absence of your dear mother and father, allow me to give you my blessing for the future."

I bowed my head and accepted her touch with immense gratitude.

After we spoke to the regent the next morning—a banal conversation that did not justify our delay in Palermo—we turned our attention to our being in a strange place for Shabbat. Though Baruch was holding up better than I had expected, subjecting him to another voyage concerned me—so we first thought of spending all of Shabbat in Palermo and delaying our departure until Sunday. But he insisted he was well enough to return home and this was what he wanted most in the world. "After all," he rasped, "I have been spared for now. But who can know how much longer I will have to be with my loved ones."

How to respond to that very real concern?

But Baruch had more to say. He was also thinking ahead. "Although the rabbi was executed, I will still follow through on my agreement to transport the crusaders out of Salerno. If for no one else, then for our poor daughters. And I want to return to Salerno with all haste, to make that happen the soonest."

I hoped that Baruch's view would prevail with his brothers. After all that had happened tragically, the removal of the crusaders from our city would be the best step toward a desirable future. I hoped that the duke's knowledge of the identity of the real killer, a fact that he could threaten to expose, would convince all the Mendozas to live up to their pledge, even coerced as it was.

And so we left Palermo early Saturday morning. The passage back to Salerno on the Ester HaMalka went smoothly—even I felt less sick than usual and simply remained on the deck, leaning on the railing beside Rafael, leaving Baruch's servants to see to him in his cabin and administer the medicine I supplied as needed—and with instructions to fetch me if he took even the slightest turn for the worse.

Standing on deck, Rafael, breaking a comfortable silence, turned to me and said, "I have been thinking about you."

"Me? Why is that?"

He gazed at me with a quizzical expression. "Despite knowing to my bones that I love you and desire to have you as my wife and unite our lives fully, Rebecca from England, I really know little about you."

"About me?" I shrugged. In truth, I never liked it when our conversations took this direction.

He nodded. "Sometimes you have hinted at topics and then left them unexplained. For example, how and why you and your father left England so precipitously. And then how you ended up in Barcelona."

I gave him my standard response to this question, hoping to head off his probing about matters I was not ready to discuss with him. "The big reason for Barcelona is family. That is where Papa was born and spent his childhood."

He shook his head. "This I already knew. I am hoping to learn more. I know your family also has connections in different places, even still back in England. So why did you choose the path you did? You have on occasion hinted at traumatic events in England that you avoid speaking of."

I shivered at his attempt to reopen that door. "I still choose not to speak of that."

He sighed. "You must realize that I grow more than ever intrigued. I look into your big brown eyes and wonder what mystery they hide."

"Oh, Rafael. Please give me time with this. I have the long habit of keeping to myself what occurred in England. I would like to open my life to you more, but I must proceed slowly. Will you grant me that?"

He squeezed my hand. "Of course. If there is any way I can help you to cross the bridge to your past, let me know. Especially because I believe it might help us to move more to the future—to a better life, more satisfying than the present. That is what I hope to build with you. Rebecca, help me find the way." He squeezed my hand.

I could start to imagine the kind of future Rafael spoke of, but I had not yet opened my heart completely to sharing my life with him. It would be him rather than any other man, this I knew. I could not find the words to respond to him, but I nodded and squeezed his hand back.

We arrived back in Salerno Sunday after a night at sea. At dinner that night, I said that I was too exhausted to talk about what had happened in Palermo.

Monday morning, before I got started on my week's work, I told Nina about the rabbi's execution. When my story was over, she regarded me with sympathy and caring. What would happen if Nina and Signora ben Levi ever got together? These two well-meaning women would smother me with kindness and affection and delicious treats—and advice. In moments of weakness, I had to admit surrendering to such care was most tempting.

eventeen

L ater Monday morning, Rafael arrived with the news that Duke Henry had summoned us to appear at his court. He commanded us to supply him with a full report of our effort to save the rabbi.

As we walked to the castle, Rafael and I saw rocks hurled through the window of the Mendoza cloth store. "Only one Jew put to death for the murder of a crusader?" The rock hurler did not hesitate to express displeasure in a destructive, raucous, drunken manner.

A clerk ran into the street. "Why are you disrupting our business in this way?"

"This business belongs to an important Jew." The crusader spat on the ground. "You all are on notice now. We demand justice for our fallen comrade. A lot more than one Jew's head. The Jews need to compensate the crusaders for our loss."

The clerk stood his ground. "This is a place of business. If you have a quarrel with what happened, take it to the duke."

"We will." The crusader shook his fist in the clerk's face.

When we arrived at the castle, we related to the duke the events in Palermo.

He shook his head. "It is good that the Mendozas will live up to their agreement to transport out the crusaders even though the executioner did not accept Baruch to replace the rabbi."

Rafael and I looked at each other and we both bit our tongues. Had we really expected any more sympathetic a reaction from the duke? If so, more fools we. We also told him about the window smashing. He did not seem troubled to hear about it or other disruptions. "Sir Thomas Dulac, one of the leaders of the crusaders, already sent an emissary. They claim more Jews were involved in the crusader's murder. That one Jew could never have been strong enough to bring down a crusader. They threaten to take their complaints to the pope. Or to take their own vengeance against the Jews. Or both." The duke took a long draught of wine from his golden chalice.

Rafael asked, "What will you do?"

The duke smiled. "This attack upon a Mendoza business after the assaults will give the family an even greater impetus to get the crusaders out of Salerno. I cannot wait."

Despite the duke's words, the transport was neither quickly nor easily put together. During the time the Mendozas gathered the fleet, the crusaders did not grow more virtuous or law-abiding, but perpetrated several more attacks and vandalism on Jews and Jewish locations.

Fear became my frequent, unwanted companion. Even Rafael, usually so stalwart, took on the tensions swirling through our city and seemed more on edge and irritable.

The other bad news we heard was, despite his brief rally in Palermo, Baruch Mendoza was once again failing and not expected to live much longer. Soon afterward, we got the final news. I greatly mourned the death of this man that I had come to admire. *Baruch Dayan HaEmet.*

❧

One week after Baruch's death, we were still trying to move our lives forward. Rafael and I were discussing his next translation while he escorted me to the hospital. Suddenly the loud argument of two large, ugly crusaders disturbed the activity on a busy market day.

After the two crusaders moved on, Rafael turned to me. "How soon do you think our lives will return to normal?"

"Normal? What is that? At least we have our work to keep us grounded. So, what about the selection of the translation projects you are next going to undertake?"

He squeezed my hand, a lovely touch of warmth. "Yes. I know you have campaigned for the work by La Trotula."

"Also, a more recent work," I reminded him. "*Practica Chirurgiae* by Rogerius of Salerno, from 1180."

Rafael groaned. "That insufferable egotist."

I shrugged. "Why let his miserable personality deter translating his surgical treatises into Hebrew?"

"Am I to assume you want the translation of the La Trotula and Rogerius texts to precede work on the Rambam's writings on sexual matters?"

"I honestly do not see why you would want to accord the Rambam's work of advice regarding a *harem* primacy over those two medical texts."

"Out of regard for the author."

"It is not as if you will not get to all of them. Merely a question of time and order."

By now we were close to the hospital. Though I did not know what awaited me there, I often found myself enmeshed in cases for hours. Because I had agreed with Rafael that I should no longer go unescorted to and from the hospital, we needed to find an expedient way to let Rafael or Manuel know when to return for my trip home.

It appeared I would be seeing only two patients for routine follow-up appointments, so Rafael and I agreed he would wait. I was about to go to the first of those when a loud disturbance in the ante-room shattered the atmosphere. Like all the other physicians present, I rushed to see who was being brought in.

A young woman was doing her best to support another young woman who was doubled over with what appeared to be severe abdominal pain. When I got closer, to my horror, I recognized Laura di Petrocelli, my dear student, as the woman providing support.

"Laura, what is wrong?" I asked when I got close to her.

"It is my cousin Benedetta," Laura cried in a loud whisper. "Please help her. Help us."

A coldness crept along my spine at the sight of her. This was no common indigestion. I needed to see the material she had brought up when she, clearly, had previously vomited, which she did again promptly. The odor of her fresh vomitus told a story that terrified me.

"Oil of pennyroyal?" I could not hold back from exclaiming. To end a pregnancy? Why else would she have dosed herself with this herb in what was clearly a toxic amount—unless someone poisoned her. "Why?" My voice had a tone of pleading.

Laura grew flustered. I needed an explanation, but first, we had to deal with the poison before it damaged her organs. Before it killed her. It might *already* be too late.

As we moved the patient to a treatment room, my frantic mind raced to come up with antidotes. When I could not recall any, all I could come up with was to flush the drug out of her system. I ordered servants to quickly bring me large quantities of boiled water.

As I waited impatiently for the water, I settled poor Benedetta into the bed where she could rest for a few moments between bouts of spasms. And, once again, I found myself praying. This time I added the hope my Jewish God would be available to listen to prayers for a young Christian woman. Surely in His infinite mercy, He would bring her through this crisis.

When the water arrived and was cooled to a safe temperature, Benedetta initially resisted drinking. But with every bit of strength and resolve, I persisted, and she did manage to drink some moderate quantity. That led to more expulsion of fluids from several bodily openings. After several more rounds of drinking and expulsions, the odor of the pennyroyal in the fluid that was released diminished somewhat, and her trembling and spasms did likewise.

Although it was clear there was still poison within her, I saw with relief that she appeared to be improving. While giving her a few minutes of respite from having to drink more water, I called to have the bed remade with fresh linens and to have Benedetta washed and given clean and dry garments.

I also took this opportunity to question poor Laura. "Can you tell me how this has happened?"

Laura swallowed tears. "You remember I spoke to you about Benedetta refusing to even speak with me?"

I nodded.

Laura sniffled. "She at last told me what had transpired. She was raped several months ago. By a crusader." Her voice broke on the last.

"Her family discovered her secret and threw her out of their home. She came to me and I snuck her into my chamber. I was going to find a way to help her. To come to you and ask for your help."

"But the pennyroyal. Surely you did not—"

She shook her head. "I did not. Magistra, I do not know how she got hold of the pennyroyal. I came home to find her so sick."

Laura held her cousin's hand and stroked her face, while I tried to give her more liquids to further clean out her body. However, she was no longer taking any, and her pulse, heartbeat, and breathing, which had been improving, were now all degrading.

Benedetta managed to open her eyes and weakly whispered, "Laura. You have been better to me than any sister." She was giving up! "The four of us had such a nice life planned. I hope that you and Roberto will have that."

"No, Benedetta. You cannot give up. I am your sister of the heart, and I forbid you to give up." Laura's voice grew alternately loud and soft.

In vain. With a moan and a gasp, Benedetta left this life. Laura shook her, yelled at her, threatened her, but could not bring her back.

Then my student and I allowed ourselves to weep—tears of pain mixed with anger for her suffering such agony. For the ruinous ending of a young woman's life. Benedetta and all the other young girls whose lives had been destroyed by crusaders and other brutes, who thought as little of these females as they would of a rabbit who ran past them in the woods. I thought of how I would want the crusaders to be punished to make them realize what they were doing to people's lives.

By the time I left the bedside and managed to take a completely shattered Laura with me, I felt hollow from exhaustion and despair. Would any more Salernitans fall victim to the crusaders' evil before we finally managed to cleanse our city of this pestilence?

Though I had become sadly aware of the decline in the quality of our lives in Salerno, I had still found much about life in the city to feel thankful for. Benedetta's death felt like the last straw. Could I ever again regard this city as a haven?

Until now, I had dismissed any thought of leaving Salerno. Suddenly, it took root in my heart to live in a different place. In our long history, we Jews had often been forcibly expelled from what we thought were our permanent homes. Sometimes, we saw the oncoming disaster and made the decision to leave before it was too late, managing to avoid the worst of the consequences. Perhaps this was one of those times and places where we needed to choose to depart our home under our own terms.

Home. At this low moment, my heart ached for a place I could call home. A place where I could feel safe to continue to grow old as a healer and a Jew. Copious tears watered these thoughts.

My thoughts now turned to Laura. I asked her if she had a place to go, and she shook her head. "I cannot go back to my home, for I know that my family will join Benedetta's in condemning her, blaming her and also me, her closest companion, for what happened to her. Please, let me go home with you until I can decide what to do."

Thus I had Laura with me when I rejoined Rafael in the hospital's waiting room. I explained what had happened as succinctly as I could. Without a word, Rafael put his arm around my shoulders, and I just leaned against him.

⋟⋞

Life must always go on, such was the fundamental commandment of our faith and tradition. For the sake of the living and the dead. For the many generations past and, God willing, those to come.

Rafael, Laura, and I walked in silence back to my house. When I saw some crusaders on our streets, even though they were not doing anything out of the ordinary, I struggled to keep from shrieking at them like some demented hag. I now had a sense of why and how Malka Freya had done what she did.

When we arrived back at my home, I could at last feel some relief in an enclosed, controlled environment.

I told Nina that Laura would be staying with us for a while.

Nina made up the bed for her in a small chamber we had for guests. Exhausted, Laura bade us both good night and thanked me for giving her a place to be alone.

When she had gone, Rafael said, "You have both been through such an ordeal. What can I do to help?"

"You have done so much," I whispered. "Thank you. I think I will follow Laura and grieve quietly tonight. Tomorrow, we can think of how to go forward."

We parted on that note. There was much to do, much to think about. But, for tonight, I hoped for the peace of sleep.

The next morning, a wan, tearful Laura told me she would go to her home to tell her family what happened and to ensure that her cousin had proper funeral rites. "Maybe they will surprise me with their humanity after all. Maybe her family will mourn what they have lost. Maybe my Roberto will step up and show me his worthiness as a man."

When she came back to my home later, it was clear none of the hopeful possibilities had come true. "I have spoken with Father Angelo about Benedetta, and he will oversee her funeral. This is important to me. As for the rest—may I stay with you until I can straighten out my life?"

"Of course. I am honored to have you in my home." We hugged and wept together.

❧

Later that day, Rafael returned to see how we were doing. As we sat in the parlor, I told him that Laura would be part of my household for the immediate future. "I am sure you will be able to help her," he said.

"I think that we will help each other. But Rafael, what is next for you?"

"After this unwanted hiatus," he said, "I am eager to get back to work. And, you, Magistra, will be happy to hear I have decided to pay heed to you."

"I am glad you actually listened to something I said," I replied, trying to act as I usually would. "Which of my words have you heeded, pray tell?"

"To thank you for all you have done, I will next turn my attention to a medical text. Either the work by La Trotula or the treatise on surgery by Rogerius of Salerno."

Not enough to banish my sadness, but I needed to reach for the hope for the future that Rafael extended. "So, my words really have had an effect on you."

"Your words always have an effect on me," he countered, his voice low and raspy. Part of our usual banter and yet not. "Which should we translate first?"

"There are good arguments for both. La Trotula's work is older, but that of Rogerius is of more general value," I said. "I shall need to give the matter more thought." I did my best to smile, which instead brought tears to my eyes again.

"You have had such shocks." He gently covered my right hand with his left. "I am sorry."

After a long pause, he covered my left hand with his right and went on, now with a lighter tone. "Speaking of choices . . ." I had learned to recognize when he was going to propose marriage, and I wished he would not, especially now. Turning him down would only further dampen my spirits.

Just as I was about to go through my usual response, Nina burst into the room. "Your papa is here!" She was so excited that she did not notice Rafael's lifting of his hands from mine as the two of us rose abruptly.

"Papa?" I clutched my throat. "Papa!" Was something terribly wrong? Though Barcelona was not so far, Papa did not make the trip to Salerno as often as he had when I first settled here, and never without sending word ahead of time.

A moment later Papa came into the room. He seemed to have aged greatly since I had last seen him. How could I have let months pass without being with Papa? And then both of us, tears in our eyes, embraced.

As if knowing my thoughts, he said, "It has been too long."

I held his hands in mine. "You are here now, dear Papa. I cannot tell you how happy I am to see you. However, you came so suddenly—is something wrong?" I shivered in anticipation of his response. Though I could see he was frailer than I had ever before seen him, he could not be dying. I prayed that he had not come to bid me farewell.

As we all sat down, Papa nodded. "Yes, there is a reason for my voyage now. But first, dear daughter, I am happy to bring you greetings from our family in Barcelona. And good evening to you too, my dear Rafael."

He went on, "Unfortunately, the tidings we hear from England are not good. Our people are suffering. They are leaving that accursed country and coming to us destitute. The Jewish community in Barcelona is overwhelmed with our kin seeking refuge."

"What has happened, Papa?"

"That horrible King John, with whom we had the misery to cross paths, is oppressing the Jews there worse than ever. Of course he even oppresses his own people, so what hope can the Jews have?"

My heart sank at the mention of the monarch's name. Before John was king, he had initiated much of the misery that caused Papa and me to leave England. This even though, under the reign of the previous king, Richard, Coeur de Lion, John had been kept some-what in check.

"I remember John Lackland all too well," I said.

Papa grimaced. "Claiming the crown and having power has given him even more opportunity for malice. Toward everyone, but he has the Jews especially in his sights."

Hearing Papa speak with such despair, my heart twisted.

"Unfortunately and unwisely, your cousin Sara had been deter-mined to stay in York, and not abandon to John the home she made with her late husband Menachem. I feared she would not be con-vinced of the danger until it was too late, but she finally agreed, for the sake of her four young children. So we did get them all out and to Barcelona. However, all of this has had a tremendous impact on her such that she is now in so low a condition, I fear that she will not live much longer, but will leave her children as orphans."

"Dear Lord," I whispered.

Rafael nodded. "This accords with what I have heard from England. What exactly can we do?"

Papa smiled. "I like a man who gets to the heart of the matter. Since you, my darling daughter, know much of the England they left, including their language, the family wants you to come and help the young ones adjust to their new life in Barcelona. And, more generally, with the continuing influx of new refugees from England, as a skilled physician and compassionate woman, you could be an immense resource for the community." And with a sad look, he went on, "I would do more, but my health does not permit me to undertake much—"

That last bit cost Papa a great deal to admit, but I could see now, even more than before, how he was diminished in energy. I stood up and paced the room a moment, trying to grapple with his words and the immediate onslaught of thoughts and memories they evoked. Sara, widowed, with four young children in trouble, as well as others of our people. England. That horrible King John. York. *How awful it must be for Ivanhoe that Richard, Coeur de Lion, died so young and his dreadful brother is now the ruler. And how awful that the Hohenstaufens are corrupting the lovely, tolerant lands they conquered. York, and Salerno, and even Palermo—so many places we once regarded as home, now turned hostile.*

Papa knew my feelings about England, how hard it had been for me to leave, so I understood that he would not reawaken my thoughts of it lightly. And he also knew of the rich and rewarding life I had in Salerno—at least until recently. I now realized I also felt a debt of honor and caring for my family from York and the other Jews we had left behind. And that debt extended as well to my family in Barcelona, who had provided support and caring when Papa and I were in need. Of course I could help resettle my cousins and the other English refugees. Being a refugee myself—more than once—how could I not help others? Thus, if Papa asked me to make this move, I felt a strong responsibility and moral requirement to do so.

And, there were my deep thoughts yesterday of how Salerno was becoming unbearable. But thinking concretely of the fundamental disruption of my life that a relocation would cause, especially when I was still exhausted, mentally and spiritually, from our efforts for the Egyptian rabbi and now from the tragedy of Benedetta, was also daunting.

"I know the family can count on you," Papa's voice entered my tumultuous thoughts.

I made up my mind immediately. "Of course I shall go, Papa."

"My darling daughter!" he said with deep relief. He inclined his grizzled head. "How long will it take to be ready?"

I started thinking about how to do this. "I must make a few arrangements with the hospital, for someone to care for my patients, and the Scuola, for someone to teach my classes and to work with my students." *Though my favorite student is now devastated and homeless from her personal loss.* I swallowed hard. "I will need at least three days."

"That would be wonderful."

I turned to Nina, whose face had gone ashen. "Of course, I know I can count on you to keep everything going here at home."

"No! You will need to find another to take care of the house!" *What is she saying! Is she abandoning me when I need her the most?* She went on, "I cannot take care of this house because I am going with you. I can help with your cousin and her children and the others, and, of course, I will be there to take care of you." She clamped her mouth into an expression of great stubbornness.

What she said made good sense. Even if it did not, when Nina decided on something in this manner, there was no point in attempting to dissuade her.

"This sounds like an excellent plan," Papa agreed. He favored Nina with a brief smile, and she responded with a small curtsey.

Next was my commitment to Laura, now also a guest in my house. I asked her to join us in the sitting room. "Though I will be away from Salerno, I insist that you stay in my home for however long it serves you."

"Leaving Salerno?" she echoed. "Why? Where are you going?"

"For family reasons, I am obligated to go to Barcelona almost immediately. I do not know when or if I will return to Salerno."

Her eyes flew open wide, and then she clasped her cheeks with the palms of her hands. "Please, may I go to Barcelona with you? I am alone in the world except for you, my dear Magistra. There is nothing anymore for me here in Salerno. And seeing the crusaders is a daily reminder of all that has happened, so leaving Salerno would be a blessing for me."

I would never have imagined that Laura would be willing to leave the place of her birth. However, as I thought of what she said, I understood her request. Perhaps the best way for her to heal was to leave this place. At least for now.

I hugged her. "Yes, dear girl, you are welcome to join us. And with your knowledge of healing, you could also help."

"And I will go with you too," Rafael added. "My relatives in Barcelona have wanted me to deal with matters there. I can also be helpful on the journey."

Papa beamed. "Wonderful. I thought I would have to hire an escort, but I will not have to with you along."

Rafael deciding to come with us was a surprise. One I liked.

With all that settled, Nina offered to show Papa to his chamber, the one reserved for him alone, so that he could settle in for what would be a short visit. And Laura left to go back to her home to gather the few of her possessions remaining there she would be taking with her to Barcelona.

❦

Rafael and I were now alone. Rafael! I was certainly pleased that he would be joining me to help in Barcelona. Now I thought of the feelings for him that had developed over the past several weeks, feelings that became more conscious to me during my conversation with Signora ben Levi. I had begun to want to let Rafael in, to want to find a way for us to deepen what there was between us.

But, lingering in my thoughts was still the memory of my knight. The memory of him, yes, though perhaps not the all-encompassing love. Thoughts of him no longer brought pain—neither the stabbing, unbearable pain from when we first parted, nor the lingering ache that had accompanied me through the years. Rather, the memories had now, much to my surprise, become more of a melancholy souvenir of past days.

All these thoughts rushed to me in the space of a few breaths. I could now look at Rafael with a fresh perspective, surprising myself with a new curiosity as to how I might react.

He cleared his throat. "We have been through the fire together, yes? More than ever, I am impressed with everything about you."

He placed his hands on mine, as they were before Nina came in with news of Papa's arrival—when I was ready to reject yet again his proposal of marriage. The touch was the same—the wonderful warmth and tingling that I had felt when we met ten years before—yes, certainly still there, but also, something richer, deeper. . .

"As confounding as all these events have been, we were side by side through it all. Together, we will make sense of it, if there is any sense to be made."

He paused briefly, then went on, "Let us truly be together as we face these questions and more. Nothing would make me happier than if you, whom I love above all, would agree to be my wife."

"Rafael. Oh, my dear Rafael, this is not a good time." My usual response to his proposals. I sighed and withdrew my hands from his. He looked at me intently but with a calm patience.

I closed my eyes and breathed slowly, delving with deep feeling into my heart for several long moments.

Then, without a conscious, rational decision, I looked into his eyes and softly said, "But then, perhaps this is the perfect time . . . I love you Rafael, and I will be your wife."

For a long heartbeat Rafael had no reaction, as if he needed time to process the words I had spoken. But then he broke into the most ecstatic smile. "At last. I am the happiest man in the world. I love you." He leaned over and placed his hands on my shoulders and kissed me tenderly, his lips, warm and sweet, covering mine in wondrous contact. Time ceased to exist.

He eventually pulled away. "Come. Let us summon your father and tell him our news."

I smiled. At this fraught time, we could provide Papa and Nina with news that both would rejoice at hearing.

Papa had just reentered the kitchen and was asking Nina something when we came in. He looked from me to Rafael almost as if he could sense what we would tell him.

Rafael cleared his throat. "Sir, long ago you granted me permission to ask your daughter for her hand in marriage." He looked at me. "Now she has finally agreed."

Nina let out a whoop of joy. With a beaming face, Papa took our hands in his. "Amidst great turmoil, this moment of superb happiness comes. Rafael, you shall be as a son to me."

How wonderful to give Papa this pleasure after so much pain. "I am counting the moments until you both stand under the *chuppah,* the bridal canopy. All the family in Barcelona will rejoice with us at your wedding."

"Yes," I said. "Let us do this as our first official act there." And Rafael nodded in agreement.

❧

Now that we had made the decision to move to Barcelona for an indeterminate amount of time, I rushed to arrange what I had to in Salerno. I saw to it that my hospital patients had competent physicians assigned to them, and likewise for my classes and students.

Rafael and I both left our homes in the care of Leah Sara Garcia and
Avvocato di Rienzi. With these commitments seen to over the next
several days, we bade farewell to this city that had meant so much to
me.

❦

Soon after we arrived in Barcelona, it was my wedding day. The sight
of Papa's expression—his joyful smile during the ceremony—brought
me comfort. After some years of disappointing him in this arena, I
could give my father this gift.

Yet it was the expression on Rafael's face that has always been with
me. This strong, handsome, fabulous man gazed at me with such love
and tenderness that my knees grew weak. How could I have denied
him and myself for so long? The waiting was now over. In a very real
sense, my new life began when I exchanged vows with Rafael under
the chuppah.

BARCELONA, 1225 CE

*And so, my darling daughter, you have the story of my life in Salerno,
including how I met and married your father. Every day I bless the
miracle that he came into my life and continues to share it. You know,
of course, that we have stayed in Barcelona, where you and your three
younger brothers and sister were born and have always lived, and we
never returned to resume our home in Salerno. You also know that my
wonderful student Laura became, over the years, an excellent healer,
a great friend to me, and a wonderful "aunt" to you. It was fortunate
that she found a lovely man, her husband Andres, and has made a
good life with him and their seven children here.*

I am pleased that you got to know your grandfather Isaac before his

*death. You gave him so much joy in his old age. The same with my dear
Nina, who loved all of us and who lived out her days with us as bossy
and busy as ever.*

*Now, though I am your mother and would love to keep you safe
always with me, I understand that it is time for you to follow your
dreams. Go forth with my blessings, and, always, my love.*

Afterword

I n so many ways, *Rebecca of Salerno* is an homage to Walter Scott and his creation of Rebecca in his 1820 novel *Ivanhoe*. I discovered this classic book when, in my forties, I wrote my doctoral dissertation in language education at Rutgers University. For years, I had loved studying language and classical literature, but, as a Jewish woman, I felt myself to be either invisible or, on the rare occasions when my peers did show up, a villain. While researching images of Jews in literature, I was delighted to discover Rebecca—the earliest positive image of a Jew I found in European literature.

Scott's Rebecca is a highly idealized figure—beautiful, brilliant, courageous, skilled at healing, loyal, multilingual, and a devoted daughter. She sets a very high bar for women to live up to. What's most important for me, though, is that Scott, in a great story, provided an image that Jewish girls and women could identify with. In more current parlance, a character we can see ourselves in. I was so taken by Rebecca that I could not stop thinking about what happened to her after Sir Wilfred of Ivanhoe (and Scott) abandoned her—this book is the result.

What inspired Scott to create Rebecca? Although we may never know the definitive answer, there is an urban legend that she was patterned after Rebecca Gratz, an American Jew who lived in the

Philadelphia area in the late eighteenth to early nineteenth centuries, and who was heavily involved in significant charitable work. Gratz was believed to have made a great impression on Scott's friend, the writer Washington Irving.

Walter Scott's *Ivanhoe* holds up today as a great story, well told—for reading and/or listening. And the six-hour 1997 production from the BBC is well worth watching (which cannot be said of the 1952 filmed version).

William Makepeace Thackeray, a nineteenth-century British writer, wrote an outrageously humorous parody pamphlet called *Rowena and Rebecca*. In his version of the story, Rebecca converted to Christianity and was then wed to Ivanhoe, leaving Rowena in the lurch. Of course, neither Scott's nor my Rebecca would ever have converted.

Reflecting my passionate interest, language questions were part of my work. I have written this book in twenty-first century American English, which was not the language my characters lived in. So what language would Rebecca and her fellow inhabitants of Salerno (and elsewhere) have spoken? In 1060 CE, when the Normans conquered the Kingdom of Sicily, many of the inhabitants spoke Greek and/or Arabic. By the early thirteenth century, most of those inhabitants were (also?) speaking a language derived from Latin. As was common in that era, the Salernitan variety of the Latin language probably both overlapped with the Sicilian and had differences. In the original *Ivanhoe*, Rebecca, born and raised in England, would have spoken perfect "English" (that is, in the form that existed more than a century before Chaucer) and, reflecting her great education, Latin. From this and from the work of translating texts I have her doing in this story, I "imagine" that Rebecca was a gifted polyglot—along with her many other virtues and talents.

While doing research on the era, I was thrilled to discover the medical school in Salerno—La Scuola Medica Salernitana—which functioned from the eighth century to the nineteenth. At this institution during medieval times, men and women, Jews, Christians, and Moslems could indeed study together. Since Rebecca had been a healer in *Ivanhoe* and intended to continue this work, it was a natural path for her to go to Salerno for her education and professional life.

Rebecca starts the novel in flight from England, in search of a new home where she can live her life in relative safety, peace, and fulfillment. When she discovers Salerno, she believes that she has found that place. Indeed, Norman Sicily was hospitable to the Jews for several centuries. At the end of the novel, Rebecca understands that is no longer the case and, yet again, flees to Barcelona, a place that beckons with greater hospitality—at least in that era.

In each period and place of dispossession, some of the Jews sensed what was coming and had the wherewithal to take the brave and drastic step of leaving while they still could. For many others, however, whether because of not recognizing what was happening or not having the opportunity to leave proactively, the resulting transition was one of dire, and often fatal, consequence. In my story, Rebecca twice falls in the first category. My family, in Poland, tragically fell into the second, with most murdered in the Holocaust and with both of my parents enduring horrendous experiences. That they survived and produced follow-on generations is a miracle that, too, has been one repeated over the millennia.

❦

Writing a historical novel necessitates many decisions. Questions of language use are especially salient for me, a long-time language learner and teacher. Early in the writing process, I decided *not* to limit the vocabulary I used to words that existed in the early thirteenth century. In reflection of that reality, I have chosen to use the word "pogrom" in the book. Although it did not come into English until much later it is, alas, a precisely accurate word to describe events repeated over centuries.

Rebecca of Salerno is a work of fiction. However, included among the characters are historical figures: William of Capparone; Pope Innocent III; Richard, Coeur de Lion; King John of England, also called John Lackland (and other names); La Trotula; Rogerius; Abraham ibn Hasdai; and Maimonides. More generally, the events and tenor of the times that form the context for Rebecca's story here—in England, Barcelona, and Salerno—are based on the history. Any and all historical inaccuracies are my errors or else, in a few cases, due to story ideas I chose to stay true to my vision.

Acknowledgments

I am grateful to have many people to thank for their help and inspiration with this book. My husband and I visited the delightful and still thriving city of Salerno, Italy in 2015. There I was excited to discover the Museo Virtuale dedicated to the Medical School and have a conversation with Giovanni Amatuccio, the director—in French, the one language we have in common. Anyone can "visit" the museum and learn about the fascinating school it commemorates: www. museovirtualescuolamedicasalernitana.beniculturali.it.

Diane Claerbout, a student of medieval history, has been a consistent inspiration. Rina Barouch-Bentov became a muse when she did not run away in horror when I approached as a stranger and told her that she immediately struck me as resembling my vision of the heroine of my novel. That she is a scientist researching viruses, now during the COVID-19 pandemic, only increases her similitude to the physician Rebecca, enhanced further by her warmth, enthusiasm, and generosity.

Early readers were Lorri Lewis, Heather Silverman, Brian Kunde, and Sara Zeff Geber, PhD. Sara invited me to a meeting of the Bay Area Independent Publishers Association, where I first met Brooke Warner of She Writes Press (SWP). Working with Brooke and the SWP community she has created is an ongoing education and pleasure. Thank you to Samantha Strom, my shepherding project manager, and to my SWP writing sisters. Thank you, also, to my generous, entrepreneurial, creative BAIPA chapter! I apologize if I've left anyone out of this list.

Finally, my most profound praise and thanks to my loved ones—children, offsprings-in-law, and grandchildren—Greg, Caryn, Lindsay, John, Ben, and Matthew—who inspire me every day. And to my husband Lee—whose tech prowess, close reading, faith in me, and encouragement have been and continue to be the greatest gifts and blessings.

About the Author

© Marlephoto

Like her heroine Rebecca, Esther Erman was a refugee. A naturalized citizen, she early developed a passion for language, which led to her earning a doctorate in language education, writing her dissertation about the Yiddish language, and working with international students on many levels. A multi-published author, Esther now lives in the San Francisco Bay Area with her husband. When they're not traveling—especially to be with family in other parts of the US and in England—she loves to bake, quilt, and add to her monumental book collection.

SELECTED TITLES FROM SHE WRITES PRESS

She Writes Press is an independent publishing company founded to serve women writers everywhere. Visit us at www.shewritespress.com.

Dark Lady by Charlene Ball. $16.95, 978-1-63152-228-4
Emilia Bassano Lanyer—poor, beautiful, and intelligent, born to a family of Court musicians and secret Jews, lover to Shakespeare and mistress to an older nobleman—survives to become a published poet in an era when most women's lives are rigidly circumscribed.

Mountain of Full Moons by Irene Kessler. $16.95, 978-1-63152-860-6
Elisha—a thirteen-year-old unmarried girl living in Ancient Israel—is different from her tribe: she composes and sings her own songs; she talks to an angel; and she tells other women to stand up for themselves. How can she exist in her society where women have no path but to marry and have children?

Bess and Frima by Alice Rosenthal. $16.95, 978-1-63152-439-4
Bess and Frima, best friends from the Bronx, find romance at their summer jobs at Jewish vacation hotels in the Catskills—and as love mixes with war, politics, creative ambitions, and the mysteries of personality, they leave girlhood behind them.

Odessa, Odessa by Barbara Artson. $16.95, 978-1-63152-443-1
A multigenerational immigrant story of a family, joined by tradition and parted during persecution, that remains bound by a fateful decision to leave Odessa, a shtetl near the Black Sea in western Russia, to escape anti-Semitism.

Song of Isabel by Ida Curtis. $16.95, 978-1-63152-371-7
In ninth-century France, a handsome officer in the King's army rescues twelve-year-old Isabel from an assault by a passing warrior. When the officer returns to her father's estate several years later, sparks fly and emotions tangle.